FLIGHT FROM A DARK EQUATOR

Robert Howel is sent out to Latin America on behalf of the International Red Cross to investigate the alleged massacre of Indians. The head of a London relief organization has also asked him to contact Liz Sayers, one of their field-workers who appears to be in some kind of trouble, and persuade her to return to England.

He finds Liz in a remote province of Colombia, a country in the grip of a fierce dictatorship and showing all the signs of an impending revolution. Liz, it turns out, is in trouble and causing trouble, by being involved with university students and urban guerrillas, many of whom are languishing in prison.

Howel falls in love with Liz, and his efforts to get her back to England before disaster overtakes her become more and more personally motivated. Parallel with his emotional involvement is his growing consternation as he discovers the true nature of an American missionary's brand of evangelism: in the name of Civilization, the CIA and business interests, he aims to destroy the local Indians by compelling them to work in a tin mine until it, too, has become completely exhausted.

Against the background of intrigue, violence and bloody convulsion now affecting Latin America, Norman Lewis tells a story of considerable suspense.

NORMAN LEWIS

Flight from a Dark Equator

COLLINS

St James's Place London

1972

William Collins Sons & Co Ltd
London · Glasgow · Sydney · Auckland
Toronto · Johannesburg

First published 1972
© Norman Lewis 1972

ISBN 0 00 221264 1

Set in Linotype Pilgrim
Made and Printed in Great Britain by
William Collins Sons & Co Ltd Glasgow

1

ONE February day in the changeless equatorial year two secret, powerful men climbed down from a Douglas DC6B at Los Remedios airfield, where a Mercedes Benz of striking antiquity was waiting to take them to the governor's palace in this provincial capital.

Both these men, described respectively in their passports as Engineer and Surveyor, were professional manipulators of long experience of Latin American politicians, and both were impressed by the old black Mercedes. They had been carried to their last meeting with a potential dictator in a Rolls-Royce with a gold-plated radiator, and they detested vulgarity.

This favourable impression increased with every moment that passed. At the road blocks they encountered, soldiers who had settled into trancelike positions jerked to their feet as if pulled into the air by wires, to salute and wave them on, and streets were cleared of traffic and pedestrians at the mere sight of the car, which possessed no siren, and was devoid of escort.

At the palace there was no question of their being left to kick their heels in anterooms; instead, they were conducted instantly into the governor's presence in a small room in his modest suite. Furnished as it was in the soothing ugliness of local Victorian style, it was a room that rarely failed to comfort and reassure visitors from overseas who had had all their stomachs could take of posturing strong men. General Alberto Cervera Lopez y Balseyán went with the room. He was a small, tight man who took after an English ancestress by the name of Harvey, and had what the engineer would have described as the face of a keen fisherman from an old *Saturday Evening Post* cover by Norman Rockwell. The surveyor noticed the quick, finicky movements of small white hands which were never still, and the General's frequent habit of touching nearby objects with the tips of his fingers as if to reassure himself of their reality.

A middle-aged maid brought glasses of thick sherry and flinty biscuits, and with this a brisk exchange of compliments came to an end and the serious discussion began.

Both men had studied the copious data available on every aspect of the General's past and present activities, his opinions, character and his likes and dislikes, and they accepted with gratitude the view of him summed up in the counsel: 'Talk to him like you would to a business man, not a politician. Come to the point. Don't wrap it up. Say what you have to say in the least possible number of words. He'll like you all the better for it. And remember his English is better than yours.'

'General, I'm glad to say my department has decided to recommend a loan.'

'Recommend?'

'Sorry. That's our way of putting it. You'll get the three millions requested.'

The General had said nothing about three millions. He had hoped for five, but there seemed no point in mentioning it now.

'That would be satisfactory.'

What a marvellous man, the engineer thought, and how refreshing to know exactly where you stood. Compare Lopez, for example, with that mangy old tiger of the Dominican Republic, Trujillo, who forced you to go through the farce of hanging round for weeks on end in the Jaragua Hotel, Trujillo City, trying to locate the go-between through whom a deal had to be done. He eased his haunches into the comfortable depths of the old-fashioned sofa, and explained,

6

'You'll be getting the maximum amount my department is empowered to recommend on its own initiative. I'm not saying Congress mightn't do a little better at some later date. If things go as well as we all hope they will.'

The General had narrowed his eyes in concentration as if to remove a very small fish from a hook. Now he smiled suddenly.

'I'm sure we need have no doubts on that score.'

'You can regard this as an expression of our confidence you'll be elected, General. Two-thirds of the amount will be paid when this becomes a fact, but you're to receive one-third in advance. As this might be regarded in some quarters as irregular, we thought it unsuitable to make a bank transfer. Instead we brought it with us in cash.'

All three men smiled slightly, and the General nodded.

'There are one or two small provisos,' the engineer said.

'Hardly that, even,' the surveyor said. 'Requests.'

Lopez smiled again, encouragingly. 'Of course.'

The engineer took up. 'My government is perturbed by the recrudescence of guerrilla activity in Latin America.'

'There is none in this country,' the General said, betraying for the first time his Latin background by a wholly non-Anglo-Saxon gesture of someone flicking away a troublesome fly or mosquito.

'Not at present, but our intelligence tells us there soon will be. An 8th October Movement for Colombia has already been formed.'

'The eighth of October. The date of the death of Guevara, if I'm not mistaken. An interesting man. I would have much enjoyed meeting him.'

It amazed the surveyor that the General could think of Guevara as interesting, but the mere novelty of his attitude increased, if anything, his respect. 'We'd like to see it nipped in the bud,' he said.

'And what would you suggest?'

'You could make a start by putting the screws on your student groups.'

'By the most remarkable coincidence,' Lopez said, 'I've already decided to do that.'

'Besides urban guerrillas, you can expect some trouble in the mountains. A band is already about to cross the frontier, coming from Ecuador.'

'That is more important,' the General said. 'This province contains thousands of square kilometres of mountainous area, much of it unexplored.'

'We have a man in this outfit working for us. They plan to work on the Indians. I hate to seem pessimistic, General, but this has to be treated as something new.'

'I read the Guevara diaries with great interest,' Lopez said. 'They contained many useful hints. Guevara seems to have failed precisely because he neglected to take account of the Indians in Indian Country. The lesson may have been learnt.'

'Is this a situation you can deal with on your own, General?'

'No.'

'Could we help?'

Yes.'

'How?'

'With helicopters.'

'You're asking for the moon, General.'

'Have you any idea of the nature of the terrain?'

'A little,' the engineer said.

'Then you must realize it's the only way. You have a mission at the capital.'

'They'd send our ambassador home if they even knew we were talking to you.'

'I'm not prepared to make a fool of myself by sending a handful of men on foot into those mountains. How soon could they send the helicopters?'

8

'I guess I'd have to refer back to settle that one.'

'Assuming agreement is reached, how soon could they be here?'

'I don't know there's much point in counting our chickens before they're hatched.'

'How soon?' the General said firmly.

'Maybe a couple of weeks. If we could get an agreement, they'd be sent with advisers.'

Lopez picked up an empty silver inkwell, tapped with a fingernail on its surface, and put it down.

'Advisers would be less welcome.'

'They'd be part of the package deal. Sorry, General, I don't make the rules.'

'Very well, I accept your terms.'

The surveyor, absorbed until this moment with the details of a picture painted in insipid colours on glass, and entitled *L'Enlèvement d'Hélène*, now drew in a quick, deep breath, and went into action.

'You have a tin mine at Ultramuerte that isn't doing anything for anybody right now, General. We understand that with an injection of capital, this could become a big producer.'

'What is your proposal?'

'One of our mining corporations would like to buy a fifty-one per cent shareholding.'

Tin, the General decided. That was the real motive of this visit. More trouble in Bolivia, where the government had fallen and the workers had occupied the mines once again; prices rising and world reserves calculated to give out by 1992. Tin ore was the one huge asset this province possessed. 'The mine is very antiquated,' he said. 'It has been closed for nearly ten years.'

'The intention would be to modernize it. I'm assuming that labour paid at local rates would be available.'

'We have an abundance of Indians who will work for

fifty cents a day.' A splendid idea had occurred to him by which two birds could be killed with one stone. His expression remained unchanged.

'Without trades-union interference?'

'We have no trades unions. The shareholding would be forty-nine per cent.'

'The shares would have to be the right price.'

'I will make enquiries,' General Lopez said.

'When might we hope to know something?'

'You'll receive my answer on the day I have your decision about the helicopters.'

2

Six weeks later to the day the same plane brought Robert
Howel to Los Remedios, where he was met at the airport
by Cedric Hargrave, the Latin American organizer of SUC-
COUR. Hargrave took him to the immigration shed where
an official sat, huddled and neckless, in a strangely vulturine
posture behind an opening of the kind seen in many French
post-offices. Hargrave had warned him that he would be
photographed at this point by a secret camera. Fifty yards
away the plane's engines had begun to thump again, and
a curtain of glittering dust swept up by its propellers fell
between them and the window. The two men stood together; Hargrave, midde-aged, unkempt, a little sun-rotted, but
entirely part of the environment; Howel, young and brisk,
a newcomer, too sharp in his movements for the latitude;
a city anxiety in his face.

The official tilted a beaked face towards them. 'Read the
notice,' he said to Howel.

The notice in Spanish and English, over the window, said
that severe penalties were imposed for withholding information or supplying incorrect information when complet-
ing the immigration form.

'Laugh and see what happens,' Hargrave said.

Howel managed a weary smile.

'Please be serious,' the immigration officer said, 'and read
the notice.'

'I've read it already.'

'Then please read it again.'

He watched Howel, his head cocked sideways, in birdlike
speculation, and as Howel raised his eyes, pretending to

read, his hand groped under his desk.

'You spoiled the first photograph he took,' Hargrave said. He turned his back on the officer to reduce the likelihood of his overhearing. 'As you see, they have quite a security set-up.'

'I've been through all this rigmarole before in the capital.'

'You're in South America now,' Hargrave said. 'They're always dreaming up something new to flummox travellers. The local police chief gets his ideas from James Bond. You never know what he'll do next. Have you ever been in this part of the world before?'

'I haven't. This is my first trip to Latin America.'

'You'll find you get used to it pretty quickly. It bothers you for the first few days, but after that you hardly notice it. Feel like a beer?'

'I feel like a number of beers.'

'Let's go down to the town, then, and find a place where we can relax. We have to pass three road blocks, by the way.'

Half an hour later they were at a window seat in a bar in one of the back streets of the town. Hargrave was trying to master a nervous cough that made his eyes water. What was this man doing here? Why had he descended so suddenly upon him, out of the blue?

Beyond the window Los Remedios, the provincial capital, was a matter of cubist shapes and hard colours, laid on in slabs and wedges and tufted with crisp shadows. In the immediate foreground, on the pavement, a man with an Eskimo's face prodded with a stick at a large rattlesnake with which he hoped to attract attention to a display of medicines.

'Average temperature, ninety degrees, night and day,' Hargrave said. 'No winter or summer, and no rainy season. It rains when it feels like it. One thanks God for air-conditioning.' He laughed again, with a quick, dry sound, almost another cough, that seemed to be offered as a constantly repeated apology for the human abnormalities and the climatic defects of the environment. He was roughly as Howel, piecing together all the accounts, had expected him to be: a young-old man, masking many defects under an expression of urgent enthusiasm, with a beard of the kind that somehow managed to reduce the latitude between good and evil in a face.

Hargrave snapped his finger for two more beers.

'You've chosen quite a time to arrive. We have a provincial governor who's expected to make a bid for the presidency any time now. The betting is he'll go for power on 1st May. It's a sort of a tradition if there's going to be a coup. Big day locally. Bit like Christmas and Easter rolled into one. Processions and so forth. Probably have the tanks out and a bit of random bombing if there's a revolution.'

He paused with a secret smile, his eyes narrowed, as if sniffing a rare bouquet of intrigue. 'That's unless the Liberals manage to clobber him first. The governor's a Conservative, so by law his deputy has to be Liberal. No love lost between them even if they're all smiles in public. Personally I'd back the governor. A very ruthless man. Went to Downside or Ampleforth, I believe. Most of them do. You'll find local politics a trifle complicated. We're promised a spot of bother with the guerrillas in the near future, by the way. It's a great life if you don't weaken.'

A rolling cloud of dust pressed momentarily on the window as a car passed, and as it cleared the man with the rattlesnake rematerialized, scowling, portentous and momentarily inflated, like a genie released from a bottle.

'It's a great country,' Hargrave said desperately, and from a depressed corner of his mouth. For a moment he had assumed an American accent that suited the remark. 'This pub is called Te Esperaré a tu Vuelta, because traditionally prisoners come here for their first drink when they're released from prison just down the road. Not—by the way—political prisoners. Once inside, they never come out. Shootings are a matter of regular occurrence.' He pointed with something like pride to the several holes in the blood-red ceiling. 'New ones. They weren't there when I was here last week.'

These bullet holes, Hargrave seemed to say, belong to me. It was something to be suffered with quiet pride, like the frosts of the Antarctic explorer, or the foolish tyranny of the recruit's barrack-room. Shots fired in boredom, the rattlesnake on the pavement, the banditry in the faces all round them, the fierce dust, the heat like the embrace of an insistent mistress—these things could be displayed as the embellishments of a meagre life.

Howel's gaze returned through the harsh bars of sunshine and the dancing motes to the far side of the road, where several black bundles of rag appeared to have been stuffed into an angle of a wall.

'Indians,' Hargrave said. 'Probably sick. You see them lying about the place. A couple got eaten by dogs the other night. Caused a lot of hoo-hah, and the local paper got fined for reporting it. Gives the place a bad name.'

'Aren't we doing anything about it?' Howel asked.

Hargrave gave him a startled look. '*We*,' he said, 'were two at the time. This country is as big as half Western Europe. Be like trying to stick your finger in the hole in the dyke.'

'Did you put it in your report?'

Hargrave explained patiently. 'This is a single incident. One of hundreds. You have to draw a line somewhere.' He coughed another sharp, apologetic laugh. 'I hear you spent a year with the ICRC,' he said.

'I was on loan,' Howel said. 'Still am. They wanted someone with investigational experience. I expect to be going back to s u c c o u r when I get back from this trip. For a while, at least.'

14

Hargrave took a chance. 'Would that have anything to do with your presence here? Charles didn't say.'

'With my presence in Colombia. I was down in Planas looking into this business with the Guahibo Indians—nothing came of it, of course—and Charles thought I might look in on you while I was about it. He doesn't seem to have had much idea of the distances involved.'

'I'm sure the ICRC wouldn't mind giving you a few days' leave,' Charles had said. 'Naturally we will provide all the expenses. Perhaps you could let us have a report about the situation at Los Remedios while you're about it. If you can find the time. The main thing is to bring Liz Sayers back.'

'I don't see how I can if she doesn't want to come.'

'Robert, you must persuade her. Do anything you have to. Just bring her back.'

He fixed Howel with his genial but shifty eye, and once more Howel was amazed at this man's almost hypnotic power to enlist sympathy. Perhaps it was because he felt things deeply. 'Why all the panic?' Howel asked.

'She's in some dreadful scrape. I'm quite convinced of that. I had a long talk with Smalldon as soon as he got back. He was discretion itself—far too discreet—but from what I could gather things are very unsatisfactory indeed. I gather she's even been in trouble with the authorities.'

'Send her an air ticket, and order her to come back,' Howel said.

'It wouldn't work. Somebody has to go and fetch her.'

'I don't want to do it, Charles. For one thing I don't have the authority—besides which, I just don't enjoy meddling in other people's affairs. Surely there must be somebody else who can handle the thing for you?'

'There isn't. We haven't anyone with your experience and tact. Besides which, we couldn't afford to send someone all the way from London. It's a chance in a thousand that you're going to be in the area. I do hope you'll change your mind.'

And in the end Robert Howel had agreed.

'We've missed you at succour,' Charles said. 'I can't tell you how thankful I am you'll be coming back.'

Dust-sodden sounds of hoofbeats reached them from the street as a party of men mounted on mules came in sight, scattering the crystalline deposits of sunshine. Howel saw a prancing tapestry of mounted figures, of lean animals, and men with straight backs and iron profiles, and above all, a satanic indifference of expression. These men rode with rifles slung on their backs, and lariats looped from their saddles.

'The governor's private army,' Hargrave said. 'Long-term convicts let out of prison to help out in the present emergency. Specialists in loot, rape and murder.'

Again the suspicion of pride in the voice.

'Sounds like a pretty sinister individual.'

'He is. All the more so because when you meet him he seems so reasonable. They say he designs his own instruments of torture, but this I do not believe. I used to see quite a bit of him in the old days, at cocktail parties, before he became inaccessible. He's no more corrupt than any other politician. Probably less. He made no bones about telling you straight out that in this country any politician expects to be able to buy votes at a dollar a time.'

'However, foreigners are left in peace?'

'Oh, absolutely, and rest assured, dear boy, that nine out of ten of them prefer to have a strong man at the helm. The geographical facts of the country make the place almost inaccessible from the capital and, believe me, it came very close to being chaos before Lopez came on the scene. I've always believed myself to be a liberal', Hargrave said, 'but if you've lived—as I have—through nearly ten years of total anarchy, I think you'd find there was a lot to be said for a strong man, too. And then again, the General's no ordinary strong man. I once heard him say that when the time came Colombia would make the transition from feudalism to modern capitalism overnight, and nothing would be allowed to stand in the way. I believe this is about to happen.'

'Has he any human weaknesses?' Howel asked.

Hargrave thought about this. 'Yes,' he said. 'I suppose he has. He's superstitious. He's very superstitious.'

Five minutes later they were back in the big American car again, in the narrow streets, heading out of town. Hargrave wound down his window a few inches to scream oaths incomprehensibly in the local Spanish at pedestrians dodging cautiously from shade-patch to shade-patch in their path.

The freckles like small birthmarks on his sun-tormented skin seemed to have been deepened by his outburst of indignation.

'In a way,' he said, 'I've lived here too long. This business of down-and-outs being eaten by dogs, and suffering as a whole—I suspect I've developed a kind of blindness. I no longer see so many things.'

Howel was ready to believe that this was no overstatement. It was a disease of the sensibilities of which he immediately recognized the symptoms.

They were in a mean street full of nimble cripples and disjointed beggars, where sellers of cooked meat were toasting fearful-looking collops of flesh over kerbside braziers. Ahead, penitents on their knees shuffled wearily over the flagstones towards the doors of a church like a Byzantine fortress.

He doesn't see, Howel thought. Doesn't feel either. Almost a husk.

Howel, fresh from a faceless Indian desert without life, colour, movement, sound; a place which fatigued even the wind and absorbed the stars by night, was glutted here, almost to the point of nausea, with sensation. But with

Hargrave it was the old trouble, the endemic sickness of the service, the slow, steady loss of love, the loss of interest, and in the end the loss of patience with the people they had set out so hopefully to serve.

'It may well apply to the feelings, the heart,' Hargrave admitted in confirmation. 'One loses the power to be affected by things. They tie a man's penis in prison and leave him until his bladder bursts. One should be outraged, but one isn't. The thing lacks reality. The imagination simply caves in.'

A dome encircled by a slow whirlwind of doves thrust into the gunmetal sky above them and a crash of church bells pulverized the hum of the car's air-conditioner. Bandoliered men on mules cantered past, and women rushed to drag their children from under their hooves.

Hargrave drove on, eyes aloof, absorbed in the important rhythms of the daily routine.

'Normally we'd take less than an hour to get out to Dos Santos, but today we're bound to have road block trouble. It'll probably take double the time.'

'Charles didn't quite seem to understand what made you move out there.'

'We got to know the local missionaries. They have the hacienda and they offered us the converted stables. The rent's lower than we were paying in the town. This is the missionary's car, by the way—Grail Williams—he's a very useful man to know.'

'He must be. Don't you have a car of your own?'

'Yes, but not an air-conditioned one. He doesn't mind anyone taking it if they want to go down town.'

'Do you find you can get as much work accomplished living out where you are?'

'Very definitely more. One obviously works better in relatively cool and congenial surroundings. The house is air-conditioned too. Got all the mod cons. I think you'll enjoy the set-up.' There was a moment of silence, and Hargrave added, 'I mean, there's no real point in being uncomfortable if one doesn't have to be.'

On the defensive, Howel thought.

The streets had suddenly closed in, and the houses had taken on a stunted, makeshift look. A few bushes appeared at the roadside, and then trees—at first with their branches hacked and mutilated for firewood, but shortly undamaged and magnificent. The sparrows of the city were now replaced by small, brilliant birds, scuffling in the red dust ahead, and as the jungle took over a blue butterfly came out of the trees and flattened itself on the windscreen as if mounted in a cabinet for display.

'You see I don't sweat,' Hargrave said. 'In consequence I feel the heat more than most. Otherwise we live a fairly spartan existence by most standards. Manage to grow most of our own food.'

'How's Liz?' Howel asked.

He felt the resistance like an electrical current, although nothing in Hargrave's profile moved.

'She's well. Very well,' Hargrave said.

'And happy?'

'Happy? Yes, she's happy.' Something tugged at Hargrave's adam's apple. 'Well, I imagine she is.'

'Smalldon didn't seem to think so,' Howel said.

'Did he tell you that?'

'He said something to Charles.'

'I suppose they didn't get on so well as they might have. There were differences of opinion.'

'I gathered as much.'

'And then of course Charles has this tendency to make mountains out of molehills.'

'But not this time, I think,' Howel said.

'So far as I know Liz is perfectly all right,' Hargrave said. 'But you'll see for yourself.' There was a pause and Howel waited for him to add something. 'Been doing some very useful work,' Hargrave said, but it was not what Howel had expected him to say.

'Pretty girl,' Howel said. 'I met her once at a party in Sloane Square. Don't suppose she'll remember me.'

They were climbing now on a red laterite road, through a series of hairpin bends, at first walled in by exuberant vegetation, and then suddenly in a sparse forest of tall, elegant trees, overlapped by a cut-out of flat, burnished mountains. Occasionally they squirted ochreous powder from their tyres over a Negroid family in rags, placed absolutely motionless outside their shack like a row of Easter Island figures, and then Howel saw his first recognizable Indians. They were going uphill at a dog-trot, hunched under real or imaginary burdens, and wearing important hats. Their children scrambled along beside them, the muscles knotted on their spindly legs.

'They won't get farther than the first road block,' Hargrave said.

'Why's that?'

'The General's new policy. He's clearing them out of the mountains. From now on, if they come down to town they'll have to stay there.'

'What's the idea?'

'They're to be assimilated. Whatever they mean by that. Actually they'll be packed off to work in plantations or mines.'

'And don't they object?'

'What do you think? In many cases the family gets split up. A father may have come down to the city to buy or sell something, and then find he can't get back. What do you imagine happens to his wife and children?'

'But surely he can leave the road and take to the mountains?'

'Not within twenty kilometres of Los Remedios, he can't.

That's to say, without the risk of being shot at. That's part of the General's security measures. You have to keep to the road. There wouldn't be any point in the road blocks, otherwise.'

'I suppose you could get me all the facts involved?' Howel said.

Hargrave showed his surprise by a faint change in his expression, noticeable even in profile.

'If you want them.'

'I've got to put in a report.'

'For the ICRC?'

'For Charles too. He's suddenly become interested in Indians. I'll explain what it's all about later.'

Hargrave's expression in profile found Charles guilty of eccentricity.

'Mind you, in the long run it's probably the best thing. They lead wretched lives up there. The coffee planters grabbed all the land worth having generations back. Personally I'm not at all sure that the reason given is the true one. I have a very shrewd suspicion that Lopez wants the Indians out of the mountains so that the guerrillas can't get to work on them.'

The road block was at the top of the pass; two halted lines of cars, coming and going, with no signs of movement.

'We've struck a bad one today,' Hargrave said. 'This is getting worse than usual. Lucky we're not in the incoming file. We'd be here for ever.'

They pulled in behind the last car. Soldiers were busy down the line eight cars ahead. 'They've suddenly become very thorough,' Hargrave said. 'Looking for concealed weapons, I suppose.'

They both climbed down. Three thousand feet above the city the heat was bearable. Ahead, half a dozen volcanic slagheaps with completely smooth sides had been raised against a harsh, granular sky. A roadside hedge was formed

21

of Jewish candlesticks of cactus. It had rained within the hour and they trod on flattened muscles of sand where a quick deluge had passed and instantly dried.

Two small, dark, jabbering soldiers, under the orders of an NCO who was slightly larger and paler than themselves, had taken the spare wheel out of a car and were stripping off the tyre, while an officer who was larger still, and quite white, looked on at a distance. A group of Indians had been herded aside where they squatted passively, drawing on endless reserves of resignation, the women separated from the men and with their backs to them. Cries of excitement came from the soldiers searching the cars. That night or the next day Howel would begin his South American notebook with a few early impressions of the two races. Indians, calm, phlegmatic, silent, self-controlled. Half-breeds, lively, emotional, spontaneous. Query diet, as well as hereditary factors?

A scuffle broke out.

'They've found a couple of Indians who were hitching a ride,' Hargrave explained.

The doors of a small ramshackle van had been opened and one of the soldiers reached in. He took a fistful of black hair, twisted his hand in it and yanked, and an Indian woman came out and fell sprawling on the ground, a baby bundled on her back. His hand still in her hair, the soldier tugged her to her feet. By this time the shawl holding the baby had loosened, and it was slipping from her back.

It'll break its neck, Howel thought. He ran forward and grabbed the soldier by the arm, and the soldier instantly let go the Indian woman, shifted his rifle to his right hand and jabbed Howel with the barrel in the pit of the stomach. Howel felt the impact of the blow, and the entry of the barrel with its massive foresight between his ribs, but there was no pain. He found himself folded into a crouching, foetal position, breathless and gulping in an attempt to trap

22

and swallow the air he could not breathe. His heartbeat was in his ears, with the slow, solemn tick of a grandfather clock. He was rocking on his heels like an absurd, ill-balanced ornament on a mantelshelf, staring down through the opalescent stars of the tears fused on his lashes at red earth pimpled with small anthills. Titters enlaced to encircle him, then closed in to form a chaplet pressing on his eyes, as his mouth fell open to release a gush of watery saliva.

Then he was sitting on a bank, Hargrave bending over him, and at the end of an unintelligible sentence.

'I seem to have passed out.'

'You did,' Hargrave said, 'and no wonder. He hit you really hard. Still feeling groggy?'

'A bit. Queasy, that's all. I'll be OK.' He wiped his eyes, and the landscape lost its haloed edges.

'A tremendous stroke of luck,' Hargrave said. 'Williams just came through. He's fixing it for you.'

'Williams?'

'Grail Williams. The missionary. I was telling you about him.'

'Of course. What's he fixing?'

'To get them to let you go. The officer was going to take you in for an act of rebellion. He was hopping mad.'

The landscape tilted away a little, then swung back. The clock ticking in Howel's ears suddenly stopped. 'What am I supposed to have done?'

'Obstructed a member of the armed forces in the execution of his duty, one of the most serious crimes you can commit. You came very near to seeing the inside of that prison in Animas Street. Here comes Williams.'

A man who seemed a giant in the context of the puny Colombian soldiers was striding towards them. He had the face of an astronaut, with big nordic features, and hair cropped to a pale stubble. The Colombian officer, a head shorter, hurried beside him, and Williams's hand, resting

23

on his shoulder, seemed to be pressing him into the ground.

Williams enclosed Howel's hand in his, gave it a slow, considerate squeeze and released it. 'Mr Howel, welcome to Los Remedios. Cedric told us all about you, and we're certainly proud to have you visit with us. I've told Juan you're a UN observer, and he's kind of worried. Wants to apologize for the misunderstanding.'

Howel felt that some sort of correction was needed here—to avoid any possible later charges of false pretences, but he hadn't the strength to make it. He tried to smile, seeing Williams through rippling water. The head also, he thought, of one of the Roman emperors, he forgot which—having about it a certain marble nobility, yet with this an inevitable suggestion of sightlessness.

The officer gave him the dregs of the fawning smile he had just turned on the missionary, and as Williams's hand fell upon his shoulder again, appeared to sink farther into the earth.

'I've arranged with Juan,' Williams said, 'that you can follow me up to Dos Santos, and you won't have any more trouble with road blocks. They've given me a Seguridad Militar numberplate at last, and that passes us straight through.' He spoke with a deep voice and the controlled power of a bass singer. 'Shall we go, then?' He dismissed the officer with a slight shove and began to walk back to his command jeep, which stood a little farther on in the middle of the road in a respectful space created between the two lines of waiting cars.

They sped on at 70 mph, boring into the saffron fog of dust from the jeep's wheels, slowing to be saluted and waved on at the road blocks. Hargrave said, 'That officer chap will get a spare part for his car out of this. Grail had some sort of special importation arrangement. One has to admit he's prepared to put himself to a lot of trouble for his friends.'

The last remark called for one of his apologetic laughs. Howel grunted a reply. An almost hallucinatory weariness had come over him. No physical aftermath remained of the episode at the first road block but a slight ache in the solar plexus, which remained sensitive to the touch. But now he remembered that he had been travelling twenty hours on horseback, by bus and by plane, since leaving a mountain village near Planas on the previous evening. He nodded off, and then awoke with a start as Hargrave braked suddenly. 'Dos Santos,' Hargrave said.

Howel saw a group of huts painted in savage colours crammed on to a small plateau of ochre and ox-blood, under a brownish sky. Behind them, as they crashed through the shattered streets, rose up an enormous house from the French countryside, grandly symmetrical in design and with a double, enormous sweep of outside staircase, in Palladian style, up to the door. Williams's jeep was parked in front of a fountain at the bottom of the steps.

'The hacienda,' Hargrave said. 'We're in those buildings to the right.'

3

WAKING up Howel found himself blinking at a striped pattern of light and shade reflected on a white wall from Venetian blinds. Faint unfamiliar sounds reached him, recalling the shrieks and hootings of animals heard at a distance, perhaps from the top of a stationary bus, from the Regent's Park Zoo. A small pink lizard with an ugly head, like a lion from a bestiary, slipped into sight on the wall, and was whisked away. He struggled to recall the events which had led to him being in this bed, then remembered. 'We conform here to the habit of the siesta,' Hargrave had said. 'It's an absolute necessity. Are you sure you wouldn't like me to make you a sandwich or something, to tide you over until dinner?' Howel had declined. 'I had something on the plane.' He had gone to bed shortly after five in the afternoon, and now he picked up his watch from the bedside table, and found that it was a quarter to eight. As he put it down, there was a rap on the door and Hargrave appeared. 'How are things this morning?'

'Fine, thanks. This morning, is it? God!'

'I know you slept well, because I gave a knock earlier. Nothing but musical snores. How are you feeling after the fracas?'

'Perfectly OK.' Howel ran a surreptitious hand over the pit of his stomach, where the soreness had almost gone.

Hargrave led the way downstairs. There was a smell of fresh carpentry and impermanence about the place that Howel found wholly familiar. He began to wonder if it wasn't something deliberately cultivated by people who went overseas for SUCCOUR: a hastily erected stage-scenery of pictures waiting to be hung and possessions in un-

26

packed tea-chests that assured them of eventual escape.

'You said you were just back from India. Did you enjoy it?' Hargrave asked.

'You couldn't enjoy it. It may have suited my temperament. India's absolutely predictable. However grim the situation may be, there are no surprises. You know what to expect.'

'You'll find this a somewhat different kettle of fish. Never know what the morrow's going to bring forth.'

'But you get used to it?'

'Eventually.'

'I don't think I could,' Howel said. 'I ought to have been a farmer. I'm in the wrong kind of job.' He thought about this and what had begun in jest ended in earnest. 'More than anything else I'd like to get my teeth into something and work at it for the rest of my life. I'd like to live and die in the same place.'

'How old are you, thirty-five?'

'Thirty-four.'

'That's a good age. You've still time. I'm fifty-five. If you stay in this another ten years it'll be too late. I'll tell you an extraordinary thing—I've come to need what this part of the world supplies in the way of insecurity and tension.'

'You're probably looking forward to those tanks and the random bombing on May 1st. '

'I probably am. Feel like some brekker, then?'

'I think I could manage some.'

Breakfast was in an enormous, whitewashed room, devoid of furniture but the table and chairs, which were crudely carpentered of cheap-looking wood. The chairs were exceedingly uncomfortable with hard, narrow seats. Hargrave, bare to the waist, sat facing him across a scrubbed and slightly splintered surface. His age, held at bay elsewhere with fair success, showed up in the loose skin draped over his chest like the folds of a garment. The meal consisted of maize cakes with fried eggs, and a sweet, thickish maize gruel. Using a blunt-nosed spoon, Hargrave scooped the yolk from two eggs and spread it slowly and with great care over a cake, until the whole surface was covered with an even yellow layer. He then picked up the cake delicately and began to eat. A slight encrustation of yolk formed at the corners of his mouth. There were no knives and forks and Howel did what he could with the spoon provided.

'Delicious, aren't they?' Hargrave said, his eyes seeming to glitter with excitement.

'They certainly are.'

'Local speciality. Grail Williams's Indian cook makes them. He sends us a fresh supply every morning.'

Hargrave began the slow process of spreading yolk on another cake, and Howel, who found the sight disgusting, averted his eyes.

'As I told you, we're vegetarians,' Hargrave said. '—Liz with occasional backslidings. She—by the way—asked to be excused. She had a heavy day with one thing and another, and had to make an early start. Eventually we hope to cut out eggs and milk, too; all animal foods, in fact. I don't propose to get on my hobby-horse at this point, nor do I expect you to have to give up meat while you're here. Williams kills his own pigs, and if you like pork he's always got a plentiful supply in his deep freeze. Which applies to bacon and ham, and the rest of it.' His smile, normally a weak one, had acquired strength and confidence, as a result, Howel supposed of this display of liberalism.

'Would you like to see some of the work?' he said suddenly. The smile had suddenly gone, leaving in its place an expression of ingratiation and anxiety.

'Whenever you're ready. Don't think of me as some sort of inspector, though.'

They went to Hargrave's study, a monastic cell of a room decorated with a map of the world from one of the Sunday supplements showing the areas likely to be affected by blast and fall-out in the event of a nuclear war. These areas had been drawn firmly and with conviction. Practically the whole of the northern hemisphere had been abolished by the cataclysm, but Howel noted that the crimson tide of fall-out had stopped several hundred miles north of Los Remedios. The titles of most of the books on Hargrave's bookshelf suggested to Howel a whimpering after certainties that eluded him— *The Interpretation of Cosmic Aid*, *The Divine Awakening*, *The Phenomenon of Astral Projection*, *Bridges to the Unknown*. He hastily rebuked himself for the censorious thought. Oceans of paper and statistics awaited him.

	National	Local
PER CAPITA INCOME	$288	$111
AV. LIFE EXPECTATION	44 Years	37.5 Years
LITERACY	44%	8%
CHILD MORTALITY	12.1%	24%
AV. NUMBER OF CHILDREN PER FAMILY	6.3	8.2
UNEMPLOYED	22%	45%
NUMBER OF LIVESTOCK PER FAMILY	1.1	.3
NUMBER OF POULTRY PER FAMILY	3	2

Howel read on steadily for an hour, sheet by sheet and table of figures by table of figures. 'What do you think of it?' Hargrave asked.

'I think it's very impressive.'

'I'm glad you do.'

'You must know everything there is to know about the way people live in rural Colombia.'

'Well not *everything*—at least a good deal.'

'Will you be doing anything with all this?' Howell asked.

Hargrave looked wounded. 'I imagine we shall eventually.

It's part of the necessary preparation.'

'What sort of field work have you been doing?' Howel said. It made him feel a little shameful and sly to ask this question to which he already knew the answer.

'Well, for example, last year we did a fairly important airlift of dried milk out to a mountain tribe who were having a thin time through the maize-crop failure.'

'Charles mentioned something about it,' Howel said. 'Didn't something go wrong?'

'They wouldn't touch the milk. It was a great disappointment.'

'Why wouldn't they?'

'Some sort of taboo, I believe.'

Howel tried to avoid a schoolmasterish tone.

'Couldn't we have sent maize?'

'There was an embargo on it. Supplies were short all round. They wanted all they could get in the city.' He suddenly seemed to be pleading. 'We bought the milk very cheaply, and Grail Williams let us have the use of his plane for nothing.'

'He's got a plane, has he?'

'The only private one in the province.'

'I'm beginning to see that he's a useful man to keep in with.'

Hargrave avoided any reply to this remark.

'Of course Liz's engaged on a very interesting project,' he said. 'She's organized the production of Indian handicrafts. It's going like—' he paused to grope after a current colloquialism and then went on—'like a bomb.'

'I'm glad to hear that,' Howel said, 'because I was beginning to fear that we might not quite be justifying our existence in Los Remedios.'

Hargrave's face had aged, with deep lines carved under the sparse beard round the corners of his mouth, and a yellow stain in the whites of his eyes. 'We've done all we could.

The local people are very quick to resent anything that looks to them like interference. We're up against corruption, indifference and pride. All we can do is to offer our help —and in the humblest possible fashion at that. Half of them think we're mad as it is.'

'Charles has asked for a report, and ICRC is interested too—from a somewhat different angle. We can't go on wasting money here if we're not performing any useful function. The only reason this office was ever started was that SUCCOUR benefited from a £20,000 legacy to be spent in Latin America. But now the money's coming to an end, and the thing is do we pull out altogether, or do we, in a manner of speaking, concentrate on the Indian field?'

'I don't think I follow you,' Hargrave said.

'The world's suddenly developed a conscience about the vanishing Indian. We could probably get half a dozen European organizations to back us in one way or another as the people on the spot.'

'I'd forget about it,' Hargrave said. 'I mean the Indian thing.'

'Why?'

'Because the Colombians wouldn't stand for it. They don't want a lot of dirty linen washed in public any more than anybody else does. They'll tell you to mind your own business or get out.'

'And you'd say they'd every right to?'

'I didn't say that,' Hargrave said. 'But I happen to know these people. I've lived in this country off and on for a number of years.'

'We're not obliged to stay here,' Howel said. 'We could go somewhere else. If the score of the operation justifies it, we could move the office.'

'Could we?' There was an eagerness in the question that took Howel by surprise. 'I suppose that mightn't be a bad thing,' Hargrave said.

'You'd be quite happy to go?'

'Oh quite.'

'What about Liz?'

An instant of rejuvenation had expired. Age and gloom were in possession of Hargrave's face again. 'I don't know about Liz. She's very absorbed in her work.'

'Well it's on the cards we'll be closing down the office anyway. Do you think she'd object to a move to Brazil, say?'

'I haven't the faintest idea. We've never contemplated the possibility. I'm afraid you'll have to ask her. My personal feeling is she mightn't be too keen on the idea.'

Liz came in to join them for an early lunch of vegetable curry. Howel found her offhand to the point of rudeness. As attractive as ever, he thought, if one could forget the sulky expression, though he found it hard to justify her popular rating as the Venus of s u c c o u r. Charles had furnished the details of her career: Dolci, VSO in Calabria, and a year with s u c c o u r in the Congo, and had insisted on hinting at a taste for promiscuous adventure with any personable member of the organization who happened to be available.

Surreptitiously studying her now, Howel found this hard to accept. Her face held no intrigue; an interesting face—striking perhaps by the standards of the past, but not those of our time. The nose, drawn with the merciless realism of an early Italian master, was long and a little sharp; the eyes were spirited but small; the full lips fell naturally into a pout. It was a face that would not have photographed well, but which appealed greatly to Howel. She seemed to have changed very much since he had last seen her, when—perhaps under the influence of drink—she had appeared frivolous. Now she spoke only to reply to his polite questionings. Their eyes never met. A bit of a neurotic, he summed her up.

32

After a hurriedly gulped-down lunch, she suddenly said, 'I suppose you want to look at my project?'

'I'd love to see whatever you're working at. If it's convenient just now. There's no hurry.'

Hargrave, exuding embarrassment, sat in his own enclave of silence probing with a long thin finger at a knot in the naked table-surface. Howel got up to follow her.

They crossed a garden where the sunshine lay in stagnant puddles. The top of the hacienda building showed above a rampart of bougainvillaea stippled and splashed with its bracts of unnatural colours. In the distance Howel heard what might have been school children singing a flattened pentatonic version of the hymn 'Dare to be a Daniel', in which the highest and lowest notes remained aloof and uncaptured. Liz led the way into another building, strangely gabled and half-timbered, that might once have been a coachman's cottage.

'The motivation of the project,' she said, 'is to help people to help themselves. Some of the Indians produce beautiful embroidery, particularly the Cholos, and we thought it might be possible to adapt this in such a way that it could be produced commercially.' She showed him a wall-case containing a cape-like garment covered by an intricate, embroidered design of eagles, jaguars and deer.

'How very beautiful,' Howel said.

'The idea was to reproduce these designs on tablecloths, napkins, and what have you. We were going to sell the stuff and turn the money over to the Cholos, or buy food for them. Whichever they wanted. We were quite ready to supply all the raw materials free of charge. They were very cheap.'

Her tone warned Howel that this was to be a tale of disaster.

'What happened?' he asked.

'It all fell through. We had two Cholo women working

down here for a month. A shop in Los Remedios was going to do the actual selling but in the end they decided they wanted what they called brighter colours, to suit the tourist trade, and the next thing was they wanted the Cholos to put Disney dogs and horses into the designs. It was just a ghastly mess. We sold about thirty-five dollars' worth of the original huipils, and then the two women we had went back to the mountains, and that was that.'

'How long had you been working on the scheme?' Howel asked.

'Nearly eighteen months.'

'Any idea of total textile sales to date?'

'Not off hand.'

'Well, roughly—a hundred dollars? Two hundred dollars?'

'More like a hundred,' she said.

'And what are you working on at the moment? Cedric said you were very busy.'

'I may be getting a couple of potters from the mission,' she said. 'They do some nice zoomorphic pots in the shape of dogs and monkeys. Actually they're very artistic.'

'Is this a commercial venture?' he asked.

'What do you mean, a commercial venture? Of course it is.' Losing her cool, he thought. '*And*, by the way,' she said, 'there's still quite a chance that Sears Roebuck may be interested in the tablecloths. They're going into costs—shipping and duty and all the rest. We should be hearing soon.'

'But nothing concrete,' Howel said.

'I told you, we should be hearing any time.'

'But even if they give you an order, didn't I understand you to say that the women who do the work had gone back?'

'Well obviously, we could get more . . . I expect you think it's all been a terrible waste of time.'

'I don't for one moment,' Howel said. 'We all have to pay for experience. You and Cedric have done everything you

34

could have done,' he went on. 'Charles admits you've had very little co-operation from London, and practically nothing in the past few months in the way of funds.' He lied: 'I know Charles is perfectly happy.' Why is she so hostile? he wondered.

'May I ask you a direct question?' she said. 'Would you mind telling me just what you're doing here?'

'I'm a bit vague myself,' Howel said. 'The rough idea is we have to decide whether to expand our commitment or to pull out altogether, and Charles wanted me to give the place the once over.'

'You're also a UN observer, aren't you?'

'Red Cross, actually.'

'Is that all?' Liz asked.

'That's all. It's enough, isn't it?' He tried a gentle, bantering tone to which she did not respond.

'You're quite sure?'

'What's this all about? What else do you imagine I could be doing?'

'Oh, don't pay any attention,' she said. 'I had a funny sort of letter from Charles the other day, and I've been wondering what it was all about. You know the kind of intrigues that go on at Sloane Square. When you're stuck out in the wilds like this you end up believing anything.'

She had calmed; the stern, capable mouth of anger had lost its boldness of contour. Howel took the plunge.

'There may be a decision to close this office down quite soon.'

'And how soon is that?'

'In a month's time, possibly.'

'Oh,' she said. It was a sound that was almost a gasp.

He pushed on. 'In which case, would you be prepared to go to Brazil? When I say Brazil, nothing's certain yet. It might be Peru.'

'I don't think I would,' she said. Suddenly her voice

35

seemed to droop with tiredness. 'The understanding was that this tour was to be for three years.'

'You weren't given any guarantee,' Howel said. 'Charles looked up the correspondence. It was hoped that the posting would be for three years, but as the whole thing was a bit of an experiment, it might be for less. That was what was said.'

'People always get a year's notice if they're going to be changed,' she said. 'Six months at least.'

'We realize that, and I know that Charles would want to do anything he could to make up for the inconvenience. You could choose your next posting. India, North Africa, South-East Asia. Anywhere you like. Or you could work at head office if you felt like it. Entirely up to you.'

'I'm not interested in making a move,' she said. 'I've got myself involved in various things here, and I'd prefer to stay on.'

'There's a fifty-fifty chance it won't be possible.'

'In that case I'll find myself another job.'

'Here—in Colombia?'

'Here, in Colombia,' she said. 'I could teach English.'

'Then I'm to tell Charles you won't be going back, whatever happens?'

'Why not?' she said. 'If you have to tell him something. I've already told him myself. I can't think why he bothers so much about me.'

'He wants to keep you in the organization,' Howel said. 'Besides which, he happens to be fond of you.' The fact had to be faced, he thought. Wild horses couldn't drag her away, and he wondered how long it would take him to find out why.

Suddenly the tension between them had snapped. He was amazed at the speed with which her moods could change, from sulkiness to open antagonism, and then to friendliness,

36

even gaiety. She had found something to joke about: the Williamses. 'Better have a siesta,' she said. 'You're invited round there tonight, and you'll need all your strength.'

Howel took her advice. He lay down but was determined to keep awake. Instead he went over a few pages of a Spanish reader he'd brought with him. The pink lizard came to watch him through eyes worn like minute sunglasses. Outside, something hooted and something hissed; hot sounds that devoured time and manufactured sleep. Thin voices from the horn of an ancient gramophone wheedled the air of 'In the Sweet By and By'. An hour passed in five minutes and Hargrave tapped on his door and opened it.

'It's five,' he said. 'I thought I'd better remind you we're going over to the Williamses at seven.'

'I'll be with you in five minutes.'

'We're going to have a dip in the river first,' Hargrave said. 'We always do in the evening. I don't know if you feel like joining us. It's very refreshing.'

'I didn't bring a swimsuit.'

'We don't use them,' Hargrave said. 'Seems silly to bother in a place like this. Wear your underpants if you're shy. It's up to you.'

A stream came rattling down through a gorge, cut a loop in the rock halfway round the plateau on which the hacienda had been built, and then poured away over a ledge and out of sight on its turbulent way down to Los Remedios. At one point, just out of sight of the hacienda building it had scooped out a pool, graining and polishing the limestone with a curiously artificial effect.

'The Williamses have a magnificent swimming-pool they're always urging us to use,' Hargrave said. 'The only cooled pool in the country. Unfortunately they have the normal mission-ary attitude towards the human body, which is only to be expected.'

'I should have thought this was much more exciting in

every way,' Howel said. It was a setting arranged by a Japanese landscape artist with the national reverence for the grotesque, completed by an enormous bonzai tree, a fir of some kind, with silvery cones the size of fingernails, and naked roots that grappled for a hold in the porcelain rock among the water splashing down from a dozen concealed spouts.

The mood was one of strained and nervous jollity. 'I suppose you'd hardly call us hippies,' Hargrave had confided early in the day, 'but we've probably succeeded in freeing ourselves from the most tiresome of the unessentials. We had quite the makings of a community when Smalldon was here.'

He said something, following it with a loud but instantly exhausted titter, and began to tear off his clothes. Liz, solemn in the face of a sacramental moment, was releasing a surprisingly ample bosom from her brassière. A moment later she stood naked at Howel's side and Howel, glancing down and then away, noted the white sickle moons of the tiny scars left by the accidents of childhood in her brown body. A tomboy, he thought, and now a very beautiful girl. More so out of her clothes—which, by his experience, was a rare thing.

'Go on,' she said. 'Don't just stand there. Take your pants off.'

It was a sort of religious ceremony, like taking off your shoes and stockings to walk up the steps of a Buddhist temple. He unzipped his trousers, let them drop and kicked his legs free in an awkward manœuvre, complicated by a trouser leg turned inside out and trapped at the ankle. He had moved a little forward, and he heard her giggle behind him, and then the splash as she dived in.

Hargrave swam past with laboured grace, pulling himself along with an antiquated breast stroke that kept his red face well clear of the water, his arms and legs looked as thin as a starved child's. He made a dash at Liz as she passed with

38

a pretence of sexual horseplay, but she easily avoided him. Howel dived in, and the chill of the water made him catch his breath. Something flashed, and writhed away from him. 'Any piranhàs?' he called to the others. Liz called back, 'Only water-snakes.'

He circled the pool, climbed out, and pulled his trousers over his wet legs. Liz, crisp and dark among small exploding lights and flickering reflections, had left the water too, and moved to a ledge across the pool. He waved to her. 'I saw a water-snake.'

'They're quite harmless.'

A sharp-winged bird, black as a swift, dropped like an arrow at the end of its flight to snatch an insect from the water's surface. Liz began a few defiant callisthenics on her ledge, while Hargrave came prancing up with a display of sun-corroded skin and ill-balanced genitalia to wrap himself in a towel.

'Marvellous girl, isn't she?' Hargrave asked.

'Very decorative indeed.'

'Said anything to her about going off yet?'

'I mentioned it.'

'What did she say?'

'She wants to stay on here.'

'I was afraid of that. Pity.'

'Why do you say that?' Howel asked.

Hargrave glanced nervously in Liz's direction, and lowered his voice. 'Mustn't let her get the idea we're talking about her.'

He began to dress. 'You'll like the Williamses,' he said loudly, 'particularly Mary. She's a very sweet woman.'

'I'm sure I shall.'

'They live rather grandly by our standards. All their food's flown in. Only eat local fruit after proper disinfection.' He tittered. 'Indirectly even their pigs eat nothing but imported food.'

'I met one or two like them in Africa,' Howel said. 'They

39

gave me my first real idea of the wealth of the USA.'

'Mind you,' Hargrave said, 'Williams is the kind of man that will do anything for you. I happened to mention the other day that our new lawn hadn't stood up to the sun. It's not grass, of course. Little plants with broad leaves. Not a bad substitute. I might have known what would happen. He's going to fix up sprinklers and connect them up with his system.'

'You told me he supplied an air-conditioning plant, didn't you?'

'Well, that's all part of the letting arrangement. You wouldn't consider taking on a house here unless it was air-conditioned.'

'And our electricity supply comes off his generator?'

'It does. We couldn't afford to put in our own. They slap two hundred per cent import duty on most manufactured goods from abroad.'

'Excellent man as this Williams may be in every way, does it occur to you that we may be a trifle too dependent upon him? It isn't a criticism. I just wonder.' Before replying, Hargrave glanced across to the ledge where Liz, having completed all the rituals of the occasion, had dressed, and was now doing something to her hair. He spoke in a low tone but with unusual emphasis.

'We *are* dependent on him, and I'll explain why. This is missionary territory. They're a fact of local life. If I want to get anything done, I can't go to the General, but Williams can, so all I can do is to go to Williams. We have to face the facts. Missionaries run the interior of this country, and half a dozen other Latin American countries as well. Supposing some official wants to go to a distant village in the mountains, and there's no road—a policeman, a doctor—supposing *you* want to go? How do you think you get there? By the missionary's plane. I've been in countries where missionaries owned slices of territory as big as Belgium.

40

You don't have to go any farther than this country. Have you heard of the Putamayo business? They haven't finished investigating it yet. A book came out last year. Spanish Capucins grabbed half a province, millions of acres. That's why General Lopez is against the RCs. That's why he's backing the Nonconformists like Williams—and Williams, of course, is backing him. The General believes that the Catholics belong to the feudal past and Nonconformism is the religion of the modern capitalistic state.

'Fantastic,' Howel said. There was something in Hargrave's expression and his tone that made him wonder, does he or doesn't he approve of this state of affairs?

'Of course it's fantastic.'

'And how do they manage to get all this power into their hands?'

'Because,' Hargrave said, 'they're the cleverest and the most hard-working men in the country. I mean in any of these countries.'

'Would you say they were sincere in their motives?' Howel asked.

'Some of them . . . I suppose you'd say most,' he added grudgingly. 'On the other hand, you don't need to be a geologist to be a missionary. You follow me?'

'Not exactly.'

'They're first on the scene when any new area's opened up. It's useful for a mining company to have someone on the spot who can tell one mineral from another.'

'Now I see what you mean.'

'They're there. They'll always be there. They're one of the local facts of existence, whether or not we always see eye to eye with them. Is there any harm in occasionally making use of their extraordinary facilities for our own selfish ends?'

'I don't know,' Howel said. 'I'd like to think about that.'

4

SMALL Indian gardeners, remarkably hatted, were at work among the stiff flames of the canna in the flower borders. Sprinklers twirled their spray over the lawns where the dew grew into silver balls that eventually began to move and roll down the gentle slopes, and the warm scented air between them and the great house was full of refracted light and the prismatic colours of soapsud bubbles. They passed a row of macaws moving along their perches like winged reptiles dragging themselves warily from the primeval ooze. Grail Williams and his wife Mary awaited them at the top of the outside staircase, and the tour of the house began.

'Mary and I rise at three every morning,' Williams said. 'We've lived among Indians for quite a while now, and we find early rising the most commendable of their habits.'

Hargrave gave Howel a quick side-glance, with a smile that said, you see what I mean.

'Mary supervises the grinding of the maize and the bread-baking, while I do my best—not always successfully—to keep up with my correspondence. Mary has her surgery from five to seven, after which we breakfast, and I get down to my translation, while Mary attends to the children's education. We have a short break round about eleven for lunch. After that our Indians and the administration of the mission seem to keep us pretty well occupied in one way or another until we retire to bed—which we usually manage to do round about eight-thirty.'

Williams and his wife exchanged smiles and little personal signals of agreement. She was tiny, with the virtue meticulously drawn in her face by a pre-Raphaelite painter.

Her husband, strong-minded for the right, visionary, percipient and sincere, towered over her. He held a scroll of paper in his right hand, which was the plans for a new and improved latrine he had been showing them, and he might have been a Roman senator about to read an imperial edict. 'Time was,' he said, 'when we used to look forward to taking our annual vacation back in the States, but I guess it's a few years since that happened. We seem to have got ourselves kind of tangled up in the life here.'

'And every year,' Mary said, 'it becomes more rewarding.'

Williams showed them pigs that weighed more than the local donkeys; cows deprived of meadows, but which, fed on dried and compressed foods, still produced abundant milk; hens that laid an oversize egg daily through their lives. A baroque summer-house had been converted into a workshop where Williams made his own furniture, and back in the main building there was a projection room where he showed the films he produced himself. An elliptical chamber with extraordinary acoustics housed the latest Sony stereo system, and a wireless room was adorned with as many dials as the cockpit of an airliner. The kitchen was the showroom of vast and gleaming labour-saving machines; the shrine—it seemed to Howel—of an idealism, rather than a place where the preparation of food ever took place. 'We live as comfortably as we can,' Williams said, but it was a profession of faith rather than an admission of self-indulgence. 'I guess there's no point in wrestling with the environment. It uses up energy that could be put to creative use.'

The missionary swung along at their side with his athlete's springy, weightless walk. Viewing his achievements, Howel felt a twinge of inadequacy, almost shame. Perhaps this was the true man of the nuclear and space age who had returned to the many-faceted renaissance ideal; a new Michelangelo, a master of all the arts and sciences of our time.

Mary had gone off to do something about coffee and sand·

wiches while Williams spoke of his missionary work. First and foremost, he was a biblical translator, a member of an organization called Preachers and Testifiers Incorporated, who specialized in scriptural translation. He had been at work for two years, and he had finished the Gospel according to St Mark, and almost finished the Epistle to Timothy.

It could take up to ten years to translate as much of the New Testament as was essential in the opinion of his organization, to put across the basic message of Christianity. 'As none of these languages is written down, a phonetic alphabet had to be devised. After that comes what is perhaps the most difficult task of all, that of teaching the people to read.' Williams smacked his lips; a sound that should have expressed satisfaction but did not. 'It must be admitted that very few show any desire to learn.'

'You're still busy with the Cholos, I believe?' Hargrave said.

'And shall be for a long time to come. They are the major linguistic group in this part of the country. The technical problems are very considerable. So many concepts are missing from their language. They are unable to think, as we do, in abstract terms. There is a terrible linguistic poverty to be filled in as best we can. To give you an example, you can't say "God is Love", in Cholo, because they have no word for God, or for love. In so far as they can conceive of a divine principle at all, this is seen as an ancestor—a female one, as they are matriarchal. In the end our text comes out, 'The great-grandmother of us all is not angry." Take as another, "'The wicked man prospereth." The best we can do with this is "The breaker of taboo snares more deer." We spend months on end trying to make these people understand heaven and hell and the evil of lives given up to idolatry, and in the end we can never be sure they really do.'

The wide forehead was suddenly corrugated in a frown,

Williams was perplexed. It was an emotion that substituted in his case for anger.

'Liz was telling me about the Cholos today. She showed me some very beautiful embroidery they do,' Howel said.

'Would you describe it as beautiful? Mary and I find their symbolism rather repellent.' The frown of perplexity smoothed out and he smiled with pretended self-criticism. 'But perhaps we're prejudiced.'

'How many Cholos are there?' Howel asked.

'Possibly eight hundred,' Williams said. 'It's difficult to say in the case of these semi-nomadic tribes. I'm afraid they're dwindling fast.'

'And how many do you expect to teach to read?'

'It could be five per cent,' Williams said. 'If we're very lucky.'

'A total of forty?' Howel said.

'If there were as many as forty, Mary and I would be thankful. Very thankful indeed. We should feel that our labours had been richly rewarded. Many of our brother missionaries working in the jungles of the Amazon are faced with far harder tasks than ours. There have been cases where an attempt has been made to bring the Bible to tribes having as few as one hundred members, and in some instances, after many years of work, the missionary has seen all his efforts brought to nought by the tribe's dying out before his translation has been completed.'

On an impulse Howel said, 'Do you happen to have heard of the Guahibas of Planas?'

'Certainly,' Williams said, 'and they're a case in point. A brother missionary was working with them with great success. Most unfortunately oil was found on their reservation, and the inevitable happened.'

'What was that?' Howel asked, beginning to suspect that Williams, in this remote corner of the provinces, might be able to supply facts that had eluded him in the capital.

45

'They were pushed back into the forest,' Williams said. 'It always happens.'

'Where they presumably died of starvation,' Hargrave said.

'I would say so,' Williams said. 'A high proportion of them, anyway. They were also lost to the Lord's word. What I'm saying is that Winthrop Shapp, a very good friend of mine, lost five years of his labours translating the scriptures. He finished with St Mark the week before the settler invasion took place. It was a terrible tragedy.'

They were now back in the living-room, where they admired the wall cases filled with Williams's collections of geological specimens. Mary had reappeared with coffee and sandwiches in variety, and Hargrave, turning away, had slyly raised the corner of one he had taken to make sure that it contained no meat in any disguise.

'Speaking of the Cholos,' Williams bayed softly, 'we had a rather disturbing experience last week. A new convert told a captain that a guerrilla had visited their village shortly before he left it to come down to Los Remedios. I ought to explain that a captain is a convert who has earned promotion, in consequence of which he is given, well—let's say a shadow authority, and a few privileges.'

'Captains are always persons of mixed blood,' Mary said. 'Cholos don't understand competition, and they haven't any feeling for authority. In fact they're just children.'

'This is disturbing because it would seem to confirm a rumour that's been already going about that the guerrillas are turning their attention to the Indians. The man appeared in this village, ten thousand feet up in the Cordillera, gave presents of knives and beads to the elders, spent about a week there, and then went away. Colonel Arana, the chief of the local security police, believes he may have been spying out the lie of the land. The thing caused quite a stir here. We had the police down in the compound making

46

their enquiries for more than two days.'

'The unfortunate thing is they took the Indian back to the police headquarters with them,' Mary said. 'We haven't heard anything about him since. Did you remember to telephone Colonel Arana, dear?' she asked her husband.

'I did, but he was out. He was going to ring back.'

'It's had a most unsettling effect on our converts' Mary said. 'You see, they don't understand violence. We've done our best to encourage their love and trust, and to shelter them from—well—the harsh things in our civilization. I'm afraid that much of our work might be undone if the police were very rough with this boy.'

'Why should they be?' Williams said.

'I don't know, but one hears so many unpleasant rumours, in the end one begins to wonder whether there isn't something in them, I suppose.'

'There isn't,' Williams said. 'You can take my word for that.' He had been sipping a glass of water with obvious connoisseurship, head cocked a little to one side, eyes withdrawn. 'This has just gone through our new filtration system,' he had just said. Now he put down his glass with a gesture of emphasis in a way another man might have banged the table. 'No acts of violence are committed on the persons of any prisoners in Los Remedios. I can't speak for prisons that don't come under General Lopez's jurisdiction. Colonel Arana is directly responsible to the General, and I happen to know what his instructions are. The General happens to be a patriot and a reformer, and that's enough to guarantee him a steady supply of enemies. I don't think we should allow ourselves to become the victims of their propaganda.'

'No,' she said. 'We shouldn't. Of course I agree with you.'

'This is a poor province of a poor country,' Williams said, 'and General Lopez is pulling it up by its bootstraps. Foreign investments are urgently required and only firm government

47

can create the political climate in which such investments become possible. When I say firm government I do not mean tyranny. I happen to know General Lopez well enough to be able to tell you that that is impossible.'

Williams turned to Hargrave, moving his whole torso to do so with a kind of senatorial stiffness.

'Cedric, I'd like you to help me set Mary's fears at rest. What's your opinion of General Lopez?'

'My opinion of General Lopez is that we'd be better off with his deputy, Ramon Bravo.'

'Bravo is a Communist,' Williams said.

'No, he's not a Communist, he's a Liberal. Hardly that, even, since he got where he is. He's a man with two faces, not entirely trustworthy, perhaps. But he's not a typical strong man. Latin America has had enough of strong men.'

'I would say that that is precisely what General Lopez is not, either. I regard him as a teacher and a philosopher. As a young man he was destined for the church. You knew him well in those days, didn't you, Cedric?'

'I knew him later, soon after he went into the army.'

'Which he entered, he confided to me, only out of a sense of urgent patriotic duty,' Williams said. 'Would you agree that he was a patriot, Cedric?'

'According to his own lights.'

'An idealist, then?'

'I would have said he *was* an idealist.'

'That sounds like faint praise,' Williams said. 'I'm not getting the support I hoped for.'

Howel got the impression that this was a subject Hargrave would have preferred to avoid. He had sensed a reluctance on his part, even, to being present at his first meeting with the Williamses and an attempt had been made to get Liz to go in his place.

'But you don't believe these stories that are being put about?'

48

'Not all of them.'

'Not *all* of them. Well I should certainly think you didn't, Cedric. Tell us how you first met the General. Mary's never heard.'

Once again, Howel sensed Hargrave's reluctance.

'It's not a particularly pleasant story. I can't imagine Mary would be interested.'

'Of course she'd be interested. You're the only person we know who lived in the country during the bad times. In any case Mary's a doctor. She's not squeamish. I know Mr Howel would like to hear.'

'It was back in the first period of the violencia,' Hargrave said. 'The whole country had gone to pot. As you know, I was a mining engineer in those days. I was running a small gold mine up in Santander, and the Conservatives and Liberals were killing each other.'

'The country was divided into two warring factions,' Williams explained for Howel's benefit. 'Liberals and Conservatives. The Conservative party was the party of the landowners and the church. The Liberals were more or less the rest.'

'The army and the police supported the Conservatives,' Hargrave said. 'I suppose that goes without saying.'

'Does it?' Williams said. 'Why should it? Would the army and the police necessarily have supported one party and not the other?'

'Yes they would. Necessarily,' Hargrave said. There was a definition in his voice that Howel heard for the first time. He sounded like a man at home with his subject.

'You're suggesting to us that they acted in a very undemocratic manner, then,' Williams said.

'I don't know that democracy comes into it. These are the facts of life in Latin America. They always have been. The word democracy's never out of people's mouths in these countries. Especially politicians. But it means hardly anything. Just before the violencia started they held two elections in which only Conservatives were allowed to vote. People may have been a bit surprised, but nobody thought it fantastic.'

Williams's voice boomed softly, charged with the reverberations of quiet authority. 'I happen to have read the Constitution. Such a thing is completely ruled out.'

'Whether the Constitution ruled it out or not, it happened,' Hargrave said. 'When a man went to vote they stamped his identity card. That was the way you could always tell which side a man was on. If he'd voted, you knew he was a Conservative.'

'Did you feel any special sympathy for either of these political groups?' Mary asked Hargrave.

'Not the slightest. As far as I was concerned there was very little to choose between them. In any case I was a foreigner. Their quarrels had nothing to do with me. I was running this small gold mine at the village of Lagrimas, and the only thing that worried me was that the miners who worked for me who were Liberals started to disappear. It was a bad place for Liberals. The local priest was a very strong Conservative. He used to preach in his sermons that it was no crime in the eyes of God for a Conservative to kill a Liberal, and also that it was better for a girl from a Conservative family to go into a brothel than to marry a Liberal.'

'I don't recall this part of the story' Williams said. 'It shows up the Roman Catholic church in an extraordinary light.'

'But that wasn't what really worried the people. They took that kind of thing for granted. What they really hated about this priest was his bad manners—'

'Colombians are very polite,' Williams said to Howel.

'—his habit of riding his horse through their gardens. Taking a short cut through their flower-beds. They really hated that. He was the first man in the village the Liberals killed when they came back.'

'How terrible!' Mary said.

'It's an unpleasant story,' Hargrave said. 'Grail wanted you to hear all about Lopez's idealism and heroism, and I suppose this has to come into it.'

'You didn't tell me the Liberals murdered your priest,' Williams said.

'Didn't I? There was so much murder, in the end you forget who murdered whom. I should add the Liberals had a bit more to worry about than their flower-gardens. After five or six of them mysteriously disappeared to be seen no more, half a dozen of my miners took to the mountains. Then one day the police turned up and murdered their wives and children. Do you want me to go on?'

'Please do,' Williams said. 'I suppose it's no use closing our eyes to the fact that things like this did happen.'

'So there we were, carrying on much the same as before. We were foreigners. Nobody bothered us. We heard that things were pretty bad all round, but Lagrimas seemed to be quiet enough. The priest went on preaching hellfire and damnation for all Liberals, and riding his horse through the flower-beds. Then one day the Liberals came back, only now they were bandits. They'd been in the mountains a year, and their families had been butchered, but the strange thing was that on the surface they were as quiet and courteous as Colombians always are. Nothing in the slightest blood-thirsty in their manner. What I didn't realize then was that they'd been round to the priest on the way, and a machetero they had with them had cut him into four with two swipes of his machete. That was the first thing they did when they went to any village—kill the priest.'

'I suppose their sufferings had turned them into animals,' Mary said. 'Completely inhuman.'

'I wouldn't say that,' Hargrave said. 'The leader of the

51

band was a fine poet. They still sing his songs in the villages in Santander. He was most apologetic for the trouble he was giving me. All he wanted to do was to look at the identity cards of the men who stayed on to work in the mine to find out which ones voted Conservative at the famous elections. It turned out there were twelve. They were hacked to pieces on the spot. They left us to clean up the mess.'

'I don't think I want to hear any more,' Mary said.

'That's all there is to it,' Hargrave said, 'or practically all. Grail wanted you to know how I came to meet General Lopez in the days when he was a fiery and idealistic young captain. Lagrimas was cut off for a few weeks after that, and then Lopez crossed the mountains with a cavalry squadron and broke through to us.'

'And I believe you told me you saw a fair amount of him?' Williams said.

'Yes, I saw a fair amount of him.'

'You were impressed, weren't you?'

'Yes, I was impressed because he was not only brave but magnanimous. There were no firing squads in the village when Lopez was there. They came later.' Hargrave glanced in Mary's direction. 'I'll tell you some other time what they did to the bandit leader when they caught him.'

'But you believe he's changed? Lopez, I mean.'

'I believe he's changed. I believe the pressures of events have been too much for him.'

'I don't agree with you,' Williams said. 'Recently I've been brought into close contact with General Lopez. I can't tell you the nature of the business, because at this stage it's confidential, but my dealings with him have convinced me of his selflessness, and his dedication to his country's welfare. Also of his humanity.'

The telephone tinkled somewhere in the depths of the building.

'That may be Arana's office,' he said to Mary.

He was gone a long time, and in the end Mary went after him. He had just put down the receiver, and from a glance at his face she knew what had happened.

'Was it Arana?'

'Yes,' he said. Williams drew his wife aside and lowered his voice. 'A most unfortunate thing has occurred.'

'Don't tell me that boy's dead,' she said.

'I'm afraid he is,' Williams said. 'I can't think how it can possibly have happened. I feel very perturbed.'

5

' W E have news for you at last, General,' the engineer said. 'The helicopters requested are being unloaded at Buenaventura today. Two lovely helicopters.' He thrust out his stomach a little and smiled like a bank manager who would like to convince a customer that the loan he has arranged is a purely personal favour granted independently of the policy of the bank.

'I believe the crews are already here,' the engineer added.

Why does he say believe when he knows they are here? Lopez wondered.

'Two advisers are arriving by scheduled flight from Bogotà tomorrow. May I ask that they be considered tourists so far as your immigration people are concerned? No special treatment of any kind, please.' The engineer now sprang a mild joke. 'We had hoped to be able to spare more than two. Advisers, I mean. But it seems like there aren't enough to go round.' All three men laughed in a way that showed that they understood and fully shared each other's dislike for advisers.

The engineer inflated himself again, the tips of his fingers pressed together, beaming. 'In the end we managed to fix up a legitimate training exercise, with not only the approval but the full co-operation of your war ministry. For once the Embassy did a great job. Terrific. I understand we offered to submit precise information with map references of areas where overflights were planned, and nobody wanted to know about it.' He sipped his sherry again, grimacing inwardly at its wry medicinal taste. 'Things seem to have worked out kind of better than we expected.'

Out of sight under the inlaid ebony table that stood between them, the General was plucking delicately, like a harpist, at chords of air. 'How long will it be before the helicopters are ready to fly?'

'A few hours. They could be at the airfield here by early morning. That's if you didn't feel we might be sticking our necks out by bringing them here.'

'No,' said the General, 'I don't feel that we should be doing that at all.'

The surveyor now took over. He was an austere and less self-important sort of man than his colleague, and the General, who reacted badly to what he considered the engineer's attempts to fraternize with him much preferred him of the two.

'Our other news is less gratifying, General,' the surveyor said. 'The guerrilla band already mentioned is on the move. They plan to establish themselves in this province. Between here and the border.'

'Then the helicopters have come in the nick of time.'

'The arrival of the rural guerrillas may coincide with the uprising of urban guerrillas in this city.'

'All necessary measures will be taken,' General Lopez said. His rather thin, high-pitched, scholarly voice seemed incapable of harbouring menace. As a young seminary he had always been praised for his plainsong chanting.

'We learn that an emissary sent on in advance by the group has already established contact with the Indians.'

'At the village of Cayambo.' The General nodded, concealing the satisfaction he felt behind the benign mask of a connoisseur of homely things, a man absorbed in small, rewarding expertise.

'He presented each of the five elders of the tribe with a knife,' Lopez said, 'and gave most of the girls Woolworths' necklaces, of which he carried a large supply. After ingratiating himself in various ways he applied to be accepted as a member of the tribe and this was agreed. A blood-mingling ritual took place, and our friend was induced to take two of the tribal women as wives, although the actual ceremony was to be deferred to await a more auspicious phase of the moon. Sexual relations did, however, take place. This man is described as tall and fair and an excellent Cholo speaker. As always in these cases, the Indians were most impressed by his coloration. He went off after a week, but promised to return soon, bringing friends.'

'Why, that's fantastic, General,' the engineer said. 'How do you come to know all this?'

'We have our sources of information,' Lopez said. 'Primitive of necessity, because the country is primitive; but I think you would say that we have our ears to the ground.'

'Somebody's been doing an impressive intelligence job, General. A very fine job indeed. Were you able to ascertain whether any ideological approach was made?'

'There was, and it was a very direct one. Our friend didn't mince his words. His message was that the Indians' land had been taken from them by the Whites—which is of course true—and the time had come to fight to get it back. He and his friends would train them, and give them modern arms and help them to avenge themselves.'

'And would you say that this propaganda had any serious effect?'

'In a way,' the General said. 'The Indians are very pacific but they have had several bad harvests. They are short of food. This man was preaching to people with empty stomachs. I believe they were tempted. Four or five Indians from this one village agreed to join forces with them.'

'In that case we have a problem, General,' the surveyor said.

'A moral one,' Lopez said. 'A moral dilemma.' He sighed. 'There is no physical problem.'

Both his visitors were slightly embarrassed. They were accustomed to the use by politicians of the word moral in their public speeches alone. It was not part of the vocabulary of such informal meetings.

'I imagine you weren't able to learn anything about this party that's on its way?' the surveyor asked.

'Nothing whatever,' the General admitted.

'We may be able to fill in a few shadowy details. Little of importance though. We expect twelve of them to cross the frontier. Our informant will be with them. They all majored at one of your universities, and they seem to have taken courses in Indian studies. I was forgetting there's one exception. A Brazilian. He sounds pretty close to illiterate.'

'A Brazilian,' Lopez said. 'Why a Brazilian?'

'He's a sharpshooter. A kid who won some sort of shooting prize, and got taken up. We haven't been able to find out what this kid is doing with the band. Our informant doesn't know why he's been included. All he can tell us is that the Brazilian will only be staying a few days, and then he's leaving them and moving on. Only the leader knows what this guy's doing with them, and what his function is. A kid who won a shooting prize somewhere—maybe Recife. They went a long way to find him, and he's got an important job to do. We'd feel happier if we knew what it was.'

'Whatever the mission, it makes very little difference,' Lopez said. 'We are arranging a warm welcome. In a few days these young men will all be in prison or dead.'

'Glad you're so confident, General.'

'I am confident. Twelve men against a whole country is not enough.'

'And not only against a country. Against the free world.'

'Yes, I was forgetting for a moment the helicopters. Against the free world.'

He sighed again, privately. 'It is a pity. The brave are very few.'

6

'L I z wants to do some emergency shopping,' Hargrave said. 'Do you think you could possibly run her down to town.'

'Emergency shopping?'

'A state of alarm has been declared,' Hargrave said. 'If there's any shooting the shops will close. I'm stuck here because it's the first of the month and the Ministry of the Interior fellow calls for his bottle of whisky. There should be mail for us, and I'd like Liz to go to the bank. Remember to buy some tea if you can.' He seemed to Howel to be pleasurably excited. 'They may bring out tanks and fire a few rounds,' he said. 'If there's any excitement you can usually get a marvellous view from the cathedral tower.' Hargrave clearly saw the occasion as a speciality of the country, a spectacle to be recommended, like a Morris dance to a visitor to rural England.

'At any other time,' Hargrave said, 'I would have asked Williams for the loan of his car. Not the one with Seguridad Militar plate—he's not allowed to lend that. I mean the saloon. It might have helped slightly at the road blocks. As it is I don't feel I can. There's been a very slight cooling in the atmosphere since the other night. I may not have shown my usual tact. Williams is a very great buddy of the General's.'

The road blocks turned out to be all that Hargrave had feared, and there were several long waits while cars ahead of them were subjected to lengthy searches. Liz seemed to be in high spirits. She chatted on endlessly.

'What time do your shops shut?' Howel asked.

'At one.'

'We aren't going to make it.'

'We've got all the afternoon,' she said. 'They open again at four-thirty. It's only the bank and the post-office that really matter. The other was an excuse to get away.'

'I can't understand you.'

'You mean not wanting to get out of Dos Santos whenever I can? Wait till you've been here a bit longer. We're absolutely shut in in that place. People from our village used to go and raid the other villages all round at the time of the troubles, so nobody likes us. And that applies to the foreigners, too. They have a dance place at Milagros. It's great fun, but nobody from our village can go.'

'What I mean is I don't understand why you don't go somewhere else altogether,' Howel said. 'If you don't like the place there's nothing to stop you getting out.'

'It doesn't happen to be convenient,' she said. 'I'll go when I'm ready. Life at Dos Santos isn't a bed of roses, but I don't suppose it would be much better anywhere else. I just keep on the move as much as I can. Make excuses to go shopping. Go round the country in buses. Homer King takes me about quite a bit.'

'Who's he?'

'Grail Williams's assistant. He collects butterflies. It's a chance to get out.'

They had been held up at the second road block, and now the monkey-faced soldier with the tommy-gun waved them on. A mile ahead there were more cars pulled in by the roadside. He accelerated to 55 mph in the old Citroën *Deux-Chevaux*, and began to slow again.

'Cedric gets terribly bored, too. He goes in for prostitutes. I'm not telling tales out of school. We talk about these things endlessly. He says it's therapeutic. A way of using up the time. Nothing whatever to do with lust. He says that Colombian ones are the most civilized in the world. Any taxi-driver in the Plaza will find you one. They have a sliding scale of charges based on age and colour. You can get a black girl in her late twenties for a dollar plus the taxi fare, but you have to pay the earth for a white girl of fourteen. Some of the older ones are married women making a bit on the side. They're all very well brought up and rather prim. Cedric shocked one of them very much by showing her an illustrated *Kama Sutra*. Asked to be sent home immediately . . . Here we go again.'

A soldier who might have been the identical twin of the last waved them in behind the queue of cars, where a mist of laterite dust squeezing through the closed windows settled in an ochreous bloom on their skin.

'We're absolutely frank about all our doings and our emotions,' Liz said. 'Ronnie Smalldon was very interested in things like self-realization and mystical unity. Cedric, too. That goes without saying. We used to sit for hours on end feeling each other's vibrations when he was here. I suppose it made a change.'

Now in the distance Los Remedios showed across the plain, spilling its outskirts into a pink mirage. A party of engineers were bringing a power line to a battery of search-lights on a truck, and a saw howled in the distance where the forest was being trimmed back. An officer came to study their passports and to check the papers of the car. He had a young face, blunted with self-indulgence, and wore white cotton gloves.

'Did Cedric say anything?' she suddenly asked.

'About what?'

'About my going down to Los Remedios today.'

'No more than what had to be done when we get there. Why?'

'Oh nothing. I got the idea he might be getting allergic to my frequent shopping trips, that's all.'

'He didn't say anything about it.'

The officer was pretending to compare Liz with her passport photograph. His eye was bright and heavily-lidded like a lizard's and there was a repertoire of obscene suggestion in his smile. With evident reluctance he pushed the passport back at her and waved them on.

'Charles didn't by any chance tell you why Ronnie went back?'

'He went back because S U C C O U R couldn't afford to keep him on here any more.'

'Well, that's a comfort, I thought it was over me. I believe I must have given him quite a headache. I happen to know that Ronnie wrote asking him to have me recalled to London. He actually went to the Colombian authorities, too. I was supposed to be having an affair with somebody he didn't approve of. A Colombian. If it hadn't been for Grail Williams I might have been thrown out of the country.'

'The indispensable Grail Williams,' Howel said.

'The indispensable Grail Williams. We don't seem to be able to do much without him. There was a terrible rumpus. Ronnie made the most absurd allegations. It was easy enough to prove there was nothing in it, but you know how suspicious these people can be.'

'This man Smalldon,' Howel said. 'I can't understand him. What right had he to interfere in your affairs?' Of Smalldon he could only remember minor things; a quick, strutting walk, a lisp, a habit of clicking his tongue and rolling his eyes in feigned exasperation. A theatrical face took on flesh in his memory, and was animated by an impudent expression. A man he had not liked, and now he thoroughly detested.

'He wanted to take my life over,' Liz said. 'Never stopped spying on me. He was some sort of queer. Thank God, he's gone. I think Charles paid a lot of attention to what he said.'

'I wouldn't say that,' Howel said. 'Charles is no fool. He wouldn't let Smalldon pull the wool over his eyes.'

They had turned off at a barricade thrown across the

road, followed the arrows of a diversion and were coming into the town by a route that Howel didn't know. The ivory of the street was carved into endless recessions of arches, and inscribed with mutilated Latin : VARIEDADES, NOVEDADES, EXCURSIONES, ENTRADA, SALIDA, NO ESTACIONAR. Men with rifles on their backs, standing in tight pools of their own shadow, were posting enormous bills on which Howel could read only the word BANDO.

The drove into the plaza as the big hand on the cathedral clock jerked up to five to one, and the shops were already putting up their shutters. 'For all Cedric's talk of tanks, I can't believe anything's going to happen,' Howel said.

'We may as well park the car, and go and have lunch.'

'Somewhere where they serve real food, if possible,' he said, 'by way of a change from Cedric's salads.'

'It doesn't exist,' she said. 'Unless you don't mind an attack of dysentery, it has to be the Hotel Central. It's about as glamorous as Liverpool Street Station.'

The Hotel Central was the ghost of a colonial palace, paunchy and baroque, that breathed out an odour of stale cooking-pots and mouldering furniture. They sat for a while among a verandah full of silent and melancholic men, deep in wicker chairs, who occasionally spat into incredibly burnished spittoons. Domes and cupolas soared from a visible corner of the plaza into a sky gone leaden with heat. Long-legged cats with puny faces, their stomachs hanging like small grey purses from their spines had begun to tread cautiously through the chairs on their way to the dining-room. A female voice complained nasally in English of having been turned back by the military on a hunting trip to the mountains. 'I shall simply demand a refund. If they expect revolutions, then they should never take people's money.'

They went in to lunch.

'I'm going to have a steak,' Liz said, 'with all the trimmings.

I'm suffering from protein deficiency.'

'What would Cedric say?'

'To hell with Cedric. I'll have it rare with sauce Bordelaise.'

He ordered two steaks, which when they came were tough and threaded through with bluish veins. Globules of oil flecked with raw blood floated among the sauce. They made faces at each other. 'There are a lot of mules in this town,' Howel said.

They both laughed.

Apart from the complaining tourist, Liz was the only woman in the restaurant. The men had trooped in from the verandah in heavy silence, and gone to work in stoic gloom on the food piled on their plates. The skeleton of a cat with the face of a tiny, angry panther had attached itself to their table. General Lopez looked down from a portrait decorated with rusted palms. His hand rested on the head of a child who had just presented him with a bouquet of daisies, and paternal love flowed out from him to the four corners of the room.

A poster of the kind they had seen being put up in the street had been fixed to the wall behind them.

BANDO

DON ALBERTO CERVERA LOPEZ Y BALSEYÁN
CONTRALMIRANTE DE LA ARMADA
GOBERNADOR JEFE DE LA SECCIÓN MILITAR DE
LOS REMEDIOS . . .

'Did you know he was an admiral too?' Liz asked. 'He says by these presents he's assumed authority to search homes without warrants, seize property of prisoners, suspend Habeas Corpus, employ secret accusations, curtail freedom to enter or leave the province, prohibit meetings, and suspend the freedom of speech, and the press. The usual thing.'

Two young men with clearly razored haircuts and exceptionally neat, dark suits, padded past them on rubber-soled shoes on their way to the door. Each carried a camera in a case, slung over his right shoulder. They walked in step.

'American soldiers in civilian clothes,' Liz whispered. 'You can always tell them because they're trying to look inconspicuous. They should make them wear flowered shirts and baseball caps, and then no one would notice.'

A cracked bell somewhere struck twice with a flat and hopeless sound, and—as if in response to a signal—the city noises began to flag and die away.

'Any plans until four-thirty?' Howel asked.

'Yes,' she said. 'As a matter of fact I'm meeting a friend.' She glanced mechanically at her watch. 'I'll have to go in a moment in case I can't find a taxi.'

Her abnormal and quite unconvincing matter-of-factness told him everything, and the shock he felt took him by surprise. A structure of facile assumptions built on the frontier of the subconscious collapsed. Secret conversations he had had with himself were suddenly shown as based on self-deception. He felt humiliation and something close to self-disgust. The gay mood of the morning was explained. She had not been drawn to him. She was not gay in his company. She was going to a lover. This, he thought, must be the affair that Smalldon had got himself mixed up in.

There was a crumb of compunction for him. 'Look, I'm terribly sorry to have to leave you on your own. What will you do with yourself?'

Why couldn't she have made some mention of this earlier? he asked himself. 'It's all right,' he said. 'I'll probably go for a walk. See the sights.'

'It's utterly dead till the shops open again,' she said. 'Even when there is a revolution, they all knock off for the siesta.'

'Don't worry about me,' he said. 'I'll enjoy myself just strolling round. Everything's still new. I can always go and sit in a bar.' With a great effort he had corrected the flatness of his voice.

She got up quickly, and with a suggestion of relief.

'See you back here at about five, then.'

As she went through the door into the street he saw her break into a skipping run.

Suddenly, with the Hotel Central's string quartet whining to the last bar of 'Tales from the Vienna Woods', the death-rattle of the last overheated taxi-engine switched off in the Plaza, the last tattered persiana clapped over its black square of window, the city changed. Stripped of its human furniture, denuded almost of sound and movement, it displayed the many faces of its secret personality, its slyness, its arrogance, but above all an obsidian indifference.

Howel walked on through the thinly-sliced shade and the scalding sunshine, past the lepers crammed into the holes and corners under the great battlemented banks, past the Palace of the Captains General, garnished with silence and ostentation, past the martyrdoms in stone decorating the Cathedral's façade, carved so lovingly from the gallows-models of its day. The small side-door of the Cathedral was open to release its catacomb-whiff. He went in, and wandered aimlessly past chapel and shrine, glancing with slight interest at the tiered silver altars, the candelabras, the chalices and the grimed religious pictures with which they were stocked.

Behind the great carved mass of a pulpit he came un-expectedly on a group of three figures, and was able in the sallow twilight to recognize the two Americans from the Hotel Central, who were with a priest. Howel heard them ask his permission to take flashlight photographs, and the priest—speaking the usual excellent English—assure them that there was no objection. As Howel passed the priest looked up, and their eyes met.

He went on. There was little to see for his personal taste, but a repetition of tawdry treasure, insipid images and oppressive pictures. He was just about to leave when he heard a quick shuffle of footsteps over the flagstones behind him, and turned as the priest came up. Through the light from the door he appeared as shapeless and untidy, with a white stubble on his cheeks and chin, showing through a bad skin condition that might have been eczema. He smiled to show decaying teeth, and Howel noted the detail that one sleeve of his cassock was badly frayed.

'Mr Howel, isn't it?' the priest said. 'I'm Father Alberto. I was hoping you would come.' He held out a hand.

'I happened to see you in your car the other day with Mr Hargrave. I hope you've brought good news. Were your superiors able to reach any decision about my letter?'

'I'm afraid I haven't been told about any letter,' Howel said. He was not in the slightest surprised at the encounter. It was normal in any of the areas where S U C C O U R operated, for the local church to approach its members with charitable schemes.

'I wrote a letter to Sir Charles,' Father Alberto said. 'Mr Hargrave was kind enough to offer to forward it to London.' He smiled again, and Howel realized that this was a face that could have been transfigured by the replacement of two front teeth. 'One is never quite sure what is going to happen to the mail these days.' He hesitated. 'Mr Hargrave told me you were expected, and I hoped that you might have been bringing me the reply in person.'

The two Americans had almost come up with them, talking in reverent murmurs. They stopped to inspect an exceptionally ugly tomb. The cameras flashed, and they moved on.

'When was the letter sent?' Howel asked.

'It could have been two weeks ago.'

'It's possible that Sir Charles wasn't able to deal with it in time,' Howel said. 'He had an attack of influenza that kept him in bed for about a week before I left.'

'In that case I must go on in hope that an answer will come. It is a pity. The thing I wrote about is very urgent, but it cannot be helped.'

Howel was accustomed in his judgment of people to rely very much on first impressions. This was a face he liked. He wanted to help Father Alberto.

'Perhaps you could give me some idea of the contents of your letter, if it's not confidential. I expect to be writing to Sir Charles in the next day or so.'

'I think we should go to my office,' Father Alberto said. 'Even in cathedrals, walls have ears.'

Father Alberto's office was at the end of a tunnel-like passage that appeared to have been cut into the living rock at the back of the cathedral, and the untidiness of the man had spread like a contagion that had littered the bare room with books and covered the floor with a frothing disorder of papers. Father Alberto swept piles of vestments from the seats of two chairs, and they sat down.

'The people of this country,' he said, 'as I wrote in my letter, are the victims of terrible injustices, and somehow world opinion must know what is going on. I wrote to Sir Charles imploring his help to publicize the outrages we are suffering from.'

Howel listened patiently, preparing his sympathy, knowing there was nothing whatever to be done. It was an almost routine experience. SUCCOUR operated in poor countries; usually countries that suffered from weak or corrupt government, and it was hard to make people understand the crippling limitations under which they worked.

Father Alberto was describing the horrors of Latin American fascism and Howel interrupted him. 'I'm sorry to say there's nothing SUCCOUR can do to help. The organization is limited to purely charitable activities, and cannot interest itself in politics. Many of the countries where it's represented suffer from unjust government but beyond extending material aid there has to be a hard and fast rule not to interfere in any way at all.'

'And even the publication of details of the outrages against the human conscience which are being committed every day, would count as interference?'

'It very definitely would. Primarily s u c c o u r is concerned with natural disasters. Earthquakes, for example.'

'The acts of God, not those of man, in fact.' The bewilderment showed in Father Alberto's face. It was impossible, Howel thought, to make them understand. How could he make Father Alberto see that however eloquent his pleading it was bound to fall on deaf ears, and that human feeling in the case of such organizations as s u c c o u r was not a matter of spontaneous response to anguish, but of a decision taken in committee? 'The organization is bound to ignore causes,' he said. 'It's concerned only with effects.' He would have liked to explain why it was that a man who allowed himself to be driven by pity into breaking the rules was not humane, but inefficient.

Father Alberto, stubbornly refusing to accept defeat, was describing the plight of certain Indians.

'In the first place the government was a party to the sale of all their fertile land to foreign capitalists, and they were driven into the mountains. Minerals were found on the land where they were resettled. Oil, too, I believe. Professional killers were used to drive them out, and when they attempted to defend themselves the army attacked them.'

It was the thing that happened to Indians wherever they were in these days . . . almost a natural process. In the accounts Howel had read, only the details varied. 'I ought to explain before we go any further,' he said, 'that at the moment I'm only indirectly involved with s u c c o u r. I'd still like you to tell me all you know about this case. There are people who are trying to do something.'

68

'Some tribes have gone altogether,' Padre Alberto said. 'It is too late to do anything to help, so it is better to forget about them. In this area only the Cholos are left. The planters took their best land for coffee, and now the timber concessionaires are claiming the forest. They mark out an area on the map, and any Indian seen in it is shot on sight. All the game is being exterminated by machine-guns. Is there nothing S U C C O U R can do?'

'S U C C O U R can't interfere,' Howel said.

'Well then, let us close our eyes to these injustices. Let us pretend they do not exist. We are faced with starving people . . . a small disaster. Can't we treat these people as if they were victims of an earthquake? Can't we bring them immediate food—some cast-off clothing, perhaps? Blankets? Could not S U C C O U R carry out this work of mercy without condemnation of those who are responsible? A half ton of maize could save a single village. Cayambo, for example. It would keep the people alive until they can harvest their own crops. All we have to do is to call this a natural disaster.'

Howel had put his notebook away, and was thinking. 'How could we get the maize to them? If it could be done.'

'By plane,' Father Alberto said. 'An hour's flight. Hundreds of lives would be saved.'

'S U C C O U R might be able to do something,' Howel said, 'but I'm not sure. I can't hold out any hopes at this stage, but I'll put it to Mr Hargrave when I get back, and see if he thinks there's anything to be done.'

Beyond the citadel of palaces and banks the city was full of fairground colours and tropical fantasy. Howel, carrying the sun on his shoulders like a burden, walked on for five minutes after leaving the Cathedral, and then found a bar containing three men asleep and a hen roosting among the unwashed glasses on the counter. The proprietor slipped

69

into sight in his pyjamas, served him, then plunged back into the utter night of the room behind the bar. Howel carried his beer to a window table.

This part of the town, someone had mentioned, was a suburb added in the 'nineties by an eccentric multi-millionaire who believed that mankind had its psychological roots in the sea, and could never be entirely happy deprived of a maritime background. The architects called in had been force-fed on postcard views of Venice, and in one way or another, by the use of woodwork painted in strong ocean blues, pointed windows and arches, by actually supporting buildings on piles, and by adding a campanile here and there, a vaguely Adriatic feeling had been achieved. This strikingly contrasted with the Moorish architectural inheritance of the surrounding areas.

The only human figures to be seen were soldiers, and had it been possible to overlook their crumpled, ill-fitting uniforms, these, too, with their pirates' faces from children's adventure books, their hooked noses, lantern jaws—in one even a black eye-patch—could have been said to have picked up something of the sea's desperation and corroding boredom.

The street was on two levels with a flight of steps in the manner of a quayside from the higher level to the lower. Twenty-one soldiers sat on these steps, not in rows, but one below the other, scanning the empty seas, their faces chiselled with the ancestral indifference that in such men of mixed blood substitutes for the white man's boredom.

This was a detachment of the governor's private army of released criminals. Their mules were hitched along the wall on the lower street level, where their arms were stacked against the wall. Howel sensed that they were evil men. 'Born in sin', the phrase came to him. Men conscripted to defend and perpetuate the evils of an evil town. What a ghastly hole, he thought. Give me Europe—England, France, Italy—and you can have the rest of the world. Watching them idly, he sipped his beer until it turned warm. Behind him the customers snored softly, their heads on the table, and in the street, nothing moved. At four-thirty Howel decided to stroll back to the hotel. The town yawned and stretched. Someone woke up in the bar to put the jukebox on. The hen fluttered down from the counter, and across the road harness jingled as the soldiers mounted their mules and began to ride away.

Liz had said five, but he hoped she might be there earlier. Suddenly he was lonely. It was a recurrent sickness that he suffered from; something that lurked like malaria in the blood and was irrational and unpredictable in its attacks— a mysterious thing he ascribed to some forgotten childhood calamity, an anxiety, a craving—a sort of purpose-defeating nausea.

Liz was not at the hotel when he arrived, nor did she appear at five o'clock. By five-thirty the feeling of isolation that no amount of rational argument with himself could disperse, had increased. Until then he had been alone in the lobby, but now the wicker chairs began to fill with men exhausted from their siesta who scratched at their flies, yawned and spat, under the slowly revolving fans. A faint growl came in from the city, awakened from its sleep.

He forced himself to wait until six, and then went to the reception.

'What time do the banks close here?'

'Usually at seven, but this afternoon they are closed.'

'And the post-office?'

'All the public offices.'

'How's that?'

'There is a state of emergency.'

'And what does that mean?'

'This is more important than the state of alarm. There is a curfew. No one must circulate in the streets after dark.'

'I'm meeting a friend who should have arrived an hour ago.'

The reception clerk nodded with terrible complacency.

'I think that everyone may be late. The taxis do not function any more today.'

'Can I phone Dos Santos?'

The man picked up his telephone, put the receiver to his ear, and replaced it, shaking his head. His face was stamped with the distinction of the occasion. 'The telephone does not function. Soon nothing will function, the light also, and then the kitchen.'

Going back to his chair, Howel heard what he first thought was a distant car backfire. It was followed by two more, and then by what was unmistakably the rattle of an automatic weapon.

Immediately, in complete silence, and without signs of surprise or emotion of any kind, all the guests seated by the windows got up, carried their chairs to the centre of the lobby and sat down again. The shots had dignified everyone present. Faces were cleansed of some of their pettiness. Gestures became more composed. Slouchers threw back their shoulders. The porter passed him unhurriedly on his way to the door, which he shut and bolted. The guests, having settled, were reading newspapers again, or sipping their coffee. No one spoke.

The reception clerk came towards him, moving like a man at the head of a procession.

'Sir, is your car parked in the street outside?'

'It is.'

'Will you please to put it in the garage of the hotel?'

'Why?'

'This is the order of the police in a state of emergency. Cars must be placed under cover and in security.'

'I have to go back to Dos Santos at any moment.'

'I'm afraid that is not possible, sir. In a state of emergency cars must not circulate. The porter will show you where the garage is.'

The porter was waiting at the door and Howel drove the Citroën into the garage under the hotel, and they walked back to the hotel entrance together. Evening had filled the street with soft parched colours, and the sunshine slid up the walls in contracting geometrical shapes towards the tops of the buildings. Cats scuffled inside the dustbins put outside the shuttered shops. A huge, mangy dog passed them, galloping like a horse. Rockets were popping somewhere.

Back in the hotel the lights came on, glowing cautiously for five minutes and then with a final blaze-up, went out again. The porter strolled across to the lift and hung a notice on the gate, NO FUNCIONA. The boys came with a trayful of candles, and began, giggling softly, to place them strategically round the lobby. Howel drank whisky without pleasure, as a medicine for his nausea.

Just after seven, when it was not quite dark outside and all the candles were alight, there was a loud knocking at the door, and Liz was let in. She was breathless, brightly casual, and—Howel suspected—on the edge of hysteria.

They went to the bar, and she dropped into a chair. 'You can keep this country. Buy me a drink.'

She turned her cheek to be kissed. 'I've had a terrible day. Make it a double.'

'I suppose you were caught up in the revolution,' he said. 'I was scared stiff.'

'I was,' she said. 'I spent the whole of the afternoon hanging about waiting for this friend of mine, and he didn't turn up. You can't go into a bar or anything like that if you're a woman by yourself, so I had to sit around in a wretched park with all the beggars within miles pestering me. In the end I got fed up with it, and just as I started to come back to the hotel I heard the shooting start.'

73

She emptied her glass and Howel crooked his finger at the barman.

'There was a lot of it,' she said.

'There was a fair amount round here, too.'

'I was cut off in the university district,' she said. 'I knew it was useless trying to cut through, so I tried to work my way round the town, and then I managed to get lost, and in the end I ran into the fighting anyway.'

'Fighting?'

'Well, not actually fighting because it was all one-sided. Lopez's private army was attacking a house. They were just shooting volley after volley into it, and then they threw hand-grenades through the windows and it caught fire.'

'And what were you doing in the meanwhile?'

'Lying down in the street like everybody else. That's what you do when the shooting starts and you're caught out of doors. You lie down. The first time it happens to you, you feel a bit undignified, but you soon get over that. One poor man got hit anyway. They must have shot him for the fun of it. It was revolting.'

A group of darkly dressed men had wandered in absolute silence into the bar, like mourners at the tail-end of a funeral procession—joyless, but not necessarily committed to grief.

'It looks as though you're condemned to me for the next few hours,' she said.

'I was hoping for that anyway. I'd been trying to work out something we could have done tonight.'

'In what way?' she said.

'A restaurant with typical music or something like that.'

'That would have been nice,' she said, 'I would have enjoyed that. What a pity it has to be this dim little hotel full of commercial travellers instead. Do you mind?'

'Of course I don't.'

'Neither do I. We've had a lot of practice at Dos Santos

at whiling away long evenings. We could play one of Cedric's self-games—for example the one where you're absolutely frank with the person you're with, and cut out all the polite and meaningless preliminaries. This used to be a great favourite with Ronnie Smalldon, but it can have two disadvantages. The first is that people find out things about you that you might not otherwise feel like telling them, and then they're unfair about it, just as Ronnie was with me. The second thing is that you can't play it more than two or three times, because you get to know all there is to know about anybody— and where do you go from there?'

'I can quite see that.'

'Do you want to play, then?'

'All right. You go first.'

'Here goes then,' she said. 'How about this to break the ice? I took quite a strong dislike to you when we first met.'

'And you didn't trouble to conceal it,' he said.

'I never do,' she said. 'If I like someone I like them, and if I don't, I don't. No half-measures. I'm not a bit diplomatic. You are, aren't you?'

'I'm cowardly.'

'The trouble is my first judgments are so often wrong. They were in your case.'

'You suspected me of being Charles's spy, didn't you?'

'I still do. No, it wasn't that. I think it was because I was so sure you knew more about me than I did about you. I felt at a disadvantage. Do you realize that you have a rather disconcerting way of smiling at people?'

'I wouldn't do it if I did,' Howel said.

'A very slight, knowing smile,' she said. 'I know all about you, it says. It made me furious.'

'Thanks for telling me. I'll be on the look-out from now on.'

'But for all that I found you physically attractive. My type. Funny, isn't it?'

75

'What is?'

'It's funny that I should resent your knowing a good deal more than most people do about my private life—'

'Which I don't for one single moment admit,' he said.

'And yet I'm quite prepared to play a game with you in which I'll tell you anything you ask me. Almost anything, let's say. Anyway, I've got over my original dislike. I quite like you now.'

He laughed. 'That's a relief,' he said.

An armoured car rumbled down the street. Distracted for a moment, Howel followed the sound and suddenly a search-light swung at him, a hard shaft of light that filled the room with alabaster faces set with tin eyes. He blinked and darkness fell again, stamped with a constellation of violet lights, and behind them, the small pale flames of the candles. 'Your turn now,' Liz said.

'Go on, then.'

'You can make a start by telling me what you thought of *me* when you first met me. No holds barred.'

'We first met at a party at Sloane Square,' he said.

'Did we? Of course we did. I remember now. I remember talking to you. Actually I was quite sure we'd run into each other before, but I couldn't remember when and where.'

'It was a brief encounter,' he said. 'You spent most of the time with some male who was very much in charge.'

'What was he like?'

'He was pompous and self-assertive. Good-looking, with a loud voice. Had a habit of throwing out his chest like a pigeon. Kept on patting your bottom. You couldn't take your eyes off him. I remember wondering, why can't they wait until they go to bed.'

'That would have been Tony Llewellyn,' she said.

'In the end he went off to be sick, I imagine, and I got you on your own for a minute or two. You were leaving for the Congo, and he was planning to follow you if he could.'

'He did,' she said, 'but he only stayed a couple of weeks. We got terribly bored with each other.'

'Nobody would have said you were bored at the party,' Howel said.

'We all change. Anyway, you haven't answered my question. What did you think of me?'

'I thought you were a neurotic. I knew that you wouldn't stay with Llewellyn long, and I was trying to think of some way of getting you away from him.'

'But you didn't try to do anything about it.'

'There wasn't time. You were leaving the next week.'

'Can I have another whisky?' she said. 'What made you think I was a neurotic?'

'Instinct,' he said. 'I can pick out a neurotic anywhere, however calm they may look.'

'Because you're one yourself.'

'Inevitably,' he said.

'Had you heard I was easy game?' she asked.

'Probably,' he said.

'You mean you had. And this was part of the attraction?'

'It could have been.'

'You're not sticking to the rules of the game.'

'Sorry,' he said.

'You don't like having to fight for it.'

'Who does?'

'A lot of people,' she said. 'You'd be surprised.'

'And much as I'd like to avoid the fight, I don't,' he said. 'It goes on all the time.'

'You're very mixed up, aren't you?' she said. 'What are you afraid of?'

'Isolation,' he said, 'loneliness, abandonment. I can't put it into words, but I spend half my life running about trying to protect myself from it.'

'Just as you are now.'

'Just as I am now. And in doing so I get myself into impossible situations. As I did in your case.'

'It wasn't a situation.'

'I'd have made it one, given half the chance. I knew you were out of reach, so I wanted you. And I'm not only a glutton for punishment but I specialize in self-deception. For example, when Charles asked me to come out here I agreed—or so I believed—to do him a favour. In reality I probably fell in with the idea because you were here. But I didn't admit it to myself.'

'You do thrive on complications, don't you?'

'I don't thrive on them, but I seem to attract them. I'm a sort of unconscious addict. And now we're on the subject of complications, you may as well tell me why you won't leave this place?'

'Why should I?' she said. 'I've got myself in difficulties with a local boy. Didn't you guess?'

Howel groped for his glass and emptied it, and the barman reached forward with the bottle, refilling it in a stealthily conspiratorial way.

'I should have,' he said. 'I suppose I did.' He smiled stiffly to disperse the ugliness in his face of a disappointment now irremediably confirmed.

'This was the one I quarrelled with Ronnie Smalldon about. Sorry I lied to you. I went to see him today, and as I told you, he didn't turn up. This could be for one of two reasons. Either he's changed his mind about me—which is very possible—or he's in trouble. In either case it's bad.'

'Tell me more about him,' Howel said, bracing himself with a kind of perverted enthusiasm to confront the difficulties that lay ahead.

'Did you say you were a collector of impossible situations? Wait till you hear about this. By way of a start he's not quite ten years younger than me, with a stuffy, upper-class Latin American background. We're tremendously unsuited to each other. His people much resent my being on the scene. In this country there are honest women and whores, and I'm a whore. He wouldn't dream of asking me to go to a hotel with him, so we usually sit and hold hands in the park.'

'Usually,' he said.

'Most of the time,' she said. 'In other words, not much love-making goes on.'

'What attracts you to him?'

'He's young and beautiful,' she said. 'Very beautiful.'

'That all?'

'And he's a poet. I've never known a poet before. You're not a poet, are you?'

'No,' he said, feeling himself utterly defeated before the fight had begun, 'I'm not a poet.'

'But it won't last long,' she said. 'It has to come to an end. I suspect I'm more involved than he is. In fact I'm quite sure of it. The moment may have come.'

Howel felt that he should offer some comfort, and he did so with reluctance.

'He's probably got caught up in the state of emergency,' he said. 'Perhaps he was out in a car, or something like that, and couldn't get back.'

'I don't believe it,' she said. 'I've been trying to convince myself that something like that happened, but now I've stopped. I know they've all been at him to give me up, and he's simply given in. I wish he'd had the courage to come and tell me himself, that's all.'

Seeing the tears in her eyes, he put his arm round her, and the sad men over their thimblefuls of coffee swivelled their heads to watch for a moment, and then turned away.

'The only other possibility,' she said, 'is that he's been picked up. He's a university student, and he told me that Lopez was gunning for them.'

Make an effort, he urged himself. Make an effort. 'Even if they have picked him up, nothing's going to happen to him if he's from an upper-class family.'

'They don't go in for class-barriers here,' she said. 'Not when it comes to torture-chambers. This is a perfect democracy on the prison level.'

There was a faint, distant racket that might have been a packing case being shoved down a flight of steps into the cellar.

She started up. 'Did you hear that?' she said.

'I heard something.'

'Do you think it was shooting?'

'I think it was someone kicking an empty can over in the basement.'

'The central prison's only a block away. Cedric said you could hear them shooting the prisoners, from the hotel, when Lopez smashed the revolt last year.'

'That wasn't shooting,' Howel said.

'Whatever happened,' she said, 'it could never have worked out. I'm too old for him. Our backgrounds are too different. In his way he's very straight. Deeply conventional. If only I knew one way or another I'd feel better. It's the uncertainty I can't stand.'

'Why not ring his home as soon as the phone is working again?'

'I probably will,' she said. 'They won't talk to me, but I'll ring all the same.'

'Friend Williams will know what's happened tomorrow.'

'I wouldn't dream of going to him again. I'm supposed to have given this boy up after the fuss with Ronnie Smalldon. Ronnie went round saying he was mixed up in anti-government politics.'

'And was he?'

'I don't know. Perhaps. I don't want to talk about it any more.'

'Are we still playing the game?' he asked.

'No,' she said. 'Let's stop. I've had enough. Thinking about that prison's made me feel sick. I've had just about enough of life in Colombia. Did you hear that noise?'

'What noise?'

'That banging noise again?'

Howel listened. A cistern gurgled, a dog whined, and behind them someone put down his coffee cup and smacked his lips. 'I don't hear anything,' he said.

'My nerves,' she said. She slipped down from her stool. 'I'm going to spend a penny. Get me another drink. I've got something serious to tell you when I come back.'

She went off, walking carefully with short steps, reaching the door not by a straight line but a gentle arc. He picked up his whisky and sniffed it, thinking *that* never saw Scotland. With the failure of the electricity and with it, the air-conditioning plant, the air had turned stagnant and a faint odour of cellar-rot appeared to be rising from the blue and white tiled floor. The two giggling boys reappeared using aerosol sprays against the mosquitoes.

Twenty minutes later when she hadn't come back he went to look for her and found her in a chair in the lobby. She looked up as he came towards her, at first, he thought, without recognition, then she gave him a dazed smile and a little wave. The light, almost entirely from a single candle, illuminated her face from a new angle, endowing it with a spiritual and wistful beauty. It was a face that benefited from association with grief. Howel wondered how long she would have sat there by herself if he hadn't decided to look for her.

'I wondered where you'd got to.'

'I've been trying to make a phone call but the line's still dead.'

He dropped into the chair beside her and she let her hand fall on his.

'You were going to tell me something,' he said. 'Remember?'

'Yes,' she said. 'I went away to think about it for a minute or two, and the decision has been taken. I've finished with this boy. It had to be sooner or later, so it might as well be now.'

The quick surge of happiness he felt was quenched instantly by a built-in habit of caution. He had come to use pessimism as a prophylactic against despair. Liz was a girl who could change her mind. She was also a little drunk.

'Well?' she said. 'Aren't you going to say anything? Am I doing the right thing?'

'You oughtn't to ask me,' he said. 'I'm not the person to tell you.'

'Don't you ever say what you mean?'

'I'm sorry,' Howel said. 'I suppose I play for safety.'

'It can be mistaken,' she said. 'With me it is, anyway.'

'All right,' he said, 'I'm more pleased than I can tell you, and terribly relieved.'

'That's better,' she said. 'That's what I expect you to say. Perhaps I'm no longer out of reach. You're supposed to be happy about it, and say so. I suppose you think I'll change my mind again? It isn't that, is it? Now remember—you're to say exactly what you think.'

'No, I don't think you'll change your mind.'

'I hate people to be diplomatic with me. I like to know just where I am with anyone. Always remember that.'

'Just one thing,' Howel said. 'Have you given up the idea that your friend may have been picked up by the police?'

'Yes, I've given it up. As a matter of fact I never believed it. All I was trying to do was salvage a little pride. He wasn't picked up by anybody. He decided he didn't want to come, and he didn't even put himself to the trouble of getting a message to me. So the thing's at an end. And in case you think my judgment's been affected by the whisky, alcohol actually has the effect of clearing my brain. Well, now I've told you . . . say something—do something. Show enthusiasm.'

'This is a terribly public place,' Howel said.

'Yes, isn't it? Full of the most awful kind of public, too. And you're a shy man, too, at the best of times, aren't you? Too shy to take a good look at me the other day when I took my clothes off. Still, that's nice. That's part of your charm. And you've done something very important for me, you've given my damaged ego a badly-needed shot in the arm. My God, I can't tell you how glad I am you happened to be around today.'

'I want you to come back to England with me,' Howel said.

He got the impression that she sobered up instantly. 'Hey, wait a minute. That's not fair. You're taking advantage.'

'You've finished with this man, haven't you?'

'I've told you so.'

'Then what's to stop you?'

'Nothing,' she said, 'really. When you come to think of it. I've got into this way of digging my heels in. Living for the day. I've also stopped thinking about the future. It would be nice to have a future again.'

'Then you'll come back with me?'

'I might. Perhaps I will.'

He handled the prospect of success with care, like a fragile object. It was almost too easy. Too good to be true. Life's predicaments didn't solve themselves in this way.

'I'd like to be quite clear on one thing,' she said. 'Are you doing this for Charles, or for yourself?'

'Charles doesn't come into it. I want you to come back with me, and I want you to stay with me.'

'Do you mean live with you.'

'That's what I mean.'

'I think I'd like to,' she said. 'But in a way I'm frightened. I don't want to make any more mistakes. Darling, I've got so used to insecurity I can't imagine life without it. Supposing we made a start and then I found I couldn't settle down? You'd be hurt.'

'I'd take that chance.'

'It might be wonderful to have settled habits again. Settled habits and a quiet mind. A decently shaped life with a future as well as a past. We'd probably get on well together. The only thing is, I haven't much self-confidence left. I'm afraid of letting us down. What do you think we ought to do?'

'We could give it a try,' he said, 'and see what happens. I'd be happy with you. I think you'd be happy too.'

'It might work out,' she said. 'It would be wonderful if it did. This is too serious a conversation to be having in a place like this. Let's go away from all these people, and be by ourselves.'

'Can I go and take a room?' he said.

'I think you should.'

7

I N this forlorn pretence, lasting a matter of days, of a change of season, the heat curled up the valleys like a snake and coiled itself round the hacienda buildings. Often the mountains above Dos Santos grew a spongy mist, appearing almost as solid as a fungoid growth that spread from peak to peak, and eventually sank down almost to the rooftops in a threat to suffocate the colour-drained village.

These were the days of heavy apathy in humans, and a restlessness amounting almost to panic among the animals. The nights resounded with the distracted squawkings of birds which, frustrated in their evening migration to the upper valleys, dashed about the village, lost in the mist.

Down in Los Remedios there were plots and counter-plots. Colonel Bravo, General Lopez's deputy, had returned from a long absence abroad where he had carried out a mission of utmost secrecy. The casual, uncommitted brokers in death he dealt with had been amazed to discover the real man under the mild and philosophical exterior. After placing his order and paying his money, Bravo explained, 'My family were Liberals. Poor people who couldn't defend themselves. Unpleasant things happened in my childhood. One cannot discuss the sanctity of the vendetta with an outsider.'

The General continued to act with vigour, and a carefully staged minimum of open terror, to demolish any urban support for the guerrillas that might appear in the mountains. Two students whose families were of slight importance were shot while attempting to avoid arrest in the Plaza itself at midday, where their fate could be sure of attracting the maximum publicity. Others were conscientiously beaten and thrown into the man-devouring dungeons under the city prison. He increased security precautions by encircling the city with a barbed-wire fence, guarded by searchlights and machine-gunners placed at half-kilometre intervals. He had a long session with his personal horoscopist, and presented heavy silver candlesticks to the chapel of the Virgin of Los Remedios in the cathedral.

Meanwhile a group of guerrillas who had trained in the comparative comfort and security of Ecuador had travelled by slow train to Alcalares, the nearest frontier town in that country. Here they rested a day, bought last-minute, perishable supplies, found a local bus to take them five more miles into the mountains, and then started their long walk.

In these days Grail Williams, considered by many to be second only in authority in the province to the Governor himself, found himself in a troubled state of mind, for which he searched many times, without avail, for biblical consolation. He had been acclaimed by his organization for the success of his mission and for gathering more souls than any of his brother missionaries throughout Latin America. But now a devastating rumour had reached his ears—that a number of his supposedly devout converts were following in secret the paganism of their forefathers.

As a result of this period of stress Mary began to see her husband in a new light. She began to ask herself whether Christian watchfulness ever degenerated into suspicion and, granted that it was commendable in a Christian pastor to be firm in advancing the cause of his faith, was it ever permissible for him to be harsh?

A hastily formed Anglo-Colombian mining company had sent three British experts it employed to re-start operations at the tin mine at Ultramuerte. They were very depressed at what they found, including a blocked tunnel which, when cleared, revealed the skeletons of thirty-seven miners who had died there from starvation or asphyxiation ten years before.

Liz and Howel were lovers, but Howel discovered under-currents of reluctance and hesitation in the relationship. By nature he was a man who found it hard to be suspicious, but having invented every conceivable excuse for her silences, her changes of mood and occasional unheralded absences, something inexplicable remained. Their future together seemed as nebulous as ever.

Quite clearly the thing was to get her away as soon as possible. He tried to pin her down to a date for leaving the country, but she found excuses for putting him off. ('I can't let Cedric down.' 'She wouldn't be letting me down in the slightest,' Hargrave said. 'Are you still thinking about that Colombian boy?' 'Of course I'm not.' She flushed with anger. 'Very well then, let's take next Friday's plane.' She lost patience with him. 'Why don't you go first? I'll follow as soon as I'm ready.')

Howel, going into the past performance and future potential-ities of S U C C O U R in Dos Santos, felt hope shrivel and then disappear.

'What became of Smalldon's scheme for raising tomatoes planted in chemical solutions?' he asked Hargrave.

'Very little, I'm afraid. We had a moderate success with the crop, but we practically couldn't give the tomatoes away. It's the people in the mountains who are so urgently in need of food, and how do you imagine you'd get tomatoes to them? In these cases the only practical food is grain.'

'So I should have thought. I can't imagine what gave Smalldon the idea of tomatoes.'

'He'd been in Kerala before he came here. They grow tomatoes in Kerala so he was going to grow tomatoes here.'

The matter of Father Alberto's letter came up.

'For obvious reasons I couldn't forward it,' Hargrave said.

'No, I suppose not,' Howel said.

'Half the letters are opened and if they'd found it, we'd

have been in the soup.'

'Did you mention it in your report?'

'No, I didn't think that was a good idea, either. Father Alberto sees himself as a kind of Savonarola. He's beginning to get in people's hair. If they got the idea here we were mixed up with him in any way it wouldn't do us any good.'

'He seemed quite sincere.'

Hargrave grimaced with exasperation. The weather was beginning to get on his nerves. A slight heat-rash prickled on his neck and wrists, and he had smeared calamine lotion with clownish effect on the tiny eruptions that had appeared here and there in his cheeks. He was appalled by Charles's irresponsibility in sending out a man who spoke only text-book Spanish, and who had prepared himself to do battle with the mellowed cynicisms and the age-old corruptions of this country by handouts supplied by the London Embassy, a biography of Simon Bolivar, and John Gunter's *Inside Latin America*.

'Surely his sincerity doesn't enter into it. We ought to avoid involvement with Father Alberto because he represents a new and dangerous trend in the Church. I say dangerous because it opposes itself to the State, and it's the State we have to do business with, and not the Church.' How long did one have to live here, Hargrave wondered, before one finally learned that everyone within reason could be manipulated if only one found the right way—that every man had his price, going through life marked with the invisible tariff for his favours, although not necessarily in terms of money? How long must a raw newcomer imbibe this atmosphere before acquiring the instinct that told him when to advance, when to retreat, but before all and above all, when to let well alone?

'Many people in this part of the world—let's say a considerable minority—believe that the Church has secretly decided that, in the long run, capitalism hasn't any future in South America, and that sooner or later it will move into the Marxist camp. Whatever happens, they say, the Church is determined to survive. It's been dickering with Marxism in Cuba—watching to see which way the cat jumped—and Marxism turned out to be not half so bad as expected. This country is stuffed with theorists and intellectuals. The way they see it is the Church is smart enough to learn a lesson, but capitalism never learns anything. They call Father Alberto a Christian Marxist. At the last Holy Week he preached seven sermons in a row on the text, "And the rich he hath sent empty away." '

'And isn't the Governor doing anything about him?'

'Not up till now, because it suits him to keep in with the Bishop, and the Bishop likes to think of himself as one of the new generation of Liberals. As soon as Lopez can persuade the Bishop to withdraw his protection, that will be the end of Father Alberto.' I may not have been able to do much, Hargrave thought, but at least I know what goes on.

'In this letter Father Alberto alleges that Lopez is following a policy of deliberate starvation of the Indians. Do you believe it?'

'Put it this way, I think there's something in it.'

'Aren't we in a position to help in a situation like this? After all, we're not expected to know anything about political motives that may or may not exist. As far as we're concerned this is a simple case of famine.'

'We could try,' Hargrave said. He'll have to learn sooner or later, he thought.

'Can you see that anybody could object?'

'Not in so many words,' Hargrave said. 'It would put them in an embarrassing situation.'

'He says the worst hit area is Cayambo. What would be the best thing to send?'

'Maize. Always maize. As I told you before.'

'That's what Father Alberto suggested. And can we buy it without too much difficulty?'

'I don't think we'd have much trouble.'

'Where would we get it from?'

'Williams would probably be your best bet. He always keeps a ton or two in reserve.'

'And how would we get it to Cayambo?'

'By plane.'

'Williams's plane?'

'It's the only one.'

'We seem to be rather in his hands.'

'You don't have to buy the maize from him but you might have to pay two or three times the price. Williams wouldn't want to make a profit. You could also transport it up to Cayambo by mules. If you could get the mules. It would take you ten days to get it there.'

'I think perhaps I'd better go and talk to Williams,' Howel said.

'There's nothing to be lost.'

8

'Y o u don't mind if I call you Robert, do you?' Williams said. 'The thing is, Robert, I'd be happy to let you have all the maize you want, now or at any other time, and I guess the Cessna can usually be spared, but this is a case where, quite frankly, I have to say no. Let me explain why.'

Howel had found Williams on his verandah, probing with what looked like a surgical instrument into a small piece of machinery held in his lap. His face wore an expression of tenderness and concern.

'Cayambo,' he said, 'happens to be the principal temporary village of the Cholos, and the Cholos are resistants.' He made this announcement sound like a verdict that left no more to be said.

'What do they resist?'

Williams raised his eyebrows. 'They resist civilization. They reject all attempts to lead them towards a civilized life.'

'Is it a fact that famine conditions exist at Cayambo?' Howel asked.

'Famine is never far away,' Williams said in a voice that was proof against calamity. 'The Cholos are nomads at a low level of human evolution. They grow some crops, but their principal food is game, which becomes scarcer every year. These people have a terrible time in those mountains. We've learned by long experience that the only argument with resistants is want. When they're hungry enough they can come down here, and we'll be waiting for them with food. This they know. To take grain up to Cayambo is only to prolong the agony.'

Williams's two noisily jubilant children, one pushing the other in a wheelbarrow, came into sight, and Williams, putting aside his piece of apparatus with a quick conciliatory pat, turned to watch them with radiant paternalism. Freakishly the spongy equatorial fog of the past few days had dispersed, and the day was springlike; the mountain outlines drawn clearly in vigorous ink by a Chinese artist, a few pines afloat in patches of refulgent mist, a skein of ibis going over, drawn like smoke across the sky to some glacial lake in the Cordillera.

'Then there's nothing to be done?'

'I don't see how there can be, Robert. Not with the Cholos. I've never had to say no to s u c c o u r before and I sure hate doing it now. I'd like you to understand that I'm only refusing on humanitarian grounds. I hope you can see that.'

'I've been told off the record it's the government's policy to starve out the Cholos,' Howel said. 'Would you agree that this is so?'

'No, I wouldn't. The government would certainly like to see them civilized, though. Having savage Indians around creates problems. Some of them rustle cattle. Their argument is that the land was taken from them anyway, so why shouldn't they? Nowadays a real danger exists of the Indian being induced to shelter guerrillas, and I guess that's as good a reason as any they ought to be somewhere where the government can keep an eye on them.'

Howel was still quite unable to disentangle himself from an uneasy feeling of inferiority in his, up till then, brief encounters with Williams. Williams presented himself as not only the master but the fashioner of his environment. He had thrown back the jungle and re-assembled here in its place the comfortable realities of Cincinnati. All the inexplicable instruments in that shining science-fiction room of his full of dials and warning lights and the symphonic noises of the century to come were in his service. He could manipulate the genes of the animals he bred as easily as he could the prejudices of the Latin American politicians who were to be induced to give him a free hand in whatever enterprise he undertook. On the face of it he carried with him an aroma of omniscience—almost of wisdom.

'Would you have five minutes to spare just now, Robert? I'd like to talk to you about our work.' The children had wheeled about to come back; one close-cropped young head, and one full of golden curls; snub noses and freckles from Cincinnati. The spray from the lawn-sprinklers drifted over them full of rainbow segments, and a macaw stretched itself in a secret way, and screeched. 'Mary gives them a half-hour break from their lessons,' Williams said. 'Time for a glass of milk and a romp round. This climate is kind of hard on them. Apart from the morning and evening breaks we think it wise to keep them so far as possible in the even temperature of the house.'

'You were going to tell me about your work,' Howel said.

'Sure you won't be bored, Robert? The way I see it is, our activities running parallel in the way they do, maybe it would help.' What time was it this fantastic man began his day? Was it really three a.m.?

'We're here to tell the Indians that Jesus said, "He who believeth in me shall be saved." These are wonderful tidings indeed. In so far as the Indian has been accessible at all he is marked psychologically with the cruel servitude of the colonial past. Let me tell you about something that happened here three hundred and seventy years ago, practically to the day. All the chiefs of the Tairona tribes were found guilty of heresy and they executed them in the main square of Los Remedios. Do you know what they did to those poor souls? They had wild colts tear their arms and legs off and they burned what was left. In the presence of the Roman bishop, and with his blessing!'

Williams, whose normal tone came closer to a salesman's

brisk and cheerful banter than to a pastor's solemnity, became absolutely serious. 'We bring to these people the gentle Jesus, meek and mild, but to do this most effectively a good deal of organization is called for. These days evangelization is run like any other promotional programme. We've worked out an overall strategy that gives the best results fastest. I'd like to talk to you about this because it has a direct bearing on the present case. I'm not boring you, am I, Robert?'

'Not in the slightest.'

'The first thing we do is to set out to establish what we call dependency. Sorry to use jargon. I'm talking now of a tribe that has remained in conditions of isolation and savagery. This process can be a long or a short one, depending a lot on luck. In brief, we seek to contact the tribe and to gain its friendship and its confidence. We do this by leaving gifts such as knives, cooking pots, articles of discarded clothing, and comestibles such as sugar. When these are regularly accepted, one of our native workers goes to the tribe again and tells them that in future they must come to the mission to receive gifts. If they agree to do this— and in three cases out of four they do—more than half the battle is over. In practice they rarely if ever go back. They have no way of gaining a living from the area adjacent to the compound. In fact they're now dependent on what we give them. In the final stage we stipulate that they must enter the compound itself and agree to accept some degree of discipline, perform light tasks in exchange for what they receive, and most important of all, receive religious instruction.'

'And how long does this take?'

'Possibly six months. Possibly a year. The only case of failure we've experienced in the whole of this country has been with the Cholos of Cayambo. Only a handful have come down and accepted conversion. The rest continue to follow their idolatrous practices.'

'And they actually refuse your gifts?'

'We've given up leaving them. It proved a waste of time and money.'

Williams stopped to scan Howel's expression with a trace of anxiety. Howel was certain that no sign of criticism or doubt had showed in his face.

'Certain irresponsible sections of the press have seen fit to attack us, but the truth is that the government of every single country with savage Indians on its territory is behind us in our civilizing mission. Ask the Brazilians who civilized their Indians. They'll tell you it was the missionaries, and they'll tell you this is how it was done.'

'So the day of the Indian outside a compound or reservation is coming to an end?'

'I prefer to say the Indian who is neither integrated in, nor complementary to, our society. In twenty years—and I give thanks to Our Lord—there won't be a single one left. And Robert, don't think this is going to involve the Indian in any hardship. Quite the reverse. The habits of savagery are soon forgotten. Say, listen—do you have an hour to spare? Because if so I'd like to run you down to the compound and show you a bunch of very happy Indians—not all of them fully qualified members of our society as yet, but all of them well on the way.'

The compound was a mile away at the end of a road beautifully engineered through the jungle. 'We call it Esperanza—Hope,' Williams said. 'It is our hope that it will prove an inspiration to Latin America as an example of harmonious low-budget urban development.' A circular area possibly a quarter of a mile in diameter was criss-crossed by streets of tiny yellow houses, some of them standing in little tonsured flower-gardens. In a far corner Esperanza was still on the move, pushing forward behind a spearhead of bulldozers into a disorderly rampart of trees. A few Indian converts were in the streets, walking singly in a slow, somnambulistic manner that suggested an absence of urgent purpose. They wore yellow cotton boiler suits. Williams explained the choice of colour.

'Many of the tribes have a superstitious aversion to yellow, and this is how we set out to cure them. The insides of the houses are painted yellow too. Their eating and drinking utensils are in yellow plastic. We use the colour whenever we can. It's the same with numbers. The number nine's sacred to them, so our aim is to strip this element of sanctity away. Everything they might find unpleasing, or let us say unclean, comes in nines. For example, there are nine latrines to be kept clean.'

Stolidly the Indians marched up and down the streets. Each man separated from the other by a dozen paces. 'We divide the day into periods,' Williams said, 'in an endeavour to create a habit of respect for routine and for time. This is the exercise period. Converts are forbidden to talk to each other purely because we've found that if they do so they naturally fall into groups, and before you know where you are you have them sitting around gossiping, or even singing. This defeats the whole purpose of the thing. After the exercise period they have supervised social awareness in the Assembly Hall, and they can talk as much as they like.'

'But isn't this a traumatic experience for them? People used to total freedom suddenly subjected to this kind of regimentation?'

'It is,' Williams agreed, 'and it has to be. It's a kind of shock therapy we're giving them. The harder we hit them, the quicker the process is completed. I'd like to be able to say that we're responsible for all the techniques we adopt, but unfortunately it wouldn't be true. We've borrowed a lot from the old Jesuits. The idea, for instance, of building Esperanza on a strictly rectangular plan. Hundreds of years ago the Jesuits first noticed that the Indians always lived in circular villages, so they moved them out into square ones. Their idea was to break down the Indian's adhesion to his customs and his past in the most effective possible way, and it's our purpose too. We've managed to induce a few Cholos from Cayambo to come and live here. Cayambo is circular, so are the individual huts in Cayambo. Every chalet in Esperanza is exactly square. Up there they have two doors—one for the women and one for the men. Down here they have to make do with one. I should add that the sexes are segregated, except in the cases of what we call our old converts who've earned the maximum privileges.'

For the first time in their short acquaintance, pride entered Williams's smile. 'We learned a lot from the Jesuits, but I guess there are one or two things we could teach them too if they were still around. We found out that an Indian's position in tribal society is defined by the position of his hut—and this applies even in the case of semi-nomads like the Cholos. We get round this by never allowing the same man or family to occupy a hut for more than a month. Maybe this isn't really so important, although we're kind of proud of it because it's an original contribution. What we found most important of all in practice was to suppress all the customs connected with the burial of the dead. These can drag on for as long as five years. We have a small Garden of Remembrance in the forest and in this the dead are buried with the short form of the Christian burial service. After that no further visits to the grave are permitted. The psychological effect of this is tremendous. These people are ancestor-worshippers. In effect you've cut the man off from the spirits of the dead and his ancestors. If there's anything that's going to make an Indian stop feeling an Indian, it's this.'

It seemed to Howel as if the details of a shabby conspiracy were being revealed to him. He felt himself morally bound to dissociate himself from this trickery: to deprive it of the support of silence. He remembered Hargrave's warning. 'He's bound to provoke you sooner or later. You won't be able to stand that terrible complacency of his indefinitely. But try to avoid an open rupture, at least until we know how we stand here. If we're going to stay on and do solid, productive work we can't afford to break. He runs this place. We have to find some way of continuing to work with this man.'

Once again Williams seemed to have divined his mental objections.

'You were talking about freedom, Robert, but in reality the Indian who comes here experiences freedom for the first time in his life—let's say after he's recovered from the first shock of his break with tradition. You may not be aware of this, but back in the tribe a man spends half his waking hours in superstitious practices and fulfilling the social obligations that a savage society imposes. With us he becomes the possessor of true leisure, and apart from singing or dancing or engaging in pagan practices of any kind, he can do what he likes with it. This is freedom.'

A whistle blew somewhere and the Indians, all moved at once by an invisible hand, changed the direction of their dejected shuffling. A bigger kind of man in a blue track suit came in sight. He walked with swinging arms and a brisk military step.

'That's a captain,' Williams said. 'The captains impose such discipline as we find necessary—and let me say, it's very mild. It's OK for them to wear blue because they're half-breeds and the colour has no significance. Our war is against symbolism in any shape or form.' When Williams said symbolism, he made the word sound like an ugly form of depravity.

'We've been talking about Cayambo and we've been talking about Esperanza,' Williams said, 'so maybe we ought to consider a few figures. Infant mortality, for instance. What would you say for Cayambo—fifty per cent? I can tell you what the figure is for Esperanza. Somewhat less than five per cent.'

Howel wondered how many children were born in Esperanza.

'Or how about life expectation? In Cayambo I personally would put it at thirty-five years. In Esperanza it might be nearer sixty.'

'But how can you say that? How long does an Indian live in Esperanza?'

'Esperanza has only been in existence two years but we reckon that if an Indian comes to us when he's young enough we can give him a good enough start to carry him through to sixty.'

The captain in the blue track suit appeared suddenly to have seen them. He changed direction and was coming towards them at a light-infantry pace.

'The so-called free Indian—and you and I know that he is not free—is sickly. He is ridden not only by his superstitions but by disease. In Cayambo you won't find a human being who doesn't suffer from a bad chest. I don't even want to talk about avitaminosis. Intestinal parasites? Malaria? Tuberculosis? You name it, and they have it. The only diseases our converts in Esperanza have are the ones they bring with them. And, by the by, an average adult male weighs 126 pounds when he arrives, and 142 pounds when he leaves. Need I say more?'

The captain in the blue track suit reached them. He came to attention with a double thud of rubber-soled boots and brought his hand up to cup his eyebrow momentarily in a military salute. He threw back his head, neck stretched, to peer at them respectfully over an invisible fence; a dignified man with a Dahomean face in polished hardwood.

It was an urgent and clearly confidential matter. Williams went off with him and when he came back ten minutes later Howel sensed that something had happened in the interval to mark a turning-point in Williams's life. Ten paces away his expression was that of a man coming from a disaster, from a shipwreck—from a fire in which children had been carbonized. By the time he joined Howel he had forced himself back into a straitjacket of calm, with only a vestige of pain in his smile.

'Sorry for the delay, Robert. Suppose we go and look at the dormitories now.'

'What did you think of it?' Hargrave asked.

'A broiler farm for human beings,' Howel said.

'You didn't tell him that?'

'No, I didn't tell him that. I ought to have done, but I didn't.'

'I can imagine you showed by your manner you weren't impressed.'

'I expect I did. He's an insensitive man. Unfortunately. This is slavery, under another name.' Howel's fury was growing. He had always been the one to deride others for sitting on the fence, for failing to face up to evil when it masqueraded under an outwardly respectable form. The most he'd managed in Williams's case had been a petulant silence. Can I be afraid of the man? he asked himself.

'Almost every post in the Upper Amazon has got its Williamses,' Hargrave said. 'There are dozens of them. Hundreds. This is what happens to the pennies in the plate. What happened to *our* pennies.'

'He actually used the word processing,' Howel said. 'He processes Indians. How do they end up when the processing's finished?'

'They're turned into plantation fodder. Or mine-fodder. As

you say, it's slavery under another name. Why don't you put it in your report?'

Mary had seen the greyness in his face that reminded her of a patient lying under the sentence of cancer, and now she probed cautiously to find the cause.

'Are you still worried about that Liz Sayers business?'

Williams looked up from his papers, his eyes still far away. 'I'm far from happy about it. Particularly in the present climate of alarm. Nor am I altogether certain there wasn't more in it than met the eye, in spite of all the young lady's denials. Which reminds me, I must speak to Homer King about taking her about in the mission's car so often. Even if the excuse is butterfly collecting. I feel he should give more time to his work.'

'Smalldon was a very stupid young man, wasn't he?'

'His action was irresponsible. Although I gave General Lopez my personal assurance that there was nothing whatever in his allegations, I'm far from convinced I was justified in doing so. Let us hope that Colonel Arana never takes it into his head to investigate the foreign community, because if he does, heaven only knows what he may find.'

The long years of experience of his reactions and his moods told her that the scent in this direction was cold.

'Is there any more news about the guerrillas?'

'Wesley Scott came through this afternoon. He was flying to the mission at Pineda and he saw a party of armed men on the trail just north of the frontier.'

'Do you think they're the ones you were telling me about?'

'I don't see who else they could be. They're heading for Cayambo. Should get there in a few days.'

'What are you going to do?' she asked.

'I've already phoned Arana.'

'I'd feel very much happier if we had no more to do with Arana,' Mary said.

'And you aren't prepared to give him the benefit of the doubt?'

'I find it very hard to believe that a boy of twenty who is in perfect health when he leaves here can die from natural causes twelve hours later at the police headquarters.'

'Well, however that may be, when I passed on Wesley Scott's news. Arana didn't seem in the slightest concerned.'

'Should we be?'

'No,' he said. 'General Lopez took two days to smash the student movement. When the moment comes, he'll smash the guerrillas, too. I cannot see that our work will be affected in any way.'

It was not fear of guerrilla warfare in their area, though, that had caused Grail Williams to push away his supper after a few mouthfuls.

'Did Mr Howel enjoy his visit to Esperanza?' she asked.

'I don't think so,' he said. 'He said very little but the impression I gained was that on the whole he was unsympathetic. This is unfortunate. Mr Howel is a Red Cross observer—whether unofficial or not—and I regard it as important to us that he should not leave here with a bad impression.'

'And could he?' Mary asked.

'I've often noticed that newcomers from the States or Europe show little understanding of the problems we face. They fail to realize that we're not dealing with rational human beings, but with children. Savage children.'

'Did you show him the new clinic?'

'No. I was prevented from doing so by a rather unpleasant happening. Luis Diego reported to me that he had positive proof of the performance of a pagan ceremony. This, as you know, is something I've suspected for some time. It's been very much on my mind.'

'What did he say?'

The room temperature was 68 degrees, but Williams's

attempt to control the bitter emotions he felt had caused tiny beads of sweat to form over the bridge of his nose. His lips moved as he repeated in silence a mantra-like personal formula. 'I never feel anger, only perplexity.'

'An Indian died some time last evening. A Cholo. An old man with avitaminosis and nephritis.'

'And you weren't notified?'

'I wasn't notified. Neither was Homer King nor Luis Diego. Diego was not told until this morning. When Diego went to see the body it was quite clear to him that death had taken place many hours previously. He showed grave negligence by failing to report to any of us there and then the suspicions he must have felt. Homer King then saw the body, signed the certificate, and arranged for the burial to take place this afternoon.'

'I remember the old man,' Mary said. 'A dear old fellow. He wasn't responding to the injections. I knew it couldn't be more than a matter of a day or two.'

Williams took out a folded handkerchief, and patted the sides of his nose. 'Later in the morning Diego was in charge of a tree-felling party, and he noticed that one of the members, Pedro Morales, was behaving strangely. Morales is a Cholo.'

'He's related to the one who died at the police headquarters, isn't he?'

'Some sort of a cousin, I believe. They have these very complicated matrilinear relationships. Diego thought Morales might have been drunk, he also noticed that Morales had a small pad of chicle attached to the inside of his forearm. This made him suspect that he might have taken part in a costumbre!'

'What a terrible thing,' Mary said. 'I thought of Morales as one of our most promising Christians.'

'Diego made a few enquiries, and in the end a woman told him there *had* been a costumbre. As soon as the old man had died they'd sent for a shaman, and they'd held a fully-fledged pagan ceremony.'

'It's almost too terrible to believe,' Mary said. 'A shaman in Esperanza! How did he manage to get in?'

'I don't know,' Williams said, 'but it means doubling the guard, and probably putting up a fence. At this stage Diego decided to examine the body and found that an amulet had been inserted in it. He says that an animal was sacrificed—'

'An animal? Where would they get an animal from?'

'It was almost certainly one of our pigs—and alcoholic liquor was consumed. Diego found they've been in the habit of making this from the root of a tree. Jungle-clearing parties bring back the root, and it's been kept in the women's latrines. The women chew it when they go to the latrines, and in this way prepare a fermenting mash. They had enough liquor prepared for this occasion to make possible a drunken orgy. At some point in the ceremony the shaman took blood from the veins of all those who had participated.'

She shuddered. 'It's like a nightmare,' she said.

Williams's lips had twisted themselves into something like a smile, as if he found a sly relish in the taste of defeat. 'This, it appears, is called a soul-guarding ceremony. In effect, the participants believe they give their souls into the shaman's care. They believe that no Indian who has taken part in this ceremony can ever become a Christian, and that his conversion, if it has already taken place, becomes null and void.' He hesitated. 'Diego suggests that a similar ceremony was conducted after the young Cholo died at police headquarters, and that this may have started the whole process in motion. I've confirmed that a pig was missing from the piggery at that time, too.'

'Has Diego any idea how many Indians may have been involved?'

'No,' he said, 'and it may take days of investigation before we know. That Morales should have betrayed us comes as a severe blow. He's shown himself to be very intelligent. As you know, he'd been helping me with my translation, and I had high hopes of his eventually becoming a native teacher. After this experience I ask myself, where can we look for loyalty?'

'When the truth comes to be known we shall find that many of them stood by us,' she said. 'Things are rarely as black as they seem. We've received many blessings in our work, and God won't withhold his blessings in future.' She went to put her arm round him.

'In another five years we must move on,' he said. 'When we are called to other fields we must leave in the certain knowledge that a band of consecrated Christians will remain to carry on. Our work here is threatened by secret idolators. We must act now before it is too late.'

She was alarmed at the fierceness of his tone, wondering for the first time if her husband hated evil more than he loved good.

'I don't think there should be any question of punishment, dear,' she said. 'They wouldn't understand.'

'Sometimes punishment cannot be avoided,' he said. 'I am totally opposed to punishment for its own sake, but it may be necessary to punish the guilty to protect the innocent and the weak.'

She shook her head. 'Perhaps we've been too severe in various ways as it is. Perhaps we've tried to go too fast. Indians never punish each other, and if we punished them now it might have a very bad effect on them. It would be terrible if we made a mistake and lost much of the ground we've worked so hard to gain.'

'Yes,' he said, 'but it would be more terrible still in the long run for the work of evangelization if they were allowed to believe that we can be hoodwinked by a pretence of faith, while their hearts remain unchanged.'

9

IN the second week in April Ecuadorian frontier guards stationed in the frontier town of Tulcán received information that a band believed to be emerald smugglers were about to cross the frontier going into Colombia near the village of San Gabriel O Sucumbios. They immediately set out for the area, alerted their network of spies all along the frontier, and were able almost in a matter of hours to locate the strangers in the small village of San Miguel de Barrenda, where their presence had provoked the greatest possible curiosity and speculation. The guards now made their plans. There were seven of them, all in late middle age, underfed, underpaid; the objects of fear and contempt wherever they went. Windfalls of this kind only happened once in a blue moon when smugglers neglected to pay the expected protection money in the capital. Bands on their way to Colombia were certain to carry hoards of American dollars to buy their emeralds. The guards enlisted a dozen ne'er-do-wells in the villages and set off with them to prepare an ambush in a ravine through which the supposed smugglers were certain to pass.

The guerrillas numbered twelve men, all of them young and tough and intensively trained in the arts of guerrilla warfare. In preparation for this action they had studied all the accounts of the previous guerrilla campaigns in Bolivia, Colombia, Venezuela, Guatemala and Brazil, and they had endlessly discussed the diaries of Che Guevara, of Rolando, Pombo, Braulio, and the rest. All these campaigns had failed, gloriously or ignominiously, depending on one's point of view, and the 8th October Movement had analysed the reasons for their failure, which were the following:

The individual guerrillas had in the main been too old for the job. By the time they were thirty-five most men could no longer support the terrible strains of jungle warfare.

Their strategy had been muddled. They often gave the impression that they had no clear idea of what they intended to do when they took to the mountains.

They had allowed their health and physical endurance to become undermined—often through near-starvation—as the result of a failure to study the natural resources of the regions they operated in.

Quite unnecessarily—as in the case of Comrade Guevara— they had sought to establish themselves in impossibly difficult terrain, where progress during marches (criticized by the Movement as usually pointless) was reduced by the dense rain forest to a few hundred yards a day.

They had failed to respect rainy seasons.

Above all, no attempt had been made while operating in Indian country to enlist the sympathy of the Indians. Consequently it was easy for the government to employ these as trackers against them.

All these errors, and many more arising from them, the Movement was determined to avoid. The members of this expedition were all in their twenties, and with one exception, from Colombian middle-class or aristocratic families. The exception was Orlando Borda, a swimming instructor, who had been born in the slums of Recife in Brazil. Borda had been in charge of the men's physical training. He was an extraordinary marksman, but the real purpose of his inclusion in the group was a secret known only to its leader, Alejandro Diaz, aged 25, a landed proprietor of Bogotá, and his second-in-command, Enrique Manera, a brilliant young lawyer. Enrique had already spent a year in gaol as a suspected guerrilla, where he had undergone severe torture. Many members of the Movement, including Diaz himself, believed that Manera should have been selected to lead this expedition.

Diaz was becoming more and more preoccupied by an anonymous message in the Movement's code delivered to his headquarters the day before leaving Quito: 'YOU HAVE A TRAITOR WITH YOU.'

On April 13th at dawn the guerrillas left San Miguel de Barrenda and began their march. They were in brimming spirits, laughing and joking and singing, while Borda strummed a guitar. Diaz was unable to persuade them to be quiet. They accepted with amused toleration his precautionary order to take the road south from the village, and then, when well out of sight of it, to cut across country for a mile or two before heading north again. Their immediate goal was the village of Cayambo, which they hoped to reach in about fifteen days. Soon after nine o'clock, still noisily happy, they entered the mouth of the ravine where the frontier guards awaited them.

The system adopted by the guards was a simple one, and devoid of the slightest element of risk to themselves. They had organized an action of this kind many times before, and the occasional blunders of the past were never repeated in these days. A number of enormous boulders had lodged among the pines in the walls of the ravine and, ensconcing themselves behind these, the guards and their allies opened fire at a range of from three to four hundred yards. The guerrillas only realized that they were under fire when they saw their comrades begin to fall. None of them saw their attackers nor even realized where the shots were coming from. The guards possessed antiquated weapons, but they were excellent shots and picked off the distant running figures below with a coolness and deliberation abetted by their years. Realizing that the only hope lay in flight, Diaz gave the order to retreat, emphasizing it with an angry wave of his pistol at Borda, who squatted cradling the head of a man who had lost most of his bottom jaw. Five minutes later the survivors reached safety at the north end of the ravine. They left three dead and three wounded behind, and shortly afterwards the guards came skipping from cover to cover down the slopes. They were disappointed and angry when they searched their victims, and the wounded did not die quickly.

An hour later the six survivors stopped, panting and haggard, with death in their eyes, in the shelter of a wood, and Diaz put to them the question: did they or did they not want to go on? They all voted to continue. True they were few now, but had not the comrade who called himself Athos assured them that they had only to reach Cholo country to be joined by a flow of Indian recruits? The blond Athos had been left lying in the ravine with a shattered thigh, and now he was dead. His loss was a grievous one because it was he who had made the pact with the Cholos and no one was sure whether they would honour it when they found that Athos was not with them. The one man who now became essential to the expedition's success was Rafael Villa, a lecturer in Indian Studies at the University of Bogotá. Apart from the dead Athos. Villa was the only Cholo-speaker among them.

The first day of lassitude and shock and secret weeping passed, and the men's spirits began to improve. They awoke on the second day in a dawn that was cold and crystalline with dew, turned their faces towards the high peaks and began the march. They trudged on steadily under a clear sky and a mild sun, a little short of breath sometimes in the rarified air of these altitudes. This was another world from the savage terrain of the guerrillas, according to all the accounts they had read, and the descriptions they had had from the lips of the few who had returned. Here it seemed that there were no mosquitoes, biting or skin-boring insects, scorpions, centipedes or snakes. There were streams in abundance to quench their thirst, and before they had time to open their rations for the midday meal a small deer came trotting into sight, which Borda brought down with a single infallible shot. The deer was skinned, cut up and barbecued, and at this point Diaz intervened with a warning. He recalled the famous passage from Comrade Guevara's diary when, after the symptoms of starvation had become alarming, the baggage horse had been killed and eaten. 'Day of belching, farting, vomiting and diarrhœa; a real organ concert . . . we stayed absolutely motionless trying to digest . . . I was very ill until I vomited and felt better. I was running all over like an unweaned baby . . . stinking to high heaven.' There were to be no such orgies under Diaz's command. He rationed the meat in person.

That afternoon, after the sparse but genial forest of oak and pine, they climbed above the tree level, finding themselves in a landscape coated with grey tundra among stalagmites of rock thrusting into a violet alpine sky. It was stumbling through the dead sea sponges of this wasteland, and appearing from a height of 2,000 feet like the insect figures of explorers on an arctic glacier, that the missionary Wesley Scott first noticed them from his plane. The guerrillas heard the Cessna's engine and then saw the plane coming in very low between the peaks, almost as if to land. There was no cover of any kind, and Diaz ordered them to throw their weapons down and walk on. The plane banked to change direction, dropped to 500 feet and passed over them, then turned and flew off, and they could hear the beat of its engine on a tympanum of rock long after the sky had closed over it.

10

THEY had been inspecting a corner of the garden set aside for a demonstration of the value of fertilizer. Two patches of corn grew side by side—one on soil that had been treated with nitrates, and the other on soil that had been left as it was. There was no doubt, as Hargrave said with enthusiasm that fizzed up suddenly and then spluttered out, that the demonstration was a success. The vigorously-sprouting fertilized corn was nearly twice as large as the corn growing in the untreated and exhausted garden soil. He giggled hopelessly. None of the local peasantry had taken the trouble to come and see the demonstration. The fact was that only the richest farmer could afford to buy fertilizer.

'Have you seen todays *Noticias*?' Hargrave asked.

'I have. Fantastic, isn't it?'

The story splashed on the front page of the local paper was of an attempted kidnapping which had failed in a bloody and spectacular manner. A vice-president of the Chase National Bank of New York had paid a much-advertised visit to Los Remedios in the company of an official from the commercial section of the US Embassy, in connection with the proposed financing of a tin-mining project. The previous evening they had left their hotel together with the intention of taking a pre-curfew stroll, when they had suddenly been surrounded by armed men who attempted to force them into a car. At that moment security police had opened fire from the windows opposite where they had been concealed, and all five attackers fell, riddled with bullets.

'The inside story is that there wasn't anyone from the Chase National Bank, or the American Embassy,' Hargrave said. 'They were a couple of FBI men attached to the Military Mission who came down from Bogotá for the job. Lopez thought that if there happened to be any potential kidnappers in Los Remedios, this was the way of getting rid of them. Williams told me all about it this morning.'

Hargrave dabbed at the heat-spots on his forehead. They had found their way to the thin shade of a bean tree, under a flinty patois of small birds fidgeting in its branches. 'I wonder if we could have a word about Liz before we go in to lunch.'

'As a matter of fact I was going to speak to you about her.'

'Don't you find her manner rather strange?'

'Very strange,' Howel said.

'Well, at least that's something. I had an idea she might have been upset with me.'

'She's been very silent for the last few days. I don't for one moment think it's anything to do with you. I haven't been able to get a word out of her.'

'Any theories?'

'None at all.'

'In the ordinary way I would have expected her to be on top of the world,' Hargrave said. 'She probably told you that the Los Ecantos store sold three tablecloth sets last week, and Grail Williams says he can probably find a couple of Cholo girls to work on another order that's in the offing. It does seem as though the native handicrafts project is going to get off the ground at last. Unfortunately just at the moment when we may be packing the whole thing in.'

A hot breeze tinkled the bean pods overhead. Howel found Hargrave watching him with a melancholic droop of his lower eyelids. 'If you'll forgive me for saying so, it seems to have started since that evening you spent in Los Remedios together. May I speak frankly? Having two eyes in my head, it's been perfectly obvious to me how things are between you and Liz, and I'm absolutely delighted. But I must say I would have hoped that things would have been different. I mean that the clouds would have lifted. Also, I don't want to appear tactless, but I do feel—as we're both sufferers from the atmosphere of depression—that we ought to pool our resources in the way of information.'

'I do, too,' Howel said. 'On the occasion of the famous evening she went to meet a boy-friend, and he didn't turn up.'

Hargrave's face filled with the commiseration it was so perfectly designed to express. 'I was afraid something like that might have happened. I'm sorry.'

'Don't be sorry. I had a pretty good idea what I was taking on.'

'She was always going off somewhere on mysterious trips. Do forgive me—but I suppose you ought to know. One could only suppose she was visiting a—er—'

'Lover,' Howel said. 'Go on. I know all about it. Don't bother about my feelings.'

'He seems to have been a student, and most unsuitable from every point of view. Ronnie Smalldon did his best to break it up. I told him to stay out of it and not to waste his time, but he wouldn't listen to me. What his motives were, I can't imagine. I doubt if he knew himself. He was a queer, so it's unlikely to have been sexual jealousy. He used to say she brought out the protective instinct in him, but I must say he showed it in a most peculiar way.'

'By going to the police '

'The finance police, of all people. He had a pal in the tax-evasion department. All they did was to tip off the secret police and next day Arana himself turned up. If it hadn't been for Grail Williams, I don't know what would have happened.'

'But why all the fuss?' Howel asked.

'Because half the students are subversives, and if you go round with them you come under suspicion. Even if you're a foreigner. What I'm afraid we have to ask ourselves now is, is this thing still on?'

'She swore to me it was all over,' Howel said.

'Unfortunately it's a story we've heard before. Do you think she could still be seeing him?'

'I'm sure she isn't. Perhaps she hasn't got over him yet. I don't know. I don't much like talking about it.'

'I think the remedy would be to get her away as soon as possible,' Hargrave said.

'There's no doubt whatever about that. As you know, I'd hoped that we could have taken the plane tomorrow. Now it's next week at the earliest. Perhaps the week after. It's difficult to know what to do.'

'Would it help if I talked to her?' Hargrave said.

'I'm quite sure it wouldn't, Cedric. Thanks all the same. We're going on some sort of natural history outing this afternoon. That's if she doesn't change her mind. I'll make another attempt to pin her down.'

'I certainly wish you luck. Afraid you may find it heavy going all the same, if she isn't any brighter than she was at breakfast.'

The outing was less than a success. It was one of those hot, shapeless days under a blistered sky, a day of flat colours, and sounds without edge. Some listless botanizing produced a few orchids; crypripediums and cattleyas—all of them poor specimens with meagre, rusted blooms. There was nothing worth taking back.

Liz had very little to say. 'Did you come up here butter-fly-hunting with Homer King?' Howel asked her.

'The kind of butterflies you find in this kind of forest aren't worth having from a collector's point of view. We used to go to places like Quebradas.'

'Quebradas,' he said, 'that's right up in the Cordillera, isn't it? How on earth did you manage to get up there?'

'In the jeep,' she said. 'The going's pretty tough, but you can make it if it doesn't rain.'

'Guerrilla country, isn't it?'

'It used to be,' she said. 'They used to hide in the caves. We were looking for a butterfly called *Papillo crassus*. It's supposed to be one of the rarest butterflies in Colombia. Naturally, we didn't find any.'

Howel laughed. 'Somehow I can't imagine a grown man chasing after butterflies.'

'You should see Homer King. It's all he lives for. You only have to tell him there's a rare butterfly to be seen somewhere, and he's off like a shot. As I told you, it's a wonderful way of getting round the country.'

'I'm getting hot,' he said. 'Let's go down for a swim.'

'Could we make it some other time? When I feel a bit more energetic.'

Later he received a rebuff. 'I don't want to make love today.'

'What's the matter.'

'I'm not in the mood.'

'You're worried about something,' he said. 'You're not yourself.'

'Don't pay any attention,' she said. 'I'll get over it. Sorry to be a wet blanket.'

'I've come to the conclusion that the longer you stay here, the worse it's going to be. I can get two seats on the plane next Friday. Why don't we just go? That gives you four clear days to pack up.'

'It's impossible,' she said.

'Why is it impossible?'

'Because something's turned up to make it impossible.'

'Can't you tell me?'

'I suppose I'll have to sooner or later.'

'It's something to do with that trip you made into town at the weekend, isn't it? Did you see the Colombian boy?'

'No,' she said, 'I didn't see him, but I found out what had happened to him. He was picked up by the police.'

'The day he was supposed to meet you?' he said.

'The day after.'

'And that puts us back in square one, I suppose.'

'No,' she said, 'it doesn't put us back in square one. I haven't changed my mind about giving him up. It's a hundred to one I'd never see him again in any case, but I've got a terrible sense of responsibility.'

'Why should you have?'

'The reason I know what happened is that two friends stopped me in the street and told me. They know the police took him away, but that's all. They don't know where he is. They think he's in the Central Prison, but they're not sure, and they want me to find out.'

'How could you find out? As a foreigner.'

'A foreigner's supposed to have a better chance. If any of his friends start making enquiries they're likely to be picked up on suspicion.'

'And you said we weren't back in square one,' Howel said.

'All my life I've felt a tremendous sense of responsibility towards people,' Liz said. 'I suppose that's why I took up this kind of job. I get involved. When I've been as close to anybody as I have to Candido, I can't just turn my back on him when he's in trouble. I've told you that the affair's over, but that doesn't mean that my responsibility to help him in every way I possibly can is too. Do you understand?'

'Yes.'

'You ought to. I believe you're the sort of man who'd stick by a friend through thick and thin. I wouldn't contemplate living with you if I didn't.'

'And have you done anything about the matter?' Howel asked.

'Yes, I have. I went down to the prison to see if there was anything to be done.'

'You went down to the prison. Oh my God!'

'But I didn't get anywhere. There was a queue with a lot of weeping women. It was about an hour before I got into the office or whatever they call it, and then they told me I couldn't see a prisoner without having a special pass, and in any case there was no one in the register in Candido's name. They said political prisoners were kept in a special block, and nobody seemed to know who was there, and who wasn't.'

'Do you mean to say nobody wanted to know why you should be interested in a political prisoner?'

'They couldn't have cared less. They were just clerks. Dim little men doing their job.'

'What an escape you had,' he said. 'My God, when I think of it. Please don't do anything like that again.'

'I must find out somehow. I'm beginning to wonder if I shouldn't go straight to General Lopez himself.'

'And do you know what would happen? You'd be thrown out of the country. At the very best.'

'I'd have to take that chance.'

'Yes, but you'd also have achieved nothing.'

'That,' she said, 'would be the trouble. What *am* I to do?'

'I wish you'd come to me before, instead of taking such terrible risks,' he said.

'I didn't want to saddle you with my troubles, and in any case, I didn't see what you could do,' she said.

'There must be some way of finding out whether a man is in prison. Cedric ought to know.'

'He'd be furious.'

'No, he wouldn't. One thing, though, will you promise to keep out of this, while I see what can be done?'

'All right,' she said. 'If you'll do something straight away.'

'We'll go back now,' he said. 'And I'll talk to Cedric.

This is a corrupt country. There must be someone in the prison service who's not above picking up a few dollars on the side.'

He found Cedric seated, eyes half-closed, before a large bunch of arums which filled his room with the odour of their stems rotting in water.

'The trouble's over the ex-boy-friend, who's supposed to have been picked up and thrown into clink,' Howel said.

Hargrave's face, bland and soporific, was alerted with irritation.

'As was inevitable,' he said.

'She's been worrying about where they're holding him.'

'Didn't you tell me she'd given him up?'

'His friends seem to think she's better placed to find out than they are. It's a matter of loyalties.'

'Do you believe it's no more than that?'

'I think I do. Liz has a strong character. I'm prepared to accept her word that the affair is over, but I can understand why she should still want to do whatever she can.'

'Can you see any end to this?' Hargrave said.

'She went to the Central Prison herself a couple of days ago, to try to find out.'

Hargrave nodded his head, lips compressed, as if in agreement with some acid inner comment. 'I cannot imagine anything more stupid she could possibly do.'

'Luckily they were too busy to pay much attention to her, or so I gather. Her latest idea is to try General Lopez.'

'Liz is a beautiful, perceptive, and in some ways accomplished woman,' Hargrave said. 'She can also be a dreadful liability. It never ceases to surprise me that she hasn't got us all into serious trouble by now.'

'My feeling is we ought to make some sort of a move ourselves,' Howel said. 'If only to keep her quiet.'

'But what?'

'Don't we know anybody in the government?'

'Yes, in Finance, Highways and Public Health. They're all eminently bribable, but they happen to be in the wrong departments. We can't go and talk to them about political prisoners.'

'Any suggestion at all?' Howel asked.

'I hate to say this, but at this moment I can only think of one man who could possibly do anything for us.'

'Grail Williams, in fact.'

'How did you guess?'

'I've taken an immense dislike to him,' Howel said.

'I know you have, but you remember I warned you not to fall out with him, because I knew you'd find him useful sooner or later.'

'Isn't there anybody else?' Howel asked.

'Not that I can think of. Personally I'd have no hesitation whatever in going to him, and anyway I get the impression he wants to keep in with you. Believe me, Williams is our best bet.'

11

A s foreseen by Hargrave, Williams proved helpful. It turned
out that the deputy governor of the Central Prison was a
Colombian married to an American lady and that this
couple were members of the Los Remedios English-Speaking
Association's amateur dramatic society, of which Williams
was a leading light. If there had been any trace of coolness
in Williams's manner at any time during Howel's visit to
Esperanza, there was no sign of it now. He was most genial
and, showing not the slightest surprise that Howel should
want to meet a functionary in the prison service, he immediately wrote an introductory note.

The prison was hidden behind the bland front of one of
Los Remedios's great colonial palaces. Howel found the
deputy governor's office on the first floor over a patio in
Andalusian style, with pomegranate trees, their fruit sus-
pended like Christmas decorations in the dark and lustrous
foliage.

The deputy governor was small, round and darkly dressed,
with the soft voice of tremendous power. A faint smell of
decay lurked among the dark Victoriana of his office, as
if somewhere a long-forgotten apple was mouldering in the
corner of a drawer. He told Howel that he had been to
Downside. Grail Williams had mentioned that he had
published a volume of poetry. 'It is always a pleasure to
meet a friend of Mr Williams,' he said. 'Mr Williams has
made a splendid contribution to the cultural life of our
town.'

'I feel embarrassed to come to you with this problem,'

Howel said. 'One can't help feeling sympathy for this girl. She met the young man in perfectly respectable circumstances. At one of General Lopez's parties, to be exact. If he had any political affiliations, she certainly wasn't aware of it. She takes no interest whatever in politics.'

There was something about the deputy governor's personality that made Howel decide to state the facts of the case exactly as they were, without holding anything back.

'Very few of us can afford to, Mr Howel. Politics has become an occupation for specialists. We outsiders are allowed to see so little of what goes on below the surface. And again, in a poor country like this we can't really afford democracy, much as we should like to be able to. It still remains very much of an imported luxury. Even one day when we have it at last, I'm afraid that the prisons will still be with us.' He sighed.

He was a man who was easy to like, and he reminded Howel of a terribly effective old Portuguese hypnotist he had once seen performing in a Paris theatre. Could he even know that he presided over the fury, the anguish and the human dilapidation—if only half the reports were true—concealed in the fearful holes in the earth only thirty feet below where he sat at this moment?

The soft but powerful cajolery continued. 'Mr Williams may have told you that I'm an amateur at this job. A square peg in a round hole. I had to take it on because no one else would. Prisons are a black legacy from the past. Alas, my freedom of manœuvre is very limited. I do my best to let in a little light, a little humanity.'

He opened a drawer in his desk and took out a sheaf of roneoed papers. 'You read Spanish, I'm sure?'

'Fairly well.'

'You may care to look at this. It's the prison magazine I edit. We call it *Regeneración*. I think that's appropriate, don't you? It has some very interesting contributions by the prisoners. I find that the lyrical quality of some of the poems is very high. You will see that there is no suffocation of the spirit—and this is what we aim at. The prisoner succeeds in keeping that tiny inner flame alight. As Milton says, "Brightest in dungeons, liberty, thou art." '

The deputy governor told Howel that since receiving Williams's telephone call he had been able to locate Candido Rosas. He was in the hospital block—sent there probably for some minor ailment. They had become very health-conscious these days. And the hospital, said the deputy governor, was the best place to be in. The food was better and the beds more comfortable. He had no objection to Howel seeing Rosas if he wished to do so, and would have accompanied him himself, had he not been working to a deadline correcting the proofs for the next issue of *Regeneración*. These had to be ready that afternoon.

Howel went out again through the great doorway in the façade of opulent, honey-coloured stone and, turning into a side lane leading to the prison entrance, stepped instantly behind the scenes of the town into the raucous, sleazy world of its stage hands and small players. The entrance to the prison was through a wicket-gate outside which an immobile queue waited like down-and-outs hoping to sleep in the cheap seats of some back-street cinema. This queue was nourished by two garishly-painted cantinas, one being Te Esperarè a tu Vuelta, to which Howel had been taken by Hargrave on the day of his arrival at Los Remedios. He had since learned the legend of this bar, which was that certain criminals who found the outside world less generous and secure than that of the Central Prison, simply crossed the road when released at the end of their sentence, drank several aguadientes, then, borrowing a weapon, shot or stabbed the nearest person in sight and gave themselves up.

Inside the wicket-gate there were more resemblances to a run-down cinema, including posters of wanted men like realistic advertisements for a gangster film, and a box office into which a man had been crammed to issue tickets that might have been claimed by an usherette waiting in the darkness with a torch.

While the man was inspecting the slip of paper the deputy governor had given him, the prison official standing nearby had been doing a trick with a handkerchief which he pulled and twisted into some vague animal shape, which then with a final tug disappeared. Suddenly this man discharged a terrible peal of laughter, a warped and crackling whinny, hammered shapeless in its own echoes in the empty, vaulted space. Immediately the man in the little office let out a guffaw which was taken up by the two turnkeys waiting behind Howel at the inner prison gate. The laughter spread and followed him into the prison corridors themselves. All these warders in their dejected uniforms who trotted smirking and cackling towards him through the prison twilight had roughly the same face. It was the face of a joker—of a man who set off stink bombs or put plastic dogs' turds on chairs—and it flashed on him that they turned to laughter like the deputy governor turned to Milton, as a refuge from the sight of humanity never seen without its mask of despair. Laughter, too, was a class distinction, where the two halves of society, gaoler and captive, were hardly otherwise distinguishable in their wretchedness.

Rosas was not to be found in the hospital. Back in the reception office the clerk guffawed over his mistake. 'Fué llevado al manicomio,' he said. He put his fingers to his temple, screwed it round, and rolled his eyes. The chief warder, who had come back with Howel, threw back his head and bayed, while a group of red-eyed old women in black cringing at the office window looked on with respect.

A decade before in a reaction of conscience-searching and liberality from the horrors of the violencia, the government had voted a large sum for the reform of the prisons in Los Remedios. Much of this had been spent on the hospital, which was consequently a showpiece, with chintz curtains for the false windows painted on the cell walls, and a picture of the harbour of Rio de Janeiro in every cell. Journalists who had heard rumours of black holes under the prison—those iron wombs where it was said that men were kept in darkness and absolute silence for up to seven years and, emerging, were reborn into the world as speechless as babies—were willingly taken to the hospital and shown the X-ray equipment, the kitchens and the diet charts. Howel was one of the few outsiders who had seen the asylum, and in taking him there, the chief warder committed a grave blunder.

Howel found himself in a vast, dark room with dirty, cemented walls and floor, cages all round, and something like a horse-trough for ablutions in the middle. He was reminded of a monkey house in the worst kind of zoo, but here the stench was far worse.

In the cages men who were for the most part naked, squatted, prowled—and in one case crawled on all fours—among excrement and puddles of urine. The chief warder had escaped, and as Howel and his subordinate came in a howling went up, and the caged men began to leap about excitedly, convulsed not with rage, but with a kind of obscene merriment—usurped from the warders, it seemed to Howel, with the arrogance of insanity.

Suddenly the officer with him dodged away and ducked. Something soft struck Howel in the chest and fell to the ground. He realized they were being bombarded with excrement. He scampered back to the door. '*Donde está Rosas?*' he asked the warder.

'*Está alli.*'

Howel made out a form in the gloom of a cage at the far end of the room. He, too, was naked.

The bombardment began again and the warder pulled him away. *'Vamonos.'*

'Don't try to keep anything back,' Liz said. 'It's not necessary. When I heard he'd been arrested I had to come to terms with everything else.' Strain sharpened her features. She pulled a ring over a finger joint and pushed it back, leaving the knuckle white.

'He's in the prison asylum,' Howel said. 'It's not as bad as it sounds.'

'Isn't it?' she said. 'Did you actually see him yourself.'

'I actually saw him for a moment. I wasn't allowed to speak to him. He looked perfectly normal to me.'

'They do, don't they? If they're not in a padded cell. Did they tell you what was supposed to be wrong with him?'

'No, but I've got my own ideas on the subject. I had a long talk with the deputy governor, who seemed a very decent, humane sort of fellow. Reading between the lines, I believe it's not impossible that the prison authorities put a man in hospital or in the asylum whenever they want to keep him out of reach of the police. He can't be interrogated if he's technically mad.'

'It's a comforting thought,' she said. 'And to you he looked quite normal?'

'Absolutely.'

'You saw his face?'

'I saw his face.'

'And he showed no signs of ill-treatment?'

'None at all.'

'What was he doing?' she asked. 'Was he in bed?'

'No, he was walking about.'

'In some sort of cell?'

'In a room,' Howel said. 'An ordinary small room. With barred windows. I think he'll be all right.'

'Is this place in the political prisoners' block?'

'No, that's just the point. It's quite separate. It's a separate building at the back of the hospital. You have to go through the hospital to get to it. The whole set-up's a great improvement on the prison itself. They make a big thing of looking after prisoners' health.'

'I'm glad of that,' she said.

'My feeling was that the deputy governor's no friend of the police state,' Howel said. 'Naturally there's very little he can say, but I believe he does what he can. Oh yes, I nearly forgot—he believes there'll be an amnesty for all the political prisoners as soon as Lopez takes over.'

She wiped her eyes, and smiled. 'Thank you very much for going. I'll never, never forget it.'

12

W I T H the cool of the evening the ventriloquial clucking of frogs had come close to the house, and the toucans, no longer imprisoned by mist, were going back to the mountains under a wide yellow sky. Grail Williams and his wife sat at their window sipping iced water. Grail had just got back after spending a day in Los Remedios.

'The children were very good,' Mary said. 'They finished all the work I gave them, and made no fuss at all about going to bed. Two cases of bronchitis at the clinic, and the throat infections are responding to antibiotics. Apart from that, nothing else. Now I'm anxious to hear how you got on.'

'I saw the General,' Grail said, 'and as ever, he was more than gracious. He gave me an hour of his time, which considering the strain he's been under was most gratifying. Everything went better than I expected. All in all, it was most successful.'

'Isn't it so often the case?' Mary said. 'One feels discouraged and defeated. Everything seems to be going wrong, and then suddenly things change again, and one can't put a foot wrong.'

'It was very clear to me that the General was delighted with the co-operation we've been able to give him at what's been for him a very worrying time. He's written a personal letter of thanks to Wesley Scott and another to the organization. Had we not acted in the prompt manner we did, he said, the government might have been involved in an extensive military operation.'

'I'm glad some good came of it,' Mary said. 'I still wish we could keep from being mixed up in this kind of thing.

It saddens me.'

Williams was distracted from answering by the entry of the first of the night's moths. He cuffed it away and then pressed a wall switch, causing a length of tubular lighting outside the window to light up. This would attract all the winged insects in the neighbourhood to their extermination by a spray released automatically at ten-minute intervals by a nozzle over the lamp-holder. It was Williams's own invention.

'I've always believed in striking while the iron is hot,' Williams said. 'This seemed to me the moment to suggest the possibility of expanding our work, and the General was not only receptive, but apparently enthusiastic.'

'Once again our prayers have really been answered,' Mary said.

'All this is a little premature, as the General isn't in power yet. However he's virtually promised to give us the OK as soon as he is. What he'd like to see us do is open another half-dozen centres right through the country. While it's early to discuss details, I gathered that the government would be very happy to build airstrips. He says he refuses to leave the Indians to their fate. I believe he's being absolutely sincere when he says that he's determined to better their standards of health and education, and eventually move them into the towns. As I see it, our aims are identical.'

'It's wonderful that he should be so lacking in bigotry, isn't it?' Mary said. 'So many Catholics resent our mission.'

'Yet for all that, he's a religious man. He expressed great interest in my work in translating the scriptures, and I told him of some of the difficulties involved, such as conveying a picture of Rome to Indians who have never seen a village of more than twenty huts. I mentioned that one of our converts once asked if Cæsar was General Lopez, and he was much amused.'

'If we're to open more centres, we should want more

trained staff,' Mary said.

'I don't think so,' Williams said. 'I see the new centres more as reception points to which the Indians could be attracted in the usual way, and then passed on down to Esperanza where the real task of evangelization would begin. The General thought that with the government behind us the work could be completed within ten years.'

Mary closed her eyes, surrendering herself to a vision.

Williams's attention had been taken for a moment by the sound of his generator skipping a beat. Probably a partially blocked fuel lead, he thought, which he would rectify in a spare half-hour before supper. He came back to the events of the day. 'The visit to General Lopez turned out to be opportune for another reason. I haven't spoken to you about this before but I've been very worried about what to do about converts who betrayed their faith by taking part in a costumbre. Diego made a number of enquiries. Forty-two admit to having been present, but the real total may be as high as a hundred.'

'A hundred!' she said. 'That's almost unbelievable. I didn't dream that it was as bad as that.'

'This calls for the most energetic action on our part. If we showed any weakness we might be putting a strain on the loyalty of our other converts. I'd already decided that the forty-two renegades would have to go, but the question was where? Now General Lopez has come along to solve the problem for me. He's offered to take any assimilated Indians off our hands and find them immediate employment in industry.'

'I didn't know Los Remedios had any industries.'

'Mines,' he said. 'They used to produce millions of dollars' worth of tin a year.'

'Wasn't there a scandal of some sort about the tin mine?' Mary said. 'Didn't the government close it down?'

Mary noticed an expression in his face that she had only

seen two or three times before in their married life. He blinked, showing the whites of his eyes for a fraction of a second. When he spoke he sounded as though he had just remembered something of slight importance.

'I believe there *were* several accidents. The gear seems to have been antiquated, and the proper safety precautions may not have been observed. I understand a new company will be taking over and modernizing all the equipment. They hope to re-open part of the workings in a matter of days.'

'Is mining heavy work?' she asked.

'Not under modern conditions.'

'Nearly all our converts still have weak lungs. I don't think they'd stand up well to conditions that imposed a great deal of physical strain.'

'The work will be no heavier than timber-felling or cane-cutting. Moreover there won't be the heat to contend with.'

She noticed the use of the future, not the conditional tense.

'You've decided, then?'

'In the case of the forty-two, yes—but there may be quite a few more. If the General's scheme for our expansion materializes we're going to have to handle a large number of converts, and that means advance planning. Maybe this is the moment to clear our doubtful elements. We've always agreed that constant employment is essential, and we're going to have to look outside our own resources to find that employment. Cane-cutting only keeps them going for six weeks, and after that it's tree-felling. By my calculations we shall have run through the trees on our present concession in a matter of six months.'

'What became of the idea of starting a quarry?'

'I didn't want to do it unless I had to, because it's no use preaching "six days shalt thou labour" if that labour can't be made a reality. We'd end up with a pile of stones and nothing to do with them. This is the real solution.' He turned his head away, and appeared to have slipped into a conversation of trivial family interest with a portrait of his mother hanging on the wall. 'General Lopez has asked to be allowed to make a donation to our field fund for each Indian taking a contract, and I haven't said no. I checked with Diego yesterday and he tells me that of the 238 Indians on our register, 175 have accepted baptism and would pass our assimilation test. I may decide to let them all go.'

His private colloquy with his mother had ceased and, returning to Mary, he was surprised by her troubled look.

'Is there anything the matter, dear?'

She shook her head, but he knew that there was, and he knew what it was. There was too much of a woman's softness in her, and he was afraid that in the great battle that lay ahead, when he would need her at his side, this softness might become weakness, and in the end she might even fail him.

It was dark now, but a point of light on the mountain slopes silhouetted against the greenly-glowing sky revealed the presence of a camp of nomads who had come down, almost to within sight of the village, in search of deer. Williams considered their plight with sincerest sorrow, comforted by the thought that experts were of the opinion that within twenty years there would be no nomads left in the whole of Latin America.

Throughout their life together Williams and his wife had always worked in the closest harmony and unity of purpose, and now, disturbed by her misgivings, he began to look round for further justification for a course of action he would in any case take.

Next morning he left home early with the intention of paying a surprise visit to the timber yard where a work-party arrived in theory at 6.0 a.m. to begin its twelve-hour working day. An informant had reported to him that this party was consistently late for work.

The prize for good conduct in Esperanza was to be employed in varied and creative work, such as weaving, embroidery, and the making of cooking utensils and pots, and those who asked to be baptized and began the slow upward struggle towards assimilation were rewarded in this way. The stubbornly conservative, or those who committed crimes by Williams's standards, were sent to the timber yard where the work was hard and monotonous. Only handsaws were permitted in the yard, and with these the great forest trees were reduced slowly and painfully to hundreds of thousands of small faggots, which were examined—and if necessary measured—by the captains in charge of the work-parties for identical dimensions. No saleable hardwood remained in this part of the forest, and the wood the Indians cut in this way had always been used to stoke the mission's fires. Williams calculated that by now he had fifteen years' supply stocked in piles that from a distance were beginning to look like the skyscrapers and monuments of a strange city.

Driving out of his garage, the missionary felt a slight sense of strain, which soon began to lift. He had been at work for two hours on his translation that morning, wrestling with passages in the Epistle to Timothy, which happened to be the scriptural book he least enjoyed. Williams had even applied to his superiors for their permission to substitute another book, suggesting Galatians, but they had not agreed. Now, as a result, his converts who already suffered from an acute absence of any sense of property were to be told that having food and raiment they should be content, and that the rich had pierced themselves through with many arrows. Williams knew of many scriptural passages assuring their reader that the enjoyment of wealth was compatible with the godly life, and he vowed one day to prepare a

133

valuable anthology of these. When St Paul wrote 'money is the root of all evil', he sounded to Williams far too much like Karl Marx.

A habit of optimism saved Williams from all but the shortest depressions and he soon plunged into a chain of speculation arising from another project broached at his meeting with General Lopez, which he had not thought fit to mention to Mary at this stage.

Although the timber on the mission's original concession of 10,000 acres was nearly exhausted the General had mentioned in an earlier conversation, and confirmed in this latest, that there would be no difficulty at all in acquiring more land. In so far as there could be said to be a market-value at all, it was very low—a dollar or two per acre. Much of the land had been designated a tribal area and as such guaranteed by the constitution for the use of the Indians in perpetuity, but as it was to be presumed that the Indians would shortly have vanished, no objection would be raised to its being cleared and put to rational use. At this original meeting the General had gone on to say that, using their old tribal techniques, no one could clear the forest faster and more efficiently than the Indians themselves, and although on the previous day he had brought up the urgent need for labour for the tin mine, Williams calculated that this demand could soon be satisfied, leaving a good surplus of labour.

Grail Williams, in fact, had seen for some months the way the wind was blowing, and a week before, in anticipation of the General's benevolent attitude, had asked a friend, the director of a small paper-mill in Bogotà, to visit him at the mission. Faced with a dozen ziggurats of beautifully-stacked timber, the man had been silent with admiration.

'Well, George. Ever seen so much wood before in your life?'

'I have, but not often.'

'What would you pay for it?'

'Nothing at all. I wouldn't buy it lying here.'

'You probably wouldn't, but what's it worth.'

'In Bogotá? Maybe two hundred thousand dollars. Here? Well, you couldn't put a price on it, because nobody would want it.'

'The mission would like to go into business with you,' Williams said. 'You could start up a part-owned subsidiary down here. We'd put up half the capital for the mill and supply all the wood the company needed at half the market price in Bogotá. What do you say?'

'How long would the supply of wood last?'

'Indefinitely.'

'You could guarantee that?'

'I could.'

'I'd like to talk to the board about it,' Williams's friend said. 'I'll give you a decision within forty-eight hours.'

Next day a cable had arrived with the one word—'OK.'

Arriving at the timber yard at exactly six, Williams felt a pleasure he was quite unable to conceal from himself to find that there were no signs of the work-party. He picked up a random sample of blocks from the pile made the previous day—and, measuring them with the ruler he always carried, found that in four cases out of six the measurements failed to fall within the limits of toleration he had set. He could see that the problem was how to tighten up discipline when the forty-two men at present employed in the yard knew that they were already suffering the maximum sentences imposed.

Twenty minutes passed and Williams decided to fill in the time by driving to a nearby patch of forest where he had recently conducted an experiment in defoliation, and from which, since it was on a hillside, the timber yard could be kept under observation. Williams had sprayed the area from his Cessna with a recently evolved defoliant. The few remaining large trees that might have protected the undergrowth had been cut out in preparation, and the spray had fallen on seedlings and underbrush, which had showed signs of wilting after a few days. Now, three weeks later, he stood knee-deep in the black and shrivelled vegetation that had been seared by drifting spray, and put a match to it. It went up with a hiss and crackle of exploding resins, throwing streamers of flame and blue smoke high into the air. The experiment was a success. In this part of the forest Williams considered defoliants unnecessary, but in the lower altitudes of the true rain-forest he decided that the process of burning and clearing could be greatly speeded up in this way.

At nearly quarter to seven, his jeep parked out of sight among the trees, Williams saw the work-party come trotting into sight. He waited five minutes and then drove down to the yard. The work-party was in the charge of a junior captain called Diogenes Calixto, a man of austere Castilian presence and thinly chiselled features, with a coal-black skin.

'At what time did you start work, Diogenes?'

'At six more or less, Mr Williams. The usual.'

It was remarkable to Williams how this man's face of a conquistador could contain an expression that was so totally subservient.

'You're quite sure of that?'

'Yes, Mr Williams. It may have been a few minutes later.'

Williams stared at him in silence for a number of seconds.

'That can't be true, Diogenes. I was here myself at six, and I've been here ever since. What happened?'

'I don't have a watch, Mr Williams, sir, personally. When Junior Captain Rodriguez took the men to the mess hall the breakfast wasn't ready.'

'What are you trying to say, Diogenes? Are you trying to tell me that you didn't know the time, or that Rodriguez kept you waiting?'

Calixto's patrician features were composed in a mask of fear and servility. 'Well, as a matter of fact, Mr Williams, Rodriguez kept me waiting.'

'You're quite sure of that, aren't you? He could lose his captaincy.'

'That's the way it was, Mr Williams.'

'You should have gone yourself to find out what was holding things up, shouldn't you?'

'Yes, sir.'

'Of course you should.' Williams reached out and tugged suddenly at the unbuttoned flap of Calixto's shirt pocket. 'You committed two crimes,' he said. 'You've been slothful and inefficient, and you haven't hesitated to attempt to cover up your tracks by lying.'

'I'm sorry, Mr Williams. I really am.'

'I'm disappointed in you, Diogenes. You've let the mission down, and when you let the mission down who else is it you let down besides?'

'Our Lord, Mr Williams.'

'I'm glad you realize that. You're right, you let Our Lord down. And what do you think we ought to do about that?'

Calixto knew the answer that was expected of him.

'I ought to be punished, Mr Williams, sir.'

'I think you ought to be punished, too. The question is, what form that punishment should take. What do *you* think you deserve in the way of a punishment?'

'How would it be if you took my money away for a week?' Calixto suggested. 'A month if you like.' A tell-tale eagerness had come into the hangdog look.

Williams shook his head. 'I'm afraid that wouldn't do. It wouldn't be a real punishment at all. You're a man who has very little to do with his money. The punishment has to be something you really feel. Something that causes you pain.'

'Maybe I could fast for a few days, Mr Williams?'

'That wouldn't do either, Diogenes. You've been too used to going short of food in the past. You never had a full stomach when you were a kid. The thing to remember is, you can't fool God. The act of contrition has to be real. Something unpleasant. Something you really hate having to do.'

'I could take over cleaning the latrines. I can't think of anything else. I really can't.'

'Well, as it happens I can, Diogenes. Right now while we've been talking I've been asking for God's guidance, and he's shown me a way you can put yourself in the clear. And it isn't going to be so difficult after all. It isn't going to be so hard as I thought it might be. Mrs Williams is going on vacation this fall. It's cold in Cincinnati, and I'd like her to have a nice warm coat to wear.'

'I can buy a bearskin, Mr Williams. The skin of a young black bear. Maybe two skins.' Calixto was grasping at a straw, knowing as he made the hopeless suggestion that no such easy solution was likely to appease the missionary, and already beginning to suspect the unpleasant truth.

Williams shook his head. 'It's possum she wants. These woods are full of possum. What I want you to do, Diogenes, is to bring me a dozen nice possum skins.'

The punishment was a real one. The opossum was taboo to the Indians and Grail Williams knew that the superstitious fear they felt for it had spread to those who lived among Indians, as Calixto had done all his life, and that this feeling was so strong as to produce a feeling of revulsion, even nausea, at the mere sight of the animal.

'God wants us to do the things we don't want to do, because that's the way he saves us from our sins. God hates sinfulness. Twelve possum skins, Diogenes. By the end of the week. You're not afraid, are you?'

'No, Mr Williams. I'm not afraid.'

'And you accept the punishment the Lord has seen fit

to lay on you with a meek and contrite heart?'

'Yes, Mr Williams, I do. I accept the Lord's punishment.'
The defeat in Diogenes's face was now total.

'Good, then, and now I'll tell you what I'm going to do
about the men. They've robbed the mission and they've
robbed God. Don't think I don't know what's been going on.
Today they won't stop work at six. They'll work for an
extra hour to make up for time lost, and then another hour
as a punishment. Naturally you'll be there, Diogenes.'

'It gets dark at seven, Mr Williams.'

'I know it does, but we won't let that bother us. We'll
run a cable over from the compound and fix up lighting.'

'Do you want me to do that, Mr Williams?'

'No, I want you to stay in the yard and get on with your
work. I'll send over an electrician,' Williams said.

He was going, and he called back. 'And by the way, Diogenes, it'll be half rations tonight.'

Williams left Calixto and drove the short distance to Esperanza to visit his assistant, Homer King. King had been with
him only six months, an energetic red-headed young man
with an expression of amazement that was easily converted
to one of anger. Williams hoped that time and the tropics
would calm him.

The walls of Homer King's office were lined with cases
containing mounted butterflies and insects, and Williams
stopped to admire them. His attention was attracted by a
particularly large blue butterfly which, from some angles,
shone as though generating its own source of light.

'That's a swell new butterfly you have there, Homer.
What's it's name?'

'*Morpho cypris*, Mr Williams. A blue female. Only about
one in a thousand turns out blue, so they don't come much
rarer. Mostways they're brown. The blue coloration is on
account of the light scatter on the air-spaces in the scales.'

'That's a very interesting piece of information,' Williams said. 'The air-spaces in the scales. Just imagine that.'

A gentleness had entered King's normally rather harsh and emphatic voice. 'You see, Mr Williams, the males require the air-spaces to reach the tops of the trees, where they feed. The females satisfy the requirements of their diet down in the undergrowth. They don't have to fly much. Once again one has to marvel at the wonders of God's creation.'

'And one never ceases to marvel, Homer,' Williams said. 'You have an absorbing hobby. I did a big spraying the other day, and I saw some pretty nice butterflies lying around. You ought to come along next time.'

'I sure will,' King said.

'Hear you've been taking Miss Sayers on some of your trips these last few weeks.'

'We've been out with the nets a few times, Mr Williams. I hope that's all right.'

'Well, in future don't take the jeep. Those plates weren't issued to the mission. They're for my personal use and I'm held responsible. And another thing, Homer; Miss Sayers has me a little worried for more than one reason. Do you think she really is interested in butterflies?'

'I think so, Mr Williams. She always seems very pleased to come.'

'Where do you go?'

'Quebradas, La Laguna, Picos Altas—Sosiego, sometimes.'

'Sosiego, eh? That village is full of subversives. Colonel Arana was telling me about Sosiego. You'd better keep a look-out for Reds while you're chasing butterflies round Sosiego.'

'There's a trader we visit once in a while. That's where I bought the *Morpho cypris*. The Indians catch them round the old emerald mine at Muzzo. They have a legend about the morphos turning into emeralds, or the other way round. I forget which it is.' He made a face of contempt. 'They have so many damn-fool legends.'

'Well, Homer, I can't see any reason why I should ask you to quit taking Miss Sayers around, but I should just like to say this. She's a young lady I have a kind of feeling about. Something about her has me wondering. Just wondering, Homer.'

Williams turned regretfully from the wall-cases, asking himself if he couldn't possibly find time to fit butterfly-collection into the catalogue of his other many interests. 'How are things going with the work here just now, from your angle of view?'

'Not as well as I'd like, Mr Williams.'

'They're not going so well as I'd like, either,' Williams said.

'In fact the last few days I've had to put a number of people in the book,' King said. 'There seems to be a new spirit about. A kind of stubbornness. When I first came here it was weeks before I had a case of authority being deliberately flouted. Now it's a matter of daily occurrence. The rule we made about women not being allowed to walk behind their husbands, for example, they break it all the time.'

'I saw a couple doing it on my way over here,' Williams said.

'We had a case of a Cholo entering a chalet by the window because he'd seen women using the door. We put him down for the timber yard.'

'It begins to look like deliberate defiance,' Williams said. 'They all know the rules.'

'A woman scraped her cheeks, with a rusty nail, maybe to produce an infection,' King said. 'Leastwise I'm pretty sure she did. At the dispensary they gave her acriflavine ointment to put on it. This was the second or third time I've seen a woman going about the place with her cheeks painted yellow. I made a few enquiries, as a result of which I have a strong hunch that this painting went along with the secret worship of an idol.'

'And I would think you were right. I would say that that was exactly what it was. You've turned out a very keen observer, Homer. Very keen indeed. Did you take any action in this case?'

'There was nothing I could do, Mr Williams. You were going to work out deterrents we could use with the women. At present we don't have any.'

'I know we don't and it's a thing I've got to get down to. Where a woman's got children you could take them away from her and put them in the crèche for a day or two. That might do some good. Anyway there's no harm in giving it a try.'

'My feeling, Mr Williams, is that we've been the victims of many deceptions we don't know about,' King said. He bared his strong canine teeth slightly, as the ingredient of anger in the balance of the moment slightly outweighed that of surprise. 'I've been doing a bit of detective work on my own and I believe the rot began to set in when that Cholo died at police headquarters.'

'That may be so,' Williams said. 'How many of our converts got themselves mixed up in this costumbre thing, do you suppose?'

'The lot,' King said. A sudden release of adrenalin into his bloodstream made him grit his teeth.

Williams watched him with curiosity, deciding at that moment that King could never become his successor at Dos Santos when he and Mary moved elsewhere. He was too passionate.

'Well, no, hardly the lot, Homer. Let's say fifty or sixty per cent at the most. Anyway, whatever the percentage is, it's too high, and I'm wondering if the moment hasn't come to take a long hard look at our basic policy, and ask ourselves whether we may not be heading in the wrong direction?'

'I hope there'll be a strengthening of discipline,' King said.

142

'Whatever else we decide to do.'

'What I have in mind is more fundamental,' Williams said. 'I'm beginning to see the need for sweeping changes, but I'm not quite certain at this stage what those changes have to be. This artisanate thing we have, for example. Letting them weave cloth and make pots. Couldn't it be that all we're doing is pandering to tribalism? Maybe we weren't as smart as we thought. Maybe we shouldn't have permitted anything that could have reminded them of the old, idolatrous way of life.'

'That's certainly the way I see it,' King said.

'Do you happen to know what our stocks of raw material for the artisanate are at this moment?'

'They're very low. I was going to speak to you about it.'

'Good. That all fits in very nicely. It couldn't really have worked out for the better,' Williams said.

13

T H E Cayambo area where they would make their base lay at 11,000 feet in a high valley between the second and third great Cordillera chains that divided up that part of the country. Before reaching Cayambo, the guerrillas hoped to make contact with the Cholo Indians of Guayabero and Mapayan. Athos had visited both tribes, and both had promised him recruits. It was hoped that some of them would be armed with old hunting rifles.

Despite all the preliminary studies the organizers of the expedition had undertaken, the men soon found themselves troubled by most of the problems that had afflicted Comrade Guevara and the comrades who had operated elsewhere at one time or another and had left an account of their sufferings. Guevara had been criticized for his deliberate choice of the tropics for the scene of his operations, but the long marches and the hard climbs in the high mountains turned out to be equally strenuous. The men who had chosen the jungle had been turned in the end into walking skeletons through the sheer fatigue of hacking paths through it in the course of their endless and pointless peregrinations. The survivors of the 8th October band hauled themselves from valley to peak and peak to valley in the rarified air that put a terrible strain on their lungs as well as their muscles. Just as their predecessors had lost their way, they lost their way. Just as the others had starved and lived on disgusting foods, they starved and lived on disgusting foods. The few cans of meat, the tinned milk, and the few pounds of meal they could carry, were soon used up, and they tasted the bitter, acrid flesh of lizards, hawks, an occasional anteater, an armadillo, even a wild cat. Like all the rest, they began to suffer from fainting fits, dizziness, diarrhœa and cramps.

The physical stresses they underwent were soon reflected (as had been the case with all the others) in dissensions and personality conflicts. The democratic spirit that had existed at the outset evaporated, and Diaz the leader became authoritarian and aloof. Fuentes, the doctor and Ramos, an ex-law student, commenting on this, noted with irony the fact that the aristocratic class, represented by Diaz, which had ruled the country through four or five families since the Conquest, was preparing to do so again after the Marxist revolution had become a fact. In this emergence of something like a shadow class structure, Borda was the proletarian. He irritated Diaz, who found him, despite his swollen feet and painfully sunburned face, too lively for the seriousness of the purpose. He entertained the men when they were in the mood for it at night by singing them Brazilian songs, and Diaz knew enough Portuguese to find the words distasteful. Borda was to some extent separated from the rest by his ignorance of political theory, his inability to employ Marxist catch-phrases, and also by his mission. He made no secret of the fact that he was from the slums of Recife and of a vague early background of juvenile delinquency and petty, belly-filling crime.

The seventeenth and eighteenth days of the expedition brought its members to a low ebb of demoralization through poor map-reading on Diaz's part. They had struggled up to the headwaters of the Magdalena river through the high valley in the province of Huila between the eastern and central Cordillera ranges. The pinnacles of Purace were behind, and now sketched in ice on the sky ahead was the Sierra Nevada de Huila, rising to nearly 18,000 feet. A crossing of the Cordillera to the west had to be made somewhere between these two impossible barriers. On the seventeenth day the attempt was begun up a deep gully Diaz believed he had identified in his map, and which appeared to take them very close to the watershed at one of the lowest points. For nearly twelve hours they struggled up through this until suddenly it turned away southwards and came to an end between two mountain spurs and unscaleable precipices.

They had spent a night among freezing mists at 13,000 feet and now they were back roughly to the point from which they had set out, exhausted and famished and in most cases sick. It was a desolate early evening, but they could go no farther and they had set up camp for the night, scraped together piles of fibrous bric-à-brac, and made fires. The valley was treeless and wasted; a landscape washed over with a depressed blue, like a colour-movie made by some outdated process. Cactus grew among mauvish flints, planted regularly as if by a gardener. A mile away the river whispered in its gorge out of sight, and the blue Cordillera beyond lay all along the horizon like a low breaker caught by a camera just before it rises to curl over at the edge of the beach. A terrible wind hissed and chirped among the stones.

The men had formed their exclusive companionships. Ramos and Fuentes squatted by their own fire, and Manera had paired off with Rafael Villa, the Cholo speaker. Borda had taken his gun and mooched a short distance away in the hope of shooting a bird, appearing as a blackened, scarecrow figure against a sky slashed with lugubrious sunset colours.

Diaz sheltered from the wind in the lee of a great boulder, some distance from the others, shivering and despondent. He felt himself the object of criticism and dislike, and sensed that patience was about to collapse. He had just given an order that there would be no evening meal—that the smelly scraps of lizard and anteater flesh which was all that remained was to be kept in reserve to face the emergencies of the next day. The decision had been received in hostile silence. Adversity, Diaz noted, had brought out more vice

146

than virtue in the men.

In these moments of gloom that accompanied exhaustion at the day's end, Diaz was the subject of paranoid speculations over the anonymous letter he had received with its warning of the existence of a traitor in their midst. He was convinced of the genuineness of this message, and his black moods were occupied by internal inquisitions conducted in turn on the members of the expedition in which every action, however trivial, and what he could remember of everything they said in his presence, was examined and re-examined for the taint of treachery. While the rational Diaz, refreshed by the night's sleep, was ready to admit to himself in the morning that there was a fifty per cent chance that the spy, if there had been one, had fallen to the frontier guards' guns, at times such as these he was utterly convinced that he was still among them.

Just after dark Rafael Villa found him, with a confession to make, and a startling piece of news. From being a cheerful and determined man Villa had been reduced to a whining complainer by repeated asthma attacks brought on by the altitudes. Villa's asthma slowed down the march, and Diaz, refusing to accept them as more than an excuse to avoid carrying a fair share of the equipment, had insulted Villa in front of the rest, and called him a leadswinger. At this point Manera had befriended Villa. He had constantly sympathized with him, carried Villa's pack as well as his own when Villa had been overtaken by an attack, and shared his food with him. Manera, too, had constantly criticized Diaz, both as a man and a leader, and the two, drawn closer and closer together, had begun to consider rebellion. Then Manera had had a staggering suggestion to make. He had proposed that they should leave the expedition. His plan was that next morning at first light they should slip away and head for the village of Teruel, about 40 miles away to the northeast. From here there was a motor road to the town of Neira, on the edge of the eastern plain. This journey could not be contemplated without first taking possession of Diaz's military map, and this Manera had said he was quite prepared to do.

It was the proposed theft of the map that had suddenly made Villa see the gravity of the situation, and had brought about his change of heart, but he had pretended to go along with the scheme, and then Manera had let drop a remark that had alerted Villa to the possibility of betrayal he had not previously suspected. Villa had said that he was afraid of the vengeance of the group, and Manera had laughed the possibility off. In a matter of days or weeks at the most, he had said, the group would no longer exist. 'We'll get a pardon,' Manera had said. 'A pardon from whom?' Villa had wanted to know. 'From the government, of course.'

'So you aren't a Marxist any longer.'

'Marxism isn't adventurism. The 8th October Movement's adventurist policies only distract Marxists from the correct approach to the conquest of power. Our model must be Chile, and the adventurists must be crushed at all costs.

'Even by collaboration with a bourgeois government?'

'Even by that.'

At this point Villa, a weak but sentimental man, concluded that Manera had sold himself out.

When seized next morning just as he and Villa were leaving camp, Manera showed only slight surprise. He was immediately tried, made no attempt to dispute any part of Villa's evidence, but asked to be allowed to speak in his own defence. Manera had made a long, eloquent and persuasive speech explaining his actions. In his analysis of the operation's weakness in planning, strategy and leadership, Manera seemed to Diaz to reproduce all his own private criticisms of the ill-starred Bolivian adventure of Comrade Guevara. They were repeating with shocking fidelity, Manera said, the patterns of failure of the past, sometimes appearing on a subconscious level, even, to plan their own defeat. Manera pointed out that in his foolish subservience to outdated revolutionary models, Diaz had even wished to start the campaign with twelve men in imitation—whether conscious or not—of the twelve survivors in the Sierra Maestra who had begun the Cuban revolution. (Why not the twelve apostles while he's about it? Diaz thought.) Denying that he was a spy, Manera listed his services to the Colombian guerrilla movement, and took off his shirt to show the scars left by the torture he had undergone in prison. He had intended to desert, he said, taking Villa with him, because he preferred to live and fight for the cause rather than to sacrifice himself uselessly in an undertaking so certain to fail.

Diaz summed up, saying that whatever contributions Manera had made to the cause in the past, it was impossible to take these into consideration in a trial on the capital charge of desertion and sabotage. He added that in stealing the only detailed map they possessed Manera had showed himself prepared to do the police's work for them, knowing that without a map, the destruction of the expedition was virtually certain. Even had they survived, their presence in the mountains would have been rendered useless, because in persuading Villa, too, to desert, Manera would have deprived the expedition of its only fluent Cholo speaker, after the loss of Athos. It was an occasion not only of acute melancholy but of embarrassment for Diaz, in which for a moment he saw himself with disgust, presiding at a harsh parody of bourgeois justice in which Manera, his hands bound behind him, was the only serene and dignified presence.

Manera was found guilty by unanimous vote, with the exception of Borda, who asked to be allowed to abstain. He seemed only a little bewildered at what might have been the incomprehension of the others. In this grey morning full of sepulchral shapes and the red eye of the sun blotted in mist, Manera seemed the only free man, standing among condemned prisoners.

Diaz rubbed his scaling fingers together as he pronounced the sentence of death. Receiving it, Manera knotted his brows for a moment as if in perplexity, but the expression soon cleared. When asked if he had any last request to make he nodded, asking in a matter-of-fact way if a chain he wore round his neck could be given to a girl who had once been his fiancée, and Fuentes wrote down her name. At this point Diaz remembered a story he had once heard of Manera's harsh treatment of this girl. He wondered . . .

Sentence having been passed, the almost unthinkable problem now arose of how it was to be carried out. Manera was escorted with almost religious formality to the shelter of a rock out of earshot of the deliberations of the others. There followed an interval of leaden, eye-avoiding silence in which they all awaited an explanation of how the life was to be taken from a man now brusquely labelled traitor, but always until this moment seen as a hero. Manera, generous and uncomplaining, had always been the most popular member of the expedition, and the majestic indifference to his fate he had displayed at his trial had made it difficult, even now, to withhold respect. Where this respect was underscored with anger, it was anger directed not so much against Manera's treachery, as at the fact that he should have plunged them into this dilemma.

Diaz forced himself in the end to begin the discussion of the macabre protocol of the occasion, but he was unable to speak with the authority of a leader. Instead of giving orders he asked for suggestions. Execution by firing squad, briefly alluded to, was turned down. Fuentes, the doctor, stated flatly that his profession was to heal and not kill, and that he would kill in self-defence and no more. Borda, fingering a crucifix, refused on grounds of religious conviction. Arguing in low tones, each man struggled to avoid his share of the responsibility for what had to be done. Ramos then asked whether Fuentes could not give Manera a Pentathol injection, after which he suggested that lots should be drawn to decide who should shoot him dead while unconscious. Fuentes agreed to do this if Manera could be persuaded to agree.

It now fell to Diaz to propose this to Manera, but Manera, calm as ever, not only refused to discuss arrangements for his death, but wanted to brush the whole thing aside almost as a joke. Diaz found himself side-tracked into a situation where he was on the defensive, attacked by Manera in the most reasonable and plausible fashion for his conduct of the trial which Manera—backed by his legal qualifications—showed up as a travesty of any kind of justice.

Morally and physically Diaz had reached the lowest point of his life. He was weak, sick, running a high temperature, and self-reproachful over his failures, and despite the fact that he knew Manera to be a traitor he felt himself vulnerable to his persuasion. It occurred to him that Manera ought to be made more comfortable while awaiting his end. The cords with which Manera's wrists had been tied appeared to be cutting into his flesh. Why tie him at all? he thought. It was all part of the ritual of repression they'd inherited from the police state. Something they did without thinking, simply because it had been done to them.

The man's uncomfortable, hungry and cold, Diaz thought, but he's not the type to complain. Manera wore only his shirt and his trousers. The wind flicked and whined at them through the rocks, and the sun, strangely flattened under a rising shutter of mist, sent out no heat. Twenty yards away the others, wrapped like Indians in their blankets, had turned their backs on a reality they wished to ignore. Diaz wanted to do something for Manera. He offered him food and coffee, offered to untie his hands, wanted to light a fire. Manera refused everything. Diaz argued with him, pleaded with him; tried to persuade Manera to confess his treachery, and to ask for forgiveness, but Manera shook his head.

Suddenly Diaz felt a spasm of fury against this man, who had not only betrayed him, but now, with such insolent indifference, refused to allow Diaz to ease the burden of his soul by accepting from him the slightest act of humanity. He wrenched out his pistol and started to wave it about, shouting. It was a wild and empty gesture born of weakness, and it drew from Manera only a glance of contempt. The others, Diaz knew, would be watching now, and Manera's contempt would spread from him to them. He can see through me, he thought. He knows me for what I really am. Fury and humiliation had loosened his bowels. He pointed the pistol at Manera's head and Manera laughed outright.

Diaz pulled the trigger.

An hour after they had buried Manera and eaten what was left of the food they moved off, marching in absolute silence. The next gully they tried proved to be the one shown on the map, and a fairly easy climb of seven hours took them close to the watershed. There was water from a spring here, and they had the good luck to shoot several pigeons. When they camped for the night Diaz addressed them. Next day, he said, they would reach the first of the Cholo villages. He believed the battle was half over.

14

T H E Y swam in the new pool they had found, made love, lay together on the dimpled sand. Howel was stroking Liz's shoulder. Now that escape was certain, the beauty of Colombia was revealed to him as never before. This was a wild and innocent fairyland. 'In a way I'll be sorry to go,' he said.

'I won't,' Liz said.

He laughed. 'No, I won't either.'

'I've uprooted myself,' she said. 'I've performed the necessary amputation. Now I can't wait. Don't you think there's any chance of cancellations?'

'Not when a football team and its supporters have taken over the plane,' he said.

'I suppose you're right. What'll we do when we get back?'

'Have a holiday in a quiet place,' he said. 'Where they don't carry guns.'

'A cool place,' she said. 'Somewhere where it rains. Like Scotland. Think of a Scotch mist and all the nice grey things. What do we do after the holiday?'

'I haven't got as far as that.'

'It doesn't matter, does it?' she said. 'As long as we're together. Are you going back to S U C C O U R ?'

'For a while,' he said. 'I promised Charles I'd help him out. How do you feel about it? We could stay in London for a month or two.'

'I'll fit in with your plans,' she said. 'We'll stay in London if you want to. Whatever you like.'

A brilliant bird, swooping down from the trees to drink,

almost collided with them, and carried its shrill tocsin back into the woods.

'A dull place with nothing much to do—that's what I need,' she said. 'For a week or two, anyway. After that, it doesn't matter.'

'This is my twelfth overseas trip in six years.'

'It must be about five for me,' Liz said.

'Would you be attracted to a different sort of existence altogether? I can't think quite what, but something a lot more settled.'

'We'll see,' she said.

'I was thinking about your involvements,' he said. 'I've always suffered from them, too. After I left Biafra I didn't seem able to tear myself free. It was the same with India. I still carry India and Biafra about with me all the time. I think one should be able to detach oneself more. It strikes me as unprofessional to allow oneself to be constantly nagged by these problems that belong to the past. Things you'll never be able to do anything about.'

'I know exactly what you mean. I still worry about a dam they were building in Sicily when I was there. We all got ourselves thoroughly involved. We had problems every day. You know, about compensation for land, and the Mafia, and one thing and another. This dam was the most important thing in my life, and then suddenly I had to go somewhere else and drop everything. I think about these people and their troubles all the time. The thing is, they were my problems, and just to take the problems away altogether is about as far from solving them as you can probably get. Do you understand me? It's like that thing they tell you about feeling pain in a leg after it's been taken off.'

'Are you going to feel that way this time when we go?' Howel asked.

'A little,' she said. 'I'm bound to a little. But I don't really want to see Los Remedios again. I've had enough of shooting and curfews, and beggars being eaten by dogs.'

'You're all packed up?' he asked.

'There's nothing to do, really. I can be in a couple of days. Do you think Cedric will be going too?'

'That's up to Charles. But I expect so. Eventually.'

'Let me see,' she said. 'What have I got to do? One thing I mustn't forget is to run over to Sosiego tomorrow. Could you take me?'

'I don't see why not. When do you want to go?'

'In the morning. The storekeeper there has something for me. I usually go with Homer King, but he can't make it this time.'

'Isn't that the fellow who has some sort of menagerie?' Howel said.

'That's the one. He sells things like snakes and jaguar cubs. Homer buys most of his butterflies from him and I usually manage to pick up Indian bits and pieces for my collection.'

'I'd like to see it,' Howel said. 'Take us long to get there?'

'A couple of hours in the Deux Chevaux,' she said. 'It's nice and cool up there. We could have a picnic.'

'Marvellous,' he said. 'We'll do that. In that case I'd better spend the rest of the day clearing up my work. Leave tomorrow free.'

'Have you got much to do?'

'The report I promised Charles,' he said. 'I can't put it off any longer.' He made a face. 'I hardly know how to start.'

'You'd better be kind to us,' she said. 'Because I'm going to insist on reading it.'

The report took him all the afternoon, and it read like a message of despair. Hopeless, he thought, hopeless. And how lucky it was they hadn't had more money to spend. He remembered the flushing water-closets piled outside a waterless village in the State of Kerala.

Powdered milk supplied to mountain villages:	£45 (Wasted)
Training and equipping Indian girls to produce woven and embroidered articles for sale:	£125 (Abandoned)
Sprinkler irrigation system:	£570 (Unused through drought)
Courses in soil conservation and fertility:	£55 (Unattended)
Tomato-raising scheme:	£220 (Abandoned through lack of marketing outlets)
Training Indian girls as hairdressers and in homecrafts:	£285 (Partially successful—one girl became a hairdresser)
Library books:	£100 (3 books taken out in 2½ years)

He wrote:

Dear Charles,
    I was able to accomplish little justifying the main purpose

156

of my visit. Privately I have no doubt that the allegations were substantially exact. This is the kind of thing that happens. But by the time I arrived all was silence and oblivion.

You asked for my impressions of our work here. Not to put too fine a point on it, the project has not been a success. The failure has been above all one of resources, but perhaps also to a lesser degree of understanding, and I hope the report will help to explain why. Faced with a task that is beyond human accomplishment, people like us are bound to find escape in things like study schemes and statistics. As a result we know a great deal about our subject, but have been able to *do* very little. Both Liz and Cedric have worked hard under discouraging conditions, but I feel sure they will be revived by a change of scene.

As for the Indians, what can I say? We have arrived here at the 59th minute of the 11th hour, and we are too small and too weak—even too lacking in passion— to influence their fate in the slightest degree. But at least we can raise our voices—if they can be heard above the voice of greed—to tell the world that the extermination it is conducting in the name of progress is a wound it inflicts on itself. The Indians are going tomorrow because Progress is determined to have raw materials (which will be exhausted in 20 years), and the last "underpopulated" corners of the world. I read with amazement that at this moment an IBP team representing 57 nations is at work not 500 miles from here studying what the article describes as "the Indians' miraculous adaptation to their environment", and deciding what they have to teach the urban Westerner in this matter, who is accepted as being in the process of destroying his.

I hope that the facts and figures supplied will be of

value to someone. There is nothing to be done here that s u c c o u r can do, and it would be dishonest to pretend otherwise.'

He was taking the sheet of paper out of the typewriter when Liz came in. She shut the door behind her and sat down. Something about this visit seemed unusual, but he was too occupied with afterthoughts about the letter to more than barely register a certain formality and deliberation in her manner.

'Finished the report?' she asked.

'Most of it, anyway.'

'Very long?'

'Not so long as I thought.'

Silence. He put another sheet of paper in the typewriter.

'What are you going to do now?' she asked.

'Get off a couple of urgent letters.'

She conscientiously shifted the position of her hands, clasped over her lap. 'After that?'

'Oh, I don't know. Go for a walk. Bird-watch. Coming?'

'It's Maria's evening off, I have to put on the dinner.'

'What are we having?'

'Vegetable curry.'

'That makes a nice change.'

'You could go and try to get some bacon from Williams,' she said.

'No, thanks.'

He was checking an address in his diary. 'We can do without bacon.'

'They've given up the artisanate at the mission,' she said.

'So Cedric was saying.'

'Well, I suppose I should make a move.' She was scraping at the floor with a toe. He had found the address in his diary and closed the book, and then he felt something like a third presence in the room. He looked up, and their eyes met.

'I can't go to Sosiego tomorrow after all,' she said.

'Oh,' he said.

'There's been an emergency.'

'An emergency?' Howel said. 'I don't understand.' For all that, premonition threw its shadow over him, and he knew a little of what was coming.

'I have to go down to Los Remedios. It's about something very urgent.'

'About Candido,' he said. 'Naturally.'

'He's out of prison. They just phoned. There must have been a prison break.'

'Who phoned?'

'A friend.'

'But why should they phone you? What have you got to do with this business? If he's out all well and good, but I don't see where you come into it.'

'He's in hiding, and he's in danger,' Liz said. 'And I suppose they think there's some way I can help.'

'But you can't,' Howel said. He repressed an upsurge of something like fury before going on. 'You can do nothing whatever. Nothing, nothing, absolutely nothing.'

'I probably can't, but I still have to go.'

'Where are you going to meet these people?'

'I don't know. I don't even know who they are. Don't look so alarmed.'

'This is absolute madness. It doesn't make sense. How are you going to contact them? What instructions were you given?'

'They weren't instructions,' she said. 'No one is blackmailing me. I was simply asked if I'd go to a certain phone box and wait for a call. The whole conversation didn't last ten seconds. I agreed to do so, and even if I had second thoughts about it I'd be obliged to keep my word. It was an appeal for help. Not an order. What else could I have done?'

'Tell me just one thing,' Howel said. 'Are these people guerrillas?'

'I don't think so.'

'You don't think so, but they could be.' He clicked his tongue in exasperation.

'I think they're just boys. Very worried and very scared. Everyone's a guerrilla who happens to fall foul of the police. They want to save a friend. I want to save him too.'

'I'll come with you,' Howel said.

'No,' she said. 'I'll go by myself. And there's something very important you can do for me while I'm gone. That is if you still want to help me. You can go to Sosiego, pick up whatever it is they have for me, and then meet me in Los Remedios.'

This has to stop somewhere, he thought. It can't go on indefinitely. He tried to frame a protest, an ultimatum. Either . . . or . . . but in the end could only fling up his hands in a gesture of hopelessness.

15

SOSIEGO was corrugated iron, palm thatch, naked children, vultures, dogs, and laterite dust lying in deep, smooth drifts. Howel had learned a little of the tragic history of this Liberal village, which in 1948 had been attacked by bandits in Conservative employ who had amputated many breasts, noses and lips, as well as roasting the mayor alive, before withdrawing. The experience had imprinted its personality with a special furtiveness. Visitors were watched from cover as if for fear that they might be the advance-guard of the returning enemy. Men Howel approached for directions slunk away out of sight and he had some difficulty in finding the local store, which, hardly differing from the rest of the huts, was a thatched shelter with open sides, built under a cataract of forest leaves.

The owner, a Colombian of Lebanese origin called Sadik, had appeared from smoke-fogged depths, avoiding with a holy man's detachment the excrement of children, and of the chickens that came and went. Spectacular examples of stock-in-trade were on display; an albino monkey, immovable in the posture of Rodin's Thinker; a cage containing a collection of living butterflies as big as bats; a serpent curled in a corner like a length of cable. Howel's arrival in the village had caused something of a stir, and a line of villagers had collected outside, strangely greyish and unlit in the vertical sunshine, to stare and to comment softly on his presence.

'How did the famous massacre happen?' Howel asked.

Sadik appeared to grope in his memory. He had settled comfortably, squatting like an Indian on his heels, his arms dangling between his legs. He wore the passiveness of the tropics like a uniform. 'A man called Lupo owned everything. I don't have to say including the peasants' womenfolk. These land reforms that never come to anything . . . You know the kind of thing. There was one of those. The idea was the government would make free loans to landowners who distributed uncultivated land. Half a caballería for every family.'

One of the hands resting on its knuckles was raised for long abstracted groping in the vicinity of Sadik's flies. 'Lupo got his loan, but all the land he gave away was in strips a metre wide and three miles long. If a peasant wanted it he had to fence it.' He made a soft, guttural noise from the Levant in sympathy with someone's predicament.

A deer hardly bigger than a terrier cantered into sight, and Sadik threw it a cigarette, which it instantly chewed up and swallowed. 'Lupo said that he was willing to buy back the strips of land for ten pesos each and most of the peasants agreed. Only two kicked up a fuss and they were shot dead by the priest, who I must explain was also chief of police. In the end someone killed the priest too, so Lupo called in the bandits. Such cruelties. Aie! Aie! Aie!'

He clucked an incomprehensible order at a screen made up from illustrations, many of them of corpses, cut from the local police gazette, and a young Indian slattern came into sight, baby at breast, and squatted, back turned to them, to fan the embers smouldering among bricks on the earthen floor. 'Now we must drink some coffee in the style of my country,' he said.

'The reason I am here,' Sadik said, 'in a way is because of this thing. All the people the bandits did not kill ran away and hid in the caves of Quebradas. Most of them still stay there. They only come to this village to trade. They could not grow food in the caves so they had to hunt animals. First of all I bought their skins from them, and afterwards there was a demand for some rare animals and butterflies, which I ship down to Bogotá. This is a life I have come to accept and enjoy. As you see, I have married a local girl. Now I am nearly an Indian, but I am still very happy to be visited by my friends from the city. This is an interesting country. I am living in a house with electric light and a refrigerator, but the woods are full of ghosts. Don't laugh—women with chicken's legs. Caves by the hundreds and nobody knows what's in them.'

Overhead a bird made the sound of someone striking a match close to the ear. Sadik said, 'The old man—Lupo, I mean—died quietly in his bed, but his son's still here. They don't have Liberals and Conservatives any more. Only the National Front, and he's the president. Last year the people, who work on his farm got together and went up to the house to ask him to give them a little more than the twelve cents a day he pays them. He told them to stay to dinner and put poison in the porridge. Nine of them died on the spot and he had their bodies thrown into the river.'

'And you mean to say that this kind of thing can happen in these days and nobody does anything about it?'

'This time, for once, they did something about it,' Sadik said. 'Somebody went to the police and there was an enquiry. The verdict was they died of a collective heart attack. Two witnesses were found hanged with their throats cut next day . . . Suicide. Nothing changes.' He reached forward to refill Howel's cup. 'Were there many road blocks on the way up?'

'Only two.'

'They keep you waiting for long?'

'Too long,' Howel said. 'They weren't in any hurry.'

'Miss Sayers always comes with Mr King. Then the soldiers don't make any trouble.'

'Mr King couldn't come today.'

'Tell him when you see him I have some wonderful new

butterflies. Tell him *Metamorpho dido*. The pale form. I will write it down for you. The best I have ever seen.'

'I'll tell him,' Howel said.

Sadik unfolded Liz's note to read it again, eyes held close to the paper, his head turned from side to side to follow the lines.

'Miss Sayers says you're a very great friend. A friend to be trusted.'

'We belong to the same organization,' Howel said. 'S U C - C O U R. I expect she's told you about it.'

'I know all about her work, Mr Howel. She is a lady with a sympathetic heart. She has given her heart to the poor of this unfortunate country. Will you be seeing her again very soon?'

'This afternoon. We're meeting in Los Remedios.'

'Could I ask you, Mr Howel, as a very great kindness to give her a message from me?'

'I'll give her a message with pleasure.'

Sadik pulled himself to his feet and went to find a pencil and paper. He wrote something and handed Howel the paper. 'On this I have written only the name of the butterfly. I would like very much for you to give it to Mr King. The message for Miss Sayers is this: I am awaiting the package whenever it can be delivered.'

'Nothing else?'

'Nothing else. I am awaiting the package. That is all.'

'I won't forget,' Howel said. 'Any package she has for you will have to be handed over before May 1st because on that date we leave for England.'

'I'm sure it will be ready before then.'

Leaving Sosiego, Howel drove too hard over a road full of ruts and boulders, and eventually burst a tyre. The spare turned out to be flat. He drove on at a walking pace to the next village, where an occasional mechanic had to be fetched from his farm, arriving hours later. In the meanwhile Howel fumed and fretted. He had arranged to meet Liz at four in the afternoon in the supreme anonymity of the bus terminal waiting-room. How long, he asked himself, could she be expected to wait for him? And at what time was the evening bus back to Dos Santos, which she would eventually take if he failed to appear? Under the magnifying-glass of his growing obsession with Liz, the thing was inflated to an extraordinary crisis. She'll think I've let her down. What else can she think? Unpunctuality at any time was unthinkable to Howel. He was ruled by the inflexibilities of a family environment he had never quite been able to escape; the exactitudes of a Celtic puritanism in which a sense of responsibility had become a tenet of religion.

By the time he had got away and reached the outskirts of Los Remedios, darkness had fallen. The city, arrogantly baroque under the sun, was reformed by night by an oriental reticence which suppressed its exhibitionism, replacing it by an introspective dignity born in remote deserts. It was an hour when servants, humming nasally, threw down water on the flagstones of concealed patios; when small, flickering breezes arose to cool the skin, and the citizens, released from a thousand cells where they had been kept in close confinement by the heat, dressed themselves formally for their evening stroll, and began to pour into the streets. At any other time Howel would have responded to the charm of the city in its evening mood, but now his sensibilities were blinkered by anxiety.

The curfew had been lifted two days before, and the going was slow for wheeled traffic. Howel crawled in bottom gear through the low-life suburbs of amiable crowds: woodsmoke, meat scorching on braziers, dried dung, rank straw, and the music of jukeboxes breathed out gustily by many cantinas. When he reached the terminal, the whole area was occupied by parked buses with men hosing off the day's dust. He had to leave the Citroën on a side-street some way off and run the rest of the distance.

He found her on a bench in the terminal waiting-room, chalk-faced under a buzzing fluorescent tube, crowded by leather-faced peasants among their mountains of baggage.

'Thank God it was nothing serious,' she said. 'I was beginning to imagine all kinds of things. Someone said there were bandits on the Sosiego road last week. Let's go somewhere where we can have a drink and talk.'

They walked two blocks to Te Esperaré a tu Vuelta and settled themselves in a dim room at the back.

'They blew a hole in the wall of the prison asylum,' she said. 'Three of them got away. Two were caught and shot on the spot.'

This was the fruit his prison visit had borne, Howel understood. He had been the tool and the spy of a guerrilla organization; had been indirectly involved in violence and bloodshed. He felt a spasm of nausea and wiped the palms of his hands together, finding them sticky.

'Sadik's ready to take whatever you have for him,' he said.

She nodded. 'I knew he would be. Everything's gone off as planned. So far, thank God.'

'So Candido wasn't mad after all,' he said.

'He was faking. The asylum was the best place to be in if anyone wanted to make a break. They burned him terribly with some electrical thing they used on him but his mind wasn't affected.'

'I'm glad he got away,' Howel said.

'And now,' she said, 'the problem consists of getting him out of town and into the mountains, where he'll be safe.' Howel note the briskness, the matter-of-factness of her tone. 'They're searching the town for him now. House by house.'

'He *is* a guerrilla, then?' Howel's lips were stiff as if he were a little drunk.

'Of course.'

'And an important one, by the sound of it.'

'One of the leaders.'

'You didn't trust me,' he said.

'I swore on oath.'

'You're in this up to your neck, aren't you?' he said. 'I ought to have known.'

Even Hargrave had been able to sum the situation up, as had been clear that morning as soon as Liz had left on the bus.

'I simply didn't want to know,' Hargrave said. 'I stuck my head firmly in the sand and kept it there. Smalldon was quite sure she was actually mixed up in this business. You know what I mean. These telephone calls in the night. These mysterious journeyings. It all added up. I personally suspect she was some sort of courier. Isn't that what they call them?'

'What a God-awful mess,' Howel said.

'Smalldon always used to say that with Liz it was like watching a blind man about to step off the kerbside into the traffic. She seemed to him totally devoid of the capacity for self-protection. I've never understood how she managed to stay out of really serious trouble. I don't suppose for one single moment there was any element of romance in the thing as far as this man was concerned. I imagine he was using her. I know they do use foreigners when they can. They're less likely to come under suspicion.'

What can I say to her? Howel thought. And ought we even to be talking about these things in a place like this? He scanned the almost empty room cautiously. Two men with haunted medieval faces plotted together in a far corner, but the cockroaches scuttling about the floor between them were undisturbed. A jukebox somewhere played *Ave Maria* to the soft accompaniment of Paraguayan harps. It was the last touch of sickly, sentimental music, not the cockroaches, the brooding faces of the two customers, and the fresh bullet holes in the ceiling that made this place so indescribably sinister.

'What did they ask you to do this time?' Howel asked.

'To help them.'

'And you're going to?'

'I'll do everything I can.'

He thought for a while before speaking again. 'Yes, I suppose you have to.'

'Not only for Candido, but because I believe in what he's fighting for. Everything else in the country is awful and dead and corrupt.'

There seemed to be an objection here, but he didn't know how to phrase it. 'You're a foreigner,' he said.

'So it's not my concern. Is that what you mean? If you want to use that argument, it makes all our work meaningless. Forty per cent of the people in this province have TB. Is that any concern of yours?'

'I like to think it is.'

'You're just as concerned as if they were your own country-men?'

'I believe so. I ought to be,' he said.

'Do you expect any government ever to do anything about it?'

'I'm a realist.'

'Only the guerrillas will ever do anything. That's if they win,' she said.

'Except that they'll be the government then,' Howel said.

'If that's the view we take, we might as well give up. Why bother about anything?'

'I agree. I shouldn't have said that. I'm simply afraid.'

'What of?'

'Of losing you.'

'Why should you?'

168

'It's a miracle to me you haven't been picked up already. That somebody hasn't given you away.'

'They're too disciplined to do that,' she said. 'They stand together whatever happens.'

'I have a terrible feeling that no one can stand up to the kind of things that Colonel Arana does to them,' Howel said.

'They'd never place me in danger,' she said. 'In any case I'm going on the first of the month, so as far as I'm concerned the whole episode will be at an end. They've asked for my help and I'll give it if I can. This would be the end even if I weren't going. It would be unsafe to the organization to use me again. They've told me.'

'And what are they asking you to do?'

She started to speak, and then stopped as a cripple came in and approached them, carrying a canary in a cage. The canary hopped down from its perch to pick a "fortune" from the small pile of folded papers in a box in its cage, and pushed a bald, moulted head between the bars towards them. Howel took the paper, and gave the man a half peso. He limped away.

'They want the military security plates from Williams's car,' she said. 'They'll use them to get Candido past the road blocks.'

'Why does he have to use the road at all?' Howel said. 'What's wrong with taking to the open country?'

'There's a fence right round the town, with lights and machine-gun posts. He couldn't get through. Can you think of any way I could get the plates?'

'No, I can't. In fact I'd say it would be an utter impossibility.'

'For example, you couldn't get them off the car?'

'I couldn't,' Howel said. 'And for a number of reasons. In the first place they're bound to be fixed on very securely, and I'm not a mechanic. Secondly, so far as I know the car's never left unattended. There are other reasons.'

'Are you shocked?'

'Not really,' he said. 'Not when I think about it. Put it this way, I'm startled. I wasn't cut out to be a conspirator. I've always had a rather unreasoning respect for law and order.'

'Even when the law's rotten?'

'I said it was an *unreasoning* respect.'

'You're not morally opposed to helping Candido get away?'

'No, I'm not morally opposed. In fact I'd probably feel a sneaking sympathy for the predicament of any fugitive. I'm just afraid for my own skin.'

'Williams goes down to Los Remedios in his car at least twice a week,' she said.

'Yes,' he said. 'He leaves it in the Garaje Mirador. In a lock-up.'

'Couldn't someone in the garage be bribed?'

'I'm sure they could,' Howel said. 'But do you know how to set about bribing a man? I don't. Bribery is an art of its own. If you or I tried it, we'd come unstuck. All we'd do is to land up in the Central Prison, with Arana's men asking us just what we wanted with the plates.'

They'd probably had this possibility in mind for a long time, Howel thought. The scheme had been planned ready to meet the contingency. The unstoppable car. The car with the open sesame plates. Somebody had foreseen an emergency in which this car would supply the only solution. Perhaps it had been the reason for Liz's recruitment—that and the many missions it had almost certainly permitted her to perform for the organization.

'What happens to the car at the mission?' she asked.

'It's kept in his garage. I happen to have noticed that it's got a lock on it like a safe deposit.'

'So it's either in the garage at home, or in a lock-up in the Garaje Mirador in Los Remedios.'

'Unless he goes anywhere else.'

'And does he ever go anywhere else?'

'He must do. As a matter of fact he's going to the party at the mine at Ultramuerte tomorrow.'

'And do they have a garage there?'

'I don't know, but I doubt it,' Howel said. 'What they probably have is one of those palm-thatch shelters to keep the sun off the tyres. And the usual perimeter fence. Probably a guard on duty. Bound to be some sort of security.'

'How does any ordinary person get to Ultramuerte?' she asked.

'Any ordinary person takes the bus. They've just started a service for the technical workers. Two buses a day. It was advertised in *El Diario*.'

'You'd want a pass to get in, wouldn't you?' she asked.

'You want a pass to get into anything in this country,' Howel said. He could see what was coming, and was preparing for a last-ditch stand.

'Could *we* get a pass?'

'We could almost certainly get a pass if we applied for one,' he said, 'but it would be a very dangerous thing indeed to hand this pass over to someone else, if that's what's going through your mind.'

'Of course it's going through my mind,' she said. 'It's a wonderful idea, isn't it?'

'When you'd finished with the pass it would have to be handed in at the Gobernación, or whoever it is issues them. They're bound to keep a register. Don't think they're fools.'

'You could lose it, couldn't you?'

'You could, but the consequences might be very unpleasant. It would be very unpleasant too if somebody happened to be caught using your pass.'

'It would be unpleasant,' she said. '*Very* unpleasant. Will you help me?'

She was offering him blood, sweat and tears. I must seem

very cold and cautious to her, he thought. Not much of a hero. He sensed that to say no would be to bring everything to an end between them but that even to attempt to man-œuvre, to temporize, might be to expose himself to irremediable contempt.

'You know I'll do whatever I can,' he said.

16

TWENTIETH day: an exhausting downhill climb; an evening meal of small lizards. Twenty-first day: very slow progress along a ravine choked with massive boulders; more lizards and couple of handfuls of peppery-tasting ants' eggs. Borda shot a vixen. No one wanted to touch the rank flesh when cooked, but Fuentes and Ramos shared the liver. The worst enemy was sunburn. The men covered as much of their blistered faces as they could with strips of cotton torn from their shirts. Diaz still comforted himself with the memories of Comrade Guevara's blunders. At least we made sure we were physically fit. At least we could all swim. It was almost unbelievable that half the members of the Bolivian expedition couldn't swim a stroke, and that a couple of them had been drowned while fording rivers.

Day twenty-two Ramos slipped on a boulder and fell into the rapids. Everyone laughed, Ramos too. Had the current allowed him to stand, the water would have come up to his waist. A few yards downstream some rocks almost broke surface. While the others shouted facetious encouragements, Ramos scrambled about on these trying to resist the pressure of the water, but gashed a foot and gave up the attempt, and let himself go again, swimming when necessary, a little alarmed as the current speeded up about the chance of colliding with an underwater rock, but keeping his head and on the look-out for a safe place to climb ashore. He was soon carried out of sight among the boulders in the river bed, and never seen again. A hundred yards further down they found that the rapids ended in a 20-feet-high waterfall.

That evening the men ate a few spiny, inch-long fish they

had found trapped in a pool, and Diaz lectured them once again on the object of the expedition. They pretended to listen while they were told for the fiftieth time that support for revolution depended not upon corrupt whites and demoralized mestizos, but upon the Indians, who were the natural, instinctive and hereditary enemies of everlastingly oppressive governments, and whose dormant genius for guerrilla warfare could be revived etc., etc.

Somebody snored, but Diaz ignored the sound. Pulling out a copy of Carlos Marighella's *Mini-Manual of the Urban Guerrilla*, he read like a priest from a breviary. 'We must be ready to destroy our enemies with the greatest cold-bloodedness, calmness and decision, the North American spy, the agent of the dictatorship, the police torturer, the fascist personality, the stool pigeon, police agent or provocateur.' He grimaced at them wildly; a stripe of sunburn at each corner of the mouth gave him a hopeless, despairing expression that never varied.

Villa whispered to Fuentes that so far as he knew, apart from the execution of Manera, no one present had ever killed anybody.

The next morning the four men reached the first Cholo village consisting of about twenty huts, in which they found no signs of life. They ransacked the huts, discovering only the bones of a dog, and the dried-up remains of a parrot hanging like a feather duster from its perch. There was coyote excrement round the god-house, where the animals had come to devour whatever offerings had been left.

In the second village, remarkably similar to the first, and equally silent and abandoned, Villa complained to Fuentes of hallucinations. He had seen a woman sitting at the corner of a hut, plucking a chicken. Villa stood absorbed in the sight, his mouth beginning to water, and he took in such details as a dribble of blood from the chicken's beak, and the feathers on the ground, lightly stirred by the cold

174

breeze. Then all had vanished. Extreme fatigue, Fuentes said. He himself had been hearing noises and occasional snatches of classical music for the last few days. He gave Villa a couple of aspirins and told him to relax. The background to this was a yammering, meaningless harangue delivered by Diaz to the surrounding emptiness. Borda, humming to himself, played a childish game with pebbles.

Later that day, when time was beginning to lose all shape, they stumbled down the mountainside into Cayambo. There were many huts like wooden igloos arranged in a circle, and soon Cholo women and children and a few old men came creeping out to surround them. The cacique arrived, slow-moving in ragged deerskins, an old Colt automatic stuck in his belt. He was bloated with malnutrition, with chubby hands like a child's and eyes submerged in his puffed-up cheeks. Villa forced his private visions to leave him and delivered the short speech he had prepared, and the cacique signed to them to squat with him on the ground, and fed them with a ladle from a bowl of maize gruel brought by a young girl with a consumptive cough.

The cacique then broke the bad news to them. They could stay two nights but no longer. Then they must go. He listed a long catalogue of the calamities that had befallen the tribe since the pact made with Athos—the attacks by gunmen employed by oil-prospectors, and by slave-raiders, and the loss of many young men who had gone down to Los Remedios in search of food and had never returned. The tribe was defenceless, he said. Only the very young and the old were left, and they were burdened by the presence of many refugees from other villages that were even worse off.

Only Villa and Borda could find the strength later to discuss their feelings about this meeting with the Cholo cacique, and both agreed that it was extraordinary how much furtive embarrassment could have been displayed in an

Indian's normally impassive features. They feared that the cacique was telling them less than the truth.

Whatever the motives behind the Cholos' refusal to give them shelter, they all understood that this was the end of the expedition, and instantly what was left of cohesion and morale crumbled. With Borda the exception, all that mattered now was to reach safety. The aloof Diaz suddenly shed his dignity like an outworn garment and was full of timid questionings. Fuentes fell into a depressive silence. Villa was gloomy and suspicious. He told Borda that there was something about the atmosphere that he mistrusted. No Indian ever showed a starving stranger the door, however precarious their own food situation might be. Borda now felt himself free to disclose something of his own plans. His destination after he left them was to be Quebradas, in the mountains above Los Remedios. Quebradas appeared by the map to be about two days away. Borda said that they were certain to find food and shelter there, and he proposed to the others that they should go with him.

They slept uneasily that night, and faced the next day with a fresh crop of misgivings. A Cholo notable told Villa that the tribe had been warned by the government of the fatal consequences of harbouring guerrillas, and that even the failure to report their presence in the area would be severely punished. He also mentioned that some boys out searching for honey some days before had seen a suspicious-looking stranger watching the village through binoculars. Hearing this, Diaz became very agitated, and wanted to leave there and then, but was dissuaded by the rest. Villa had been told by the Cholos that migrant deer had appeared in the neighbourhood, and they all finally agreed, however reluctantly, that it would be wiser to rest in the village another day, and spend another night there, with the chance of eating meat, than to set out forthwith, still weak with fatigue and on empty stomachs.

An old Cholo took Borda hunting. He knew of a gorge through which the deer, migrating to the higher pastures, often passed. The two men built a hide among the trees in the gorge, and waited there until about midday, when Borda shot a small buck. They cut out a bamboo pole, lashed the animal to it, and started back for Cayambo. They were still in the forest and almost within sight of the village when they heard the helicopters pass over.

The strategy employed by the helicopters had been tried once before—in Guatemala—and with complete success. Security, economy and speed were the watchwords of the senior adviser. After Zacapa the commanding officer had shaken him by the hand and complimented him. It had been a model operation, and he was determined that this should be a model operation too.

To avoid any possibility of an accident, the first Chinook made a trial run in at 500 feet and 80 mph, and when this had drawn no fire it dropped to 150 feet, slowed to half-speed and returned. It then released a shower of coloured tinfoil shapes, after which it drew off with the second helicopter to await the inevitable rush by the villagers to collect these valuable gifts as they floated down from the sky.

Five minutes later when it was judged that the majority of the Indians would have been enticed into the open, Chinook number one came back. Some of the Indians—particularly the children—ran for their huts, but the majority waited in the hope that more treasure would be showered on them. The gunners supplied by General Lopez now opened up with the Chinook's five machine-guns, firing two thousand rounds in a matter of a few seconds, which instantly reduced the scrambling humanity below to heaps of squirming maggots. To complete its operation the Chinook lifted again to 300 feet and dropped a new and experimental kind of bomb composed of solidified petrol containing an explosive charge. From above this appeared to open in the centre of the village like a brilliant sea anemone in a corona of a thousand white tentacles. The sight, a beautiful and even peaceful one, was much admired by all the occupants of the helicopters. Where the feathery tips of these tentacles touched the huts all round, orange flames immediately went up, and as those who had taken refuge in them ran into the open, the second Chinook moved in to repeat the process.

Among the last victims was Diaz and the fire took him in its grip, and stripped him instantly of his clothing, and then his skin. His lipless mouth opened to scream, but no sound came. He fell on his back. His eyes turned to bubbling fat, and in a moment his charred belly burst open to release boiling intestines. Villa and Fuentes had died instants earlier from many bullet wounds, and now, as the burning Indians fell across their bodies, their flesh began to cook.

Chinook number one moved away to perform a brief task of tidying up, encircling the village's outskirts and pausing here and there to pick off with delicacy and precision the rare straggler or fugitive. Within ten minutes the operation was at an end, and both helicopters landed in a field and the crews got out to stretch their legs or to satisfy a little morbid curiosity.

The two advisers strolled back to the helicopters. Lee Gross was an ex-Air Force lieutenant, and Joseph Rinaldi had been an army sergeant.

'Well, it was all right,' Gross said to Rinaldi for the third time. 'We got through without getting anybody hurt.'

'We sure did,' Rinaldi said.

'You have this feeling of relief,' Gross said. 'It's natural. Nobody got hurt. That's how it has to be when I give the orders. We did what we came for, and that's fine with me.'

Rinaldi took a series of deep breaths in an effort to clear his nausea, and Gross went on talking excitedly. 'You could learn something from that strike. I'll tell you something—it was just right. I guess I'm still hyped. Why didn't you take any pictures, Joe? I could kick myself, I had to leave my camera behind. I thought you went for photography in a big way?'

'I got a lot of pictures of the type of subject already,' Rinaldi said. 'I got a whole collection. It smelt kind of bad back there.' Rinaldi had worked in his parents' Brooklyn restaurant before being drafted into the army, and the presence in the devastated village of a familiar kitchen smell had sickened him.

'When those Dacs went it was an entertainment,' Gross said. 'You should have got it in colour. You could have sold those pictures to a magazine. *Life* maybe.'

'Nobody wants to know about pictures like that any more. I've tried,' Rinaldi said. 'They've got tired of buying them. They've seen too many.'

'All the same it would have been nice to have something to show the fellows back in Panama, Joe. We did a good job. We cleared up and got out, and nobody got hurt. That's the main thing. This was like Guatemala, only better. In a small way, I mean. It was clean and quick. It was instantaneous.'

'We get more experience as we go on,' Rinaldi said. 'I guess it's better now we don't prep the area any more. The element of surprise. Pity there were only three guys after all.'

'You have to learn to expect that. We had a body count of 372 on our first op at Zacapa, and we only got two we were after. The guy that's president now shook me by the hand. He thanked me in person. We only got two guys but he was very happy. And we didn't have any Dacs those days. We had to burn all the hootches by hand.'

'I'm glad I missed it,' Rinaldi said.

'How were the gunners on your ship?' Gross asked. 'The

ones with me were terrible. Just crazy to keep firing all the time. At nothing. I took over one of the guns for a few bursts, just to show them. It was too easy. The way the pilot handled the ship it was terrific. You couldn't go wrong. These guys that were trying to make a run for it. You could come up behind them and practically tap them on the shoulder. There was one old guy I took apart. Scientifically. Just to show them how it was done. I took him apart like he was a doll. I had the chips of bone flying into the air. When I zapped him with seven point six two, he came apart. It doesn't hurt me to kill these guys, any more than it does gooks. For me they *are* gooks. Slants. I can't tell the difference. Listen, Joe, what's the matter? You're kind of quiet.'

'Nothing,' Joe said. 'I guess it's just the let-down after being hyped.'

Gross laughed. 'I don't believe that, Joe. Your trouble is you're a grunt. Once a grunt always a grunt.'

'You've got to give me a bit more time,' Rinaldi said. 'I guess I'll get used to it, the same as anybody else.'

They had almost reached the helicopters now, where the American crews and the Colombian soldiers, separated by an invisible barrier, had formed two groups to drink coffee.

'Let's go get some coffee,' Gross said good-naturedly. 'You'll feel better.'

A navigator filled their cups and Gross thanked him with the emphatic courtesy for which he was noted, and which in this case drew a quick glance of surprise.

'Well, I guess it's back to Panama tomorrow,' Gross said. 'Mission safely accomplished once again—eh? What's the first thing you're going to do when you get back, Joe?'

'Go to bed for a couple of days,' Rinaldi said. 'I'm going to finish off a bottle of wine and go to bed.'

'I'm going to take in a movie,' Gross said. 'A wild, exciting movie, maybe a Western. But nothing with too much sex in it. Nothing with too much sex.'

17

I N the high mountains, where it was autumn for a week, rain had fallen, and towards the day's end a little of its freshness had touched and alerted Dos Santos under a dramatic evening sky, striped with slate and magenta.

Mary Williams watched her husband in silence, trying to bring herself to say what she had to say. It was hard to find time to talk to him about important things. Williams had come in from a day charged with activity, only to dash off into the garden to tape the song of a rare variety of mocking-bird. He would now drink his coffee, summarize the day's events in a sort of rapid and perfunctory news bulletin, and then go off to his radio room where he would remain until it was time to go to bed. Grail, she was afraid, was changing. He had been a bold man who often offended by his directness, but now the boldness had been invaded by caution. From being a fighter, he was becoming a diplomat. He had learned to weigh his words, to head her off from the discussion of delicate subjects. She found it hard to pin him down. Mary's life had always been contained by measurable dimensions and absolute beliefs. Like the house she lived in it was uncluttered—a matter of clean, polished surfaces. Grail's new aptitude for silence, compromise and evasion filled her with unhappiness.

Williams put down his cup and glanced at his watch.

'You remember that priest, Padre Alberto, don't you?'

'Very well,' she said. 'An untidy little man with rather a sweet expression. We met him at the English-Speaking Association.'

'I'm glad to hear that they may be doing something about

him at long last. He's turned out a crypto-Communist. Preached a number of most provocative and subversive sermons in the cathedral.'

'Cedric told me about them,' Mary said. 'Rich people go to hear themselves attacked. It amuses them.'

'Possibly it was a bit of a joke at first,' Williams said, 'but the joke's worn thin. The police appear to be getting worried. It's thought he might have a following of subversives. Anyway, last Sunday he badly overstepped the mark.' He paused, 'Are you feeling well?' he asked. There was a yellowness in her face he diagnosed as a symptom of a body that had lost patience with the tropics. Her lips were white, and clear-cut half-moons of shadow had been imprinted under her eyes.

'Just tired,' she said. 'That's all.'

'He said that twenty years from now the students and churchmen who fight for an ideal will become heroes. I'm quoting his actual words.'

'I suppose it's possible,' she said. 'Times and opinions change.'

He gave her a troubled look, and waited, but she had no more to add. She must be even more tired than she admitted to being, he thought.

'Colonel Arana regards it as a deliberate incitement to rebellion,' Williams said. 'I had a long chat with him on the subject.'

'We should have as little to do with Colonel Arana as we possibly can,' she said.

'I think you're wrong there, my dear,' he said reasonably. 'The authorities are beginning to see that they can rely less and less on the Catholic Church. And not only in this country. Wouldn't it be throwing away a great opportunity if we said no to them when they turned to us for support? Shouldn't we consider above all the long-term interests of the evangelical movement?'

'I suppose we should,' she said. 'But this is one time when I find it hard to do so.'

'In the long run,' he said, 'my feeling is that nothing but good can come of this. From the mission's point of view. There is one embarrassing circumstance. Did you know that Elizabeth Sayers used to see a good deal of Padre Alberto?'

'No, I didn't.'

'She's been seen to visit him on a number of occasions.' She recognized the pause, and the loss of focus in his voice. The question when it came was put to an invisible third person; a casual enquiry that might have been about a book mislaid. 'She's never spoken to you about him?'

Had it been necessary, Mary would have lied deliberately for the first time in her life. 'She's never spoken to me about anything but her work. Apart from that we've very little in common.'

'It's a profound relief to me that she'll be going so soon,' Williams said. 'I never cease to regret that I spoke to General Lopez on her behalf. I imagine she'll be under police surveillance while she remains here. Perhaps it might be better if we saw as little of her as possible. I'm afraid we're committed to attending the official opening of the mine with the SUCCOUR people, but after that I don't think we should be seen in public with them.'

Her moment had come. Her fists were clenched so tightly that the fingernails dug into the flesh. She opened her mouth to speak, but Grail plunged into his bulletin again.

'I rang a friend of Shultz's in L.A. and told him about the assets in timber we have lying around. He agreed to a hundred thousand dollar loan to buy sawing equipment. The machinery will be shipped and be here in a month. This means that from now on timber's going to stop being a useless by-product and become our main interest.'

'After preaching the Gospel,' she said.

'General Lopez wants us to start taking over the Naqalá

Indians next month. He wants to start a coffee project in the Naqalá area. He'd like us to take a hundred families for processing. Religious instruction and basic citizenship. I believe that by cutting a few corners we might be able to accomplish this in three months.'

'But how are we going to learn their language if they only stay with us three months?'

'We can't,' he said. 'It's out of the question.'

'In three months we wouldn't be able to learn enough even to translate the Lord's Prayer.'

'No,' he said, 'we couldn't even do that.' His tone reminded her of a realistic salesman at the Los Encantos store trying to sell a utility washing-machine of local manufacture. 'We'd have to cut our coat according to the cloth. The most we could do would be to give them the rudiments of Christian belief and conduct. One's duty towards God, and one's duty towards one's neighbour. General Lopez was insistent upon the time factor, and we're very dependent upon him. I sincerely believe that if we devote enough thought to the methods we adopt, we can find a way of streamlining the approach to salvation.'

Mary said, 'I went to Ultramuerte today.'

For a moment she thought he had not heard her. 'To the mine,' she said.

Williams was a long time in replying. 'I'm sorry you did that, dear. I should have preferred to go with you.'

'Why?' she asked.

'In a day or two's time,' he said. 'It would have given the Indians the chance to settle in. Things are bound to be a little disorganized at first.'

'It was urgent,' she said. 'There was no way of contacting you. When I went to the clinic this morning they told me that three of my patients had been taken there by mistake.'

'There couldn't have been very much wrong with them,

dear. Homer and I were most careful to check on health records.'

'They were chest cases that hadn't cleared up. So I went over to get them back. You didn't tell me this place was like a prison camp.'

'Oh, come, dear. Hardly a prison camp. Of course there's a wire fence, but that's because they've valuable equipment to protect.'

'I was challenged at the gate by an armed guard who was most unpleasant and overbearing. In the end I was able to see the manager, a Mr Frazer. Have you met Mr Frazer?'

'Only for a few moments. I gather he's a capable man, and well thought of. Cedric Hargrave used to know him well.'

'He was horrible,' Mary said. 'He made no attempt to hide his hostility. I told him that I'd come to take three of my patients away, and he laughed in my face. He seemed to regard my concern for them as pure hypocrisy. Without saying so in so many words, he made it clear that he regarded us as labour recruiters for the mine. He called our Indians mission fodder. I'm afraid I became very angry.'

'This is very disturbing,' Williams said. 'I happen to know that Mr Frazer is working under harassing conditions at this moment in time. But that doesn't excuse flagrant rudeness—I shall certainly speak to him.'

'He seemed to think that you were perfectly well aware of the deplorable conditions our Indians are living in, and that you condoned them.'

'Deplorable conditions?' Williams said. 'I believe that some of the accommodation is a little makeshift, but this is temporary. I'm told that eventually the camp will be a model of its kind.'

Rebellion seemed to feed on rebellion. 'Have you seen it?' Mary said. It was the first time she had ever challenged him in this way.

'I was shown over the living quarters, but I must admit it was when the Indians were not there. I would describe them as adequate if not ideal. There may be a little crowding at first, but this should soon be remedied.'

'Our Indians are living in what they call a bunk-house.' She paused, her eyes beginning to water at the memory. 'There are three floors; fourteen rooms to a floor, and three families to a room. There's hardly any water and no sanitary arrangements. The filth and squalor are beyond belief.'

'I agree it's most regrettable, but I'm sure it's only temporary.'

'I told Mr Frazer that morality was bound to suffer when people are crowded together, regardless of the sexes, in such conditions, and he actually said one might as well forget about morality in a mining camp. He suggested that eventually, as the mining population expands, loose women might be brought in.'

'Mr Frazer sounds like a cynic. I wouldn't take him too seriously.'

'He said a fifteen per cent per annum casualty rate was to be expected through accidents.'

'I doubt it. But always remember that the death rate of the uncivilized Indian in the mountains other than from natural causes would be even higher.'

'They're *our* Indians,' she said. 'Don't you feel responsible for them?'

'For their souls,' he said. 'Yes.'

'Perhaps it's because I'm a doctor,' she said. 'I can't help feeling that their bodies count for something too.'

He looked at her in astonishment. Over the years they had shaped and trimmed each other's opinions, creating in the end a family orthodoxy of unspoken assumptions from which the present deviations were remarkable. 'Whatever happens now, we saved them,' he said. It was offered as the final irrefutable argument.

She threw in the crushing counter-attack. 'Did you know the Indians are given drink?'

He gulped. 'At this mine?' he said.

'At this mine. It's the custom. They're given a pint of liquor before they start work in the morning and a pint when they finish at night. A horrible concoction of maize-beer and rum. Mr Frazer says that the working conditions are so hard, they couldn't carry on without it. Before I came back here I stopped off to see Mr Hargrave, and he said they do it in all the mines. He said it's part of a policy of deliberate degradation. He knows because he used to be a mining engineer himself, and that was one of the reasons why he gave it up. In some mines they give the miners a daily ration of coca leaves. They stupefy and brutalize them in every way they can. It's a case of anything to keep them quiet.'

She watched his face anxiously, her lips trembling, waiting for him to speak. 'If it is true that the Indians are given alcohol I shall see General Lopez and ask him to put a stop to it.'

'And supposing he refuses to do anything about it?'

For a moment there was anger and resentment in his face, and her intuition told her that it was directed against her. His expression cleared, and then became almost bland. 'It would be a tragic situation indeed, and I confess that I should feel despondent. I should be faced with the fact that our work had suffered a very grave setback.'

'Wouldn't you say a defeat?'

'Not a defeat,' he said, 'because however agonizing their present circumstances, these Indians are saved. They have gained a priceless treasure that can never be taken from them.'

Her patience collapsed, plunging her into the ultimate heresy. 'Is a drunken, debauched Christian better off than a pagan living a good life?'

The shock steadied him; clarified his thoughts. 'A pagan

can never lead a good life,' he said. 'If we can no longer accept that, our mission ceases to have meaning.' In the normal way few of the clichés of religion came into their private conversations, but now Williams felt a little touched, as if by the spirit of prophecy. 'They will not be called into account,' he said, 'for the evils that are done to them. If General Lopez does not keep faith with us, his responsibility will be grave indeed.' He quoted. ' "Whoso shall offend against one of these little ones which believe in me, it were better for him that a millstone were hanged about his neck, and that he were drowned in the midst of the sea." '

'It's not General Lopez's responsibility,' she said, 'it's ours. We must go to him immediately and tell him that these abuses must stop, or we shall take our Indians back.'

'It could never be done,' he said.

'If you're not prepared to go, I'll go myself.'

'Even General Lopez can't stop progress,' Williams said. 'Now the wheels have been set in motion, there can be no drawing back. Too many interests are involved.'

Very close to the open window a nightjar suddenly called with a foolish mocking sound.

Mary shuddered.

18

THE prospect of movement, of action—the knowledge that, one way or another, life at Dos Santos was about to come to an end, had suddenly touched them with impatience and restlessness. At breakfast next morning, a hammer crossed with a screwdriver among the plates and cups suggested a scutcheon of change, and the odour of splintered pine and wood-shavings was as strong as the coffee. Hargrave had performed in their presence a symbolical act, stacking up ready for packing a set of the *Encyclopædia Britannica*, probably unopened since their supply to an original purchaser many years before. 'I took them over from the last vice-consul, and he got them from the one before him. No one ever seems to have got down to having shelves made to put them out. I'm hoping my old friend Maclaren Frazer may feel like taking them off my hands.' His titter showed that he knew the hope was an absurd one. 'We used both of us to be interested in extra-sensory perception,' he added weakly. The remark seemed intended to condone any eccentricity.

'So you've taken the plunge at last,' Liz said.

'I haven't much option, have I? If we're pulling out.'

'You could have stayed on until Charles makes his mind up where the new HQ is to be.'

'To tell you the truth, I feel rather like you. I've had enough of foreign parts for a bit. I had a long screed from Sarah a couple of days ago, and things don't sound too brilliant. Miles is on his way to Katmandu, and now she's been asked to take Christopher away from school. A father's guiding hand seems to be indicated. Looks like a year or so in Hartlepool.' He made it sound like a boast. 'Expect I'll be pushing off a week after you. You're on an evening flight, aren't you?'

'We take off at five.'

'Good. Give you plenty of time to see the procession first.'

'Is it worth seeing?' Howel asked.

'You oughtn't to miss it,' Hargrave said. 'It's a bit of everything. Semana Santa at Seville, jungle drums, old Inca stuff, Lourdes. Tremendous mass hysteria. The dumb speak and the cripples throw away their crutches . . . You can't possibly miss the procession.'

'Would we have time?' Howel asked.

'All the time in the world. It's all over by midday. It sets out from the cathedral at ten and finishes at twelve. That's when Lopez will declare himself president.'

'You really think he will?'

'I'm certain of it. You only have to watch the straws in the wind. By and large it's not a bad time to be leaving. I'm not too optimistic about the future.'

'How can you bear to go away and leave all those little projects of yours, Cedric?' Liz said.

'It's going to be a bit of a wrench, I admit,' Hargrave said. 'The Sonora wheat might have turned out a winner. I was working on another scheme I didn't tell you about for irrigating seedling trees with dew. Using the old Roman method. I was keeping it under my hat until I had something to show. Apart from that, let's face it, the possibilities here have come to an end. Take these maize cakes, for instance. I regard them as a sign of the times.' He had scooped the yolk from his second egg, and spread it with loving precision over the cake's adobe-like surface, patting out a final wrinkle with his spoon. Now he picked it up, bit off a fragment and chewed with a look of troubled concentration. 'These cakes suggest to me that the Williams empire is crumbling, and

Dos Santos is going downhill. They've never been the same since Grail's cook deserted. Maria does her best for us, but she hasn't a clue. Were you here when the lights went off last night? Twice.'

'Who was it said Mary might be leaving him?' Howel asked.

'I did,' Liz said. 'I'd never have believed the day would come when Mary would want to open her heart to me. She's terribly fed up.'

'Who wouldn't be with a husband like that?' Hargrave said. 'Everybody knows he's hand in glove with Lopez. What do you think is going to happen to them in the remote chance of Lopez coming unstuck?'

'I think the children were the final straw,' Liz said. 'They used to bring Indian children up from that concentration camp of theirs to play with them for an hour a day. Now they've all gone with their parents to the mine. He keeps them shut up in an air-conditioned room.'

'Poor little devils,' Howel said.

'Talking about the mine, that reminds me,' Hargrave said. 'I'm rather jittery about this party today. Ramon Bravo's going to represent the Governor, and Maclaren Frazer will be host. I'd like to talk to you about him. He's a very old friend, and I was wondering if you could help.'

'He hits the bottle, doesn't he?' Liz said.

'He occasionally drinks more than's good for him. You've met him, haven't you, Bob?'

'I believe I've seen him,' Howel said. 'In the bar at the Union. If it was the man I'm thinking of, he may have been offering to fight the barman.'

'Tall with a beard, slim build, rather untidy-looking,' Hargrave said.

'That's the man,' Frazer had, in fact, borne an uncanny resemblance to Hargrave himself, both of them tropical stage-props from a bygone age.

'Type out of Somerset Maugham,' Howel said. 'When he stopped arguing, you'd have thought he was listening to the rain.'

The description fitted Hargrave pretty well, too, he thought. In between the waxing and waning of short-lived enthusiasms, he listened to the rain.

'He's immensely likeable,' Hargrave said. The sagging outlines of his face were lifted and strengthened by a moment of wary enthusiasm. He sounded as if he were praising some new horticultural technique, while preparing himself for the scepticism of his listeners. 'Likeable, but difficult. Had rather a rough time of it in one way or another. Bit of a chip on the shoulder. I suppose one may as well admit that in a way he goes with the mine. It's got rather an off-putting reputation. They probably couldn't get anybody else.'

'Mary Williams told me all about him,' Liz said. 'She said he was quite the rudest man she'd ever met.'

'He's allergic to the missionaries. He was running a nickel mine at Rosario when the Capuchins took over the area. There were baptists there before, and any of his work-force who happened to have been converted Baptists were publicly flogged, and whenever they wanted free labour they just used to come to the mine and help themselves.'

'I find some of these stories hard to swallow.'

'Ask Frazer. He's got a collection.'

'I can't wait for his meeting with Williams,' Liz said.

'Unfortunately it might be very damaging to Frazer's prospects,' Hargrave said. 'He doesn't mean to be rude, but he has this habit of saying exactly what he thinks. I suppose it's a very commendable quality in a way. And very rare. Unfortunately it gets him into hot water. They deported him from Panama for an offence described as Public Insult. To a second cousin of the President. One has to bear in mind the fact that at the moment he's under some stress. He says he's been badly let down over this mine job. It's

turned out to be far worse than he expected it to be.'
Hargrave summed up Frazer's predicament with a sigh.
'He never put down any roots. Here today, gone tomorrow.
One needs a base, an anchor; a sense of being part of a
community.'

'This looks like being quite a party,' Howel said.

'It's got all the makings of a shambles,' Hargrave said.
'If they had to have a party at all I can't think why they
wanted to have it at the mine. Have either of you ever been
to Ultramuerte?'

Howel and Liz shook their heads.

'It's all the name suggests—beyond death. Frazer says
it's the most terrible hole he's ever been in since he's been
a miner, and he's not one for exaggeration. His electrician had
an attack of depression two days after they moved in, and
slashed his wrists. It has a special climate all of its own. The
whole place stinks to high heaven of sulphur. When they
first opened the mine up they only had criminals working in
it. It's caved in a couple of times. They've only been in operation for a week and they've had a half-dozen serious accidents
already.'

'You never hear about things like this, do you?' Liz
said. 'I mean there's never anything published in the papers.'

'They're not allowed to,' Hargrave said. 'Under the edict.
Nothing can be published that fails to sustain the mood of
national confidence. Reports of criminal or tragic incidents
are barred. Still you can't complain they're short of news.
Did you see the long interviews *El Diario* published today
with six people who'd seen the image of the Virgin move its
eyes?' He groaned, 'I nearly forgot. I ran into Chavez, the
editor, and they're preparing a terrible charade. He told me
they're bringing a happy, smiling collection of fake miners
down from Los Remedios to be photographed and chat to
the distinguished visitors. The real ones will be locked away
out of sight. Soak though he may be, Frazer's an upright

Scot and a Presbyterian, and I know him well enough to know that he isn't going to stand for it. Chavez actually boasted about it. Thought it was a tremendous joke.

'And what are we supposed to be able to do about all this?' Howel asked.

'I really don't know. I only wish I did. We'll have to play it by ear; but if only we could get Frazer into a corner somehow or other. Surround him. Keep him from seeing what's going on . . .'

19

THE complex of mine buildings at Ultramuerte had been designed by the same eccentric architect responsible for the maritime flavour of a suburb of Los Remedios situated some hundred miles from the coast. This man had been an admirer of railway stations, and the few industrial edifices he had been commissioned to build had been as close in their appearance to railway stations as he could make them.

In this case the building had been carried out in yellow brick imported at high cost by sea from Panama. The tall gothic windows made a sun-trap of the rooms, and the administrative staff, in the days before air-conditioning, worked in temperatures that rarely fell below 100 degrees Fahrenheit. A vast and purposeless concourse area in the centre of the main building opened out on a conventional station platform, and for a few weeks in 1905, until it burst a boiler which was never replaced, a miniature train carried the manager to his duties in the various parts of the mine. *El Diario*, in its coverage of the mine's opening, reported that the town's notabilities accompanied the manager on his first trip, and that apart from a top hat, he was dressed in the green uniform of a senior locomotive driver of the Colombian State Railways. The report mentioned that the tour, undertaken in the early evening, was cut short by a plague of bats. The newspaper, reflecting the national taste for fantasy and defiance, was full of praise for every aspect of this project.

Howel, Hargrave and Liz had driven down in convoy to the party with Williams and his wife, and arriving they had split up. Howel and Liz found themselves isolated close to one of the enormous chapel windows. On three sides of them Colombians sipped German champagne, or scotch poured from bottles with absurd labels, all the women beautiful, all the men with noble, imperturbable faces; products of a ruthless selection which condemned the unlovely to sterility. There were orchids galore in the jungle, but the room had been decorated with $500 worth of rosebuds flown in a refrigerated container from the USA. The slight nose-tickling odour of sulphur dioxide that hung on the air at Ultramuerte had been suppressed by the liberal use of perfumed aerosol. The view through the window was of a sepulchral landscape hammered out of metal, of grass like seaweed, and stunted trees surviving in meagre pockets of soil in the seams of ore. What appeared to be fruit hanging in their branches was a crop of bats which awaited nightfall to hunt the flying insects for which Ultramuerte was famous. It was very hot.

'Williams was quieter than usual,' Howel said.

'They're breaking up,' Liz said. 'It's definite now. Mary told me she couldn't take any more. She says he gets stranger every day. Did you hear about the parrots? Somebody wrung their necks. She said he wept like a child. The first time she'd ever seen him in tears.

'There was something about those birds that always reminded me of him,' Howel said.

'When's the bus due?' she said.

'It should have got here soon after us.'

'It's late, then.'

'They always are.'

'I know Mary doesn't want to stay long,' Liz said. 'She didn't want to come at all. What time is it now?'

Howel looked at his watch. 'Six-fifteen, nearly.'

'Do you think it could have got here without our seeing it come?' she asked.

'No,' he said. 'I can see most of the car park and it isn't there.' He twisted his head to get a better view through the window and the sun rays striking across from the beginnings of an invisible sunset frosted the dust on the glass. He could see the rear end of Williams's jeep, and it's powerful number plate between the cars parked around it. 'I'm afraid our bus has not arrived.'

'The Williamses will most likely leave at about seven. What are we going to do?'

'What *can* we do?'

'Please go and look,' she said. 'Just in case it's parked somewhere where you can't see it. I can't stand this suspense.'

'All right,' he said, 'but you stay put. If Williams happens to come over you'd better see to it that he doesn't stand where I'm standing, because he could see his car.'

'Be as quick as you can,' she said. 'I'm getting very jumpy.'

'Shall I get you another drink first?'

'No, and don't be long.'

Howel went out, going first to the front, where a score of cars, the command jeep in the middle of them, were parked under the eye of a skinny negro shouldering an antique Mauser rifle. The sun, low over the trees, had painted the landscape with a jaundiced light. In the distance a thin shouting broke into the foreground chirp and whistle of bull-frogs. A loud-hailer voice brayed wordlessly and was silent.

Howel went quickly to the rear of the buildings, where the miniature locomotive of the mine's infancy mouldered under peach-coloured rust; its funnel entwined by a magnificent convolvulus. He came back again and was just about to go in when his eye was taken by a speck of moving colour on the leaden flank of the mountain. This was the bus, still about three miles and thirty or forty hairpin bends from Ultramuerte.

He went back to Liz. 'You can relax. It's on its way. Be here in about a quarter of an hour.'

'It's cutting it terribly fine,' she said.

'We've got to hope for the best.'

'I wonder what they'll do about the guard,' she said.

'Probably bluff him. He looks half-witted.'

'I'm trembling like a leaf.'

'You've never looked calmer.'

'How hot it is,' she said, 'or is it me?'

'It's hot,' Howel said. 'It's hotter in here than out in the open. The air-conditioning must have packed up.' He could feel little areas of coolness on his face, at the temples and under the lower lip, where the sweat was breaking through.

'Couldn't we get them to switch on the fans?' she asked.

Howel stopped a waiter passing with a tray of drinks and pointed to a fan. 'No funciona,' the man said.

'No funciona,' Howel said. 'The current must be off.'

'I'm going to turn into a grease spot in another ten minutes of this,' she said. 'Is the bus there yet?'

'No, give it a chance. Here comes Cedric, by the way. You'll have to stop looking out of the window.'

Hargrave struggled towards them through the crowd, a disorderly lay-figure in an environment of almost devotional propriety. The sweat glistened in rivulets in the creases of his face but he was exultant. 'Everything's fine and dandy,' he said, his voice tuned to a slightly nasal resonance for the outworn Americanism. 'Frazer can't leave the mine, and Bill Hackett, his number two, is doing the honours. Nice chap. He's with Ramon Bravo now. Come and meet them.'

Liz hung back and Howel gave her a gentle shove forward. At that moment he had caught sight of the bus, a moving shape at the back of the ghostly landscape seen through the dust. It bumped up the road on the last few yards of its journey, its hugely-lettered advertisements calling on the world to buy more aspirins, and stopped with its broken nose pushed up against the gate. 'The bus is here,' he said quietly.

Ramon Bravo, still lithe and aquiline in middle age, his skin, nicotined by the equatorial sun, in dramatic contrast with the purest of white hair, was talking mines to Bill Hackett, the assistant manager, a lively Cockney with the gestures of a Greek. With Bravo was an exceedingly beautiful Quechua girl who smiled continuously but did not speak. Bravo having raised Liz's hand to his lips, moved nothing but his eyes. Hargrave had told Howel that he had been a poor cowboy in his youth and, conscripted into the army, had won promotion—as was then possible—as much on the score of his ability as a poet as anything else.

Hackett was in the middle of telling Bravo just what was wrong with the mine. 'Frankly, everything's haywire from whatever way you look at it. Labour for a kick-off. A bunch of Indians, as weak as kittens. Frazer gets them from a missionary. Bit of a racket. Not that poor old Frazer can help it.' He felt the change in the atmosphere, looked up and saw Williams and his wife in urgent private discussion, just out of earshot. 'That's the one, isn't it?'

'Whatever our private disagreements,' Williams was saying to Mary, 'we must stand together in public. For the sake of the mission.'

'The mission no longer exists,' Mary said.

'In that case, for the sake of the evangelical movement.

'I don't know about even that,' she said. 'I'm no longer sure that we believe in the same things. And remember that I came here on condition that we stayed no longer than half an hour.'

'We'll have to go and speak to Bravo in a moment,' Williams said. 'It's most unfortunate that the General chose him as his deputy. If he ever succeeded General Lopez he'd give us short shrift. I have a feeling that he dislikes us intensely.'

'So many people dislike us,' Mary said. 'They use us, but they dislike us. At most they think we're a necessary evil. They'd make scapegoats of us if they could.'

'We must go and speak to the Colonel now,' he said, 'or they'll think it very strange. Please try to look pleasant.

Hargrave had taken Howel aside. 'Think I ought to pop

out and see if I can give old Frazer a hand. He seemed to be in a bit of a spot.' He drew a finger across his forehead, temporarily fusing a line of heat-spots, and made a faint, whistling noise of distress. 'Pity they couldn't have called this party off. The generator must have passed out again.' He went off with a limp wave for the others just as the Williamses joined the group.

Hackett was in the process of demolishing the last of the deputy governor's hopes for the future of the mine. 'An eventual big-scale producer? I don't see how. Can't understand how anyone could believe such a thing. Not if they knew anything about mining.' He knotted his brows and spoke at an enormous speed with a kind of flat, uninvolved sincerity, like a policeman giving evidence in an unimportant case before a magistrate's court.

'That is disappointing news indeed,' Bravo said. He had the face of a clairvoyant, receptive to every change in tension, every signal, however trivial, and, studying Hackett's face through his long white eyelashes, he could find no deviousness there. 'We were told a different story,' he said. A faint American accent from nowhere in particular marked him as not born a member of the ruling class.

'This isn't a real mine at all,' Hackett said, with something close to a whine of dissatisfaction. 'It's a lot of holes in the ground. The installation's all wrong. Shafts driven in the wrong direction. Don't even follow the seams. Didn't have a clue.' His words poured out in an elided gabble, broken up in London fashion like Arabic, complete with glottal stops, and his hands moulded images of contempt. Liz and Mary Williams had drawn apart for a moment, and Liz's hand touched Mary's in consolation. The Quechua girl swept them all in silence with her wide, empty smile. It was said that Bravo had rescued her from a brothel.

A waiter came with champagne. Howel said, 'I seem to have forgotten my glass.' He went back to the window. The bus was through the gate and had just come to a stop, and the passengers were climbing down into the stagnant light. They carried haversacks and toolkits and were dressed in a miscellany of workers' uniforms. Any one of half a dozen could have been a mechanic. A kind of throbbing anxiety had begun to well up inside him. I personally haven't anything to lose, he assured himself but the tautness of his nerves remained. Muffled behind the window glass, the loud-hailer voice began its remote gargling again.

He went back to Liz. 'Anything happening?' she whispered. 'Not yet.'

Williams had leaped into the breach in the battle for confidence. He wore a salesman's confidential smile. 'Yes, but the longwall system is the obvious answer. I've just spoken to General Lopez on the phone and he informed me that a million dollars' worth of equipment is on the way. A complete longwall installation with conveyor-belts.'

'You're putting new wine into old bottles,' Hackett said. 'However much you modernize the gear, you can't take the sulphite content out of the soil. At the best of times there's a wet bulb temperature of ninety-five degrees.' His tone was matter of fact. He might have been expressing a lack of enthusiasm for a brand of cigarettes.

'I gather that it is very hot,' Bravo said.

'And damp. It could be improved by proper ventilation. What we can't do anything about is surface water percolating through the mine and turning the sulphite into sulphurous acid. Every metal object throughout the whole of the workings is corroded. You can't go up a ladder, for instance, without taking a chance that it's going to fall apart and break both your legs. This is an area of recent volcanism. You've got water at a hundred and thirty degrees coming up through the footwall.'

Bravo said, 'Would you be agreeable to repeating to General Lopez what you've just told me?'

'I'd like to tell him a lot more, if he felt like listening,' Hackett said. 'This mine's full of carbon dioxide and hydrogen sulphite, and we can't blow it away fast enough. Last week the main generator on the pump packed up and we had a couple of cases of asphyxiation. We're on the relief generator now. They had to switch the circuit supplying this building. That's why there's no air-conditioning and no light.' His matter-of-factness had worn out, and he produced a grimace of despair displaying a proletarian disorder of teeth which he had difficulty in covering again with his lips.

Perhaps through a trick of his imagination, the heat of the underground galleries and tunnels seemed to Howel to have escaped up through the rock beneath them, and to be filling the room. Liz's hand held in his was hot and damp and patches of sweat were spreading across his shirt from the hollows under his collar-bones. Even the stoical Colombians in the vicinity were beginning to murmur complaint. The smell of sulphur came with a corrosive edge through the pseudo-lily-of-the-valley of the aerosol, and Howel observed that the petals of the rosebuds in a nearby vase showed signs of blackening at the edges. He put up his hand to the neckband of his shirt, tugged surreptitiously at it, and the button gave way. An elderly Colombian began to cough quietly into his handkerchief. Liz's voice was in his ear, silencing for a moment Bravo's cold questioning and Williams's booming dissent. 'Mary wants to go. Can't you think of some way of stopping her?' Her fingernails pressed into the flesh of his hand. 'I feel faint. What are we going to do?'

'Get her away if you can,' he whispered back. 'Make some excuse. Ask her if she knows where the first-aid room is. She might like the excuse to visit it. If the thing's going to be done at all, it can't take more than another ten minutes.'

The waiters were coming now with lighted candles, and

Howel slipped away to make indirectly for the window. Through it, little could be seen but the dark outlines of cars. He noticed a pinkness haloed in the sky behind foreground sheds, and in it, sparks wandering like fireflies. He could not be certain afterwards whether the commotion in the room started before or after the wailing of the siren. Soft feminine whinnyings of consternation had broken out. A ringing voice meant to calm but which only excited began 'Señoras y Señores—', candles toppled, the whinnyings became shrieks, then the stampede for the doors began.

Howel found Liz again in the open. They were in a wide alleyway between sheds, the gloom fogged with smoke containing waving spears of torchlight, and in this space people came and went, running, like assault troops in a confused battle that was turning into a retreat. Here, in a bewildered group, appeared the fake miners in burnished helmets and spotless dungarees, now deserted by the pressmen, as well as a party of young ladies who had come to read poetry on industrial themes, who fluttered with plaintive cries in search of their chaperone.

Hargrave came up out of the smoke, his clothing wet and blackened. The pumps went again and the miners panicked and went berserk,' he said. 'We got a few out and locked them in the security compound. They've got machetes. Must have found some firewater too. One of the guards got cut up. I've been trying to do something for him.' He hiccuped violently. 'Has anyone seen Bravo? He might be able to do something. If only we could talk to them it would help. God knows how many of them are still down the mine. They set fire to all the buildings.'

'Where's Frazer?' Howel asked.

'Last time I saw him he was trying to get the rescue squad into the mine. They have to go through the compound, and the Indians will cut them up if they try. We dragged out some casualties but the women got them away from us and took them to the bunkhouse, over there. They wouldn't let us in. Tore at us with their fingernails.' He hiccuped again; a high-pitched falsetto sound that was close to a sob.

'They'll let me in,' Liz said. 'I'll go and see what I can do.'

'You want bandages and splints,' Hargrave said. 'First-aid kit. Where are the splints coming from? They've got broken arms and legs. All of them in pretty bad shape.' An oil drum in a burning hut nearby exploded with a muffled, lethargic blast, colouring his face as if with shame. He pulled off his shirt and began to tear it into strips and Howel did the same.

20

T H E man on the gate took off the chain, lifted the gate clear of the post, gave it a shove, and it swung open on its own weight. The bus backed away, stopped with a jerk, ground its gears, then heaved itself forward through the opening. Inside the compound, it swung round in a tight, creaking semi-circle, to stop facing the gate again, ready to leave. The driver switched off, took off his dark glasses to wipe the sweat from his forehead, and climbed down.

Five passengers got out followed by Juan Simon, 22, a drop-out law-student who had taken a job in a garage where he worked with zeal. Simon wore dark blue dungarees with a Texaco shield sewn on the pocket, ball-player's black boots with white inserts, and a knotted silk scarf in the colours of Los Remedios football team. In eighteen months he had turned himself into a mechanic not merely in the matter of the skills he had mastered, but in the mental attitudes, the tastes, enthusiasms, and in the witty and laconic manner of speech of the Colombian lower classes. He possessed the gift in emergency of calm and plausible effrontery, which he was inclined even to practise for its own sake. This was the first major mission that had been entrusted to him.

Simon spoke to the driver. 'How long are we staying?'

The driver tapped on his watch. 'Five minutes.'

'I've got a job to do. Half an hour. Then I'll come back with you.'

The driver jerked back his head, the corners of his mouth depressed in a gesture which meant that he would leave in five minutes whatever happened.

Simon hoped that a bribe of twenty pesos would make him change his mind if necessary. Two passengers climbed into the bus talking excitedly, and the driver went to speak to the man at the gate. Simon shouldered his kit, walked across to the car-park and found the jeep, noting, as he had feared, that the security plates were welded on to heavy brackets, and that the bolts securing the brackets would be difficult to reach without jacking up the car. His first impulse was characteristic. Fifty yards away the Negro guard was skulking behind a pile of oil barrels. He had been told that a mutiny had started in the mine, and he was afraid he might be called upon to risk his skin.

Simon shouted to him. 'Feel in the mood to give me a hand with this car?'

'Sorry. It's not allowed. I'm on duty.'

Another idea occurred to Simon. He might be able to talk the bus driver into lending him the bus's jack and waiting while he unbolted the plates. Or he could simply unlock the car door with one of the three keys he carried that between them would unlock any door, and after that jump the ignition—if none of his keys would work in the switch —and drive away. It was a bolder plan but it was simpler, and the only possible snag would be the immediate discovery of the car's loss and a telephone call to the police in Los Remedios. Simon was encouraged to remember that in the city itself only half of the phones ever worked, and that in the country it was rare indeed to find one in order.

He strolled across to the guard.

'Where's the telephone?'

The guard laughed. 'We don't go in for luxuries here.'

Simon gave him a cigarette, and started back towards the jeep.

The bus driver, back in his seat, called to him. 'Well, are you coming or not?'

Simon waved to him with his left hand. He groped in his toolkit for his key-ring with the other.

Frazer stood with his back to the security compound gate to prevent the deputy governor from forcing his way in. Bravo was dignified and unemphatic. 'As representative of the government, he said, 'I order you to allow me to pass.' Frazer glowered at him, chewing on his lips. He had just gulped down half a hip-bottle of whisky, and the effect had been, if anything, to sober him. It had certainly increased his anger. 'Order away,' he said. 'As much as you like. I'm the boss here. It doesn't matter one way or another to me personally, but I'll be the one to carry the can if you go in there and get yourself killed.'

They seemed to be at the mouth of a dark cave, its obscure walls fuming and flushed with sullen light. Overhead, bats as big as crows criss-crossed a crepuscular vault of sky. The mestizos of the rescue squad waited with their lamps and equipment, their faces luminous with fear. The back wall of this cave had been painted with a crouching frieze of palaeolithic men. They were naked, their bodies smeared with ash.

Williams broke out of the confused crowd, loping into view with Mary running a little way behind. At the sight of him, the men of the rescue squad, some of whom had seen service in Esperanza, flinched away like sheep cornered in the angle of a corral. He came up to Bravo and Frazer, his shoulders enormous and slightly hunched, his hands prepared, like a powerful ball-player about to throw himself into the action. 'I think I can deal with this,' he said.

'You've come in the nick of time,' the deputy governor said. 'Please speak to those Indians in their own language. Explain to them that many of their people are still in the mine, lost in the darkness. No one will be allowed to harm them in any way. All we want is to go into the mine and bring out those people who are lost.'

'I'd be happy, Mr Bravo,' Williams said.

He stood erect, his feet together and both arms raised

like an orchestra conductor, and then began in a powerful, resonant voice. It was a voice that challenged and imposed discipline on the anarchy of the surroundings, the joyful voice practised by the missionary trainees for many hours upon captive but severely critical audiences, before they were released to their labours in the field. The sentences came in waves, almost with the rhythm of a chant.

Frazer interrupted. 'Have you explained to them? What's that you're saying?'

'First I'm preaching the Lord's word,' Williams said. 'I'm calling sinners to repentance and grace. I'm telling them that Jesus's blood cleanses from every sin.'

'We haven't time for that,' Frazer said. 'Men are in there suffocating. Cut that stuff and tell them that what happened was an accident. It wasn't a punishment of some kind. Not an advance sample of your Hell.' He stared into the big, smooth, invulnerable face with the hatred that came so easily to a man slowly being throttled in the iron grip of his paranoia. Worse than the most corrupt politicians, he thought. As merciless as the murder gangs hired by the land-grabbers. 'For Christ's sake stop preaching at them and tell them it was an accident.' He shouted, 'Tell them it was an accident.'

'Nothing in this world is an accident,' Williams said. 'Everything is ordained by the will of God. Everything but sin.'

'Get him out of my sight before I hit him,' Frazer said. He raised a clenched fist and lowered it again, the violent impulse shattering itself on Williams's impassivity. Williams ignored him as a man might ignore a small, yapping dog. 'Mr Bravo,' he said, 'perhaps you'd be agreeable to allow me to handle this situation in my own way. I've just called for an active sign of contrition, and as it's not been forthcoming I'd like to suggest a different tactic. Right now half-a-dozen of my ex-captains are employed in this camp. If you'd agree to give them the word, I'm confident they'd have little difficulty in restoring order.'

'Please do as I requested,' Bravo said, 'and simply explain what has happened. It would be better if you talked to their shaman.'

'There is no shaman. They have always been excluded from the mission.'

'There is always a shaman,' Bravo said.

'Even if there were, as a Christian pastor I could have no dealings with him.'

Mary walked away from them suddenly and went up to the fence. She called out in Cholo, and there was an instant guttural affirmative sound from the Cholos in reply. A movement at the back of the line of naked Indians produced a shrunken little old man, who was pushed to the front. He was absurdly dressed in a white man's cast-off shirt of an old-fashioned, formal kind with many pleats and buttons.

'That's your man,' Bravo said. 'That's your shaman. Now tell him what's happened, and ask for his permission to come through.'

Mary called out again, and the old man replied in a hardly audible mumble. He hung his head, and was shivering as if from fever.

'He gives his permission,' Mary said, 'but I must come first by myself.'

'That's impossible,' Williams said. 'Out of the question.'

'I'm going alone,' she said, 'and everything's going to be all right . . . Mr Frazer, would you open the gate?'

Frazer took the key out of his pocket, and went with her to unlock the gate. With the other hand he felt for his hip flask. 'I'll come with you,' he said.

'There won't be any trouble,' Mary said. 'I couldn't possibly be afraid of that old man, he's one of my patients.'

She walked through the gate. 'Modesto,' she said, holding out a hand, and the old man came to meet her. They spoke for a moment, then she turned round to the others. 'You can come now,' she said.

It was shortly before midnight before Williams and his wife parted company. They stood for a moment in silence. Moonlight drizzled about them from the hot, tattered clouds. The silence of exhaustion had fallen on the mining area broken only by the bell-gong of the nightjar, lost in space, a sound of loneliness and unearthly melancholy.

'I must go back,' Mary said.

'I'll come back with you. There must be something I can do.'

'It's better for me to be alone with them for the present.'

'And after our long and fruitful partnership you feel unable to make any concession,' Williams said.

'As far as the mission's concerned, I can't. What I've seen tonight makes it impossible for me to even consider going on. The only thing is, I shan't be going home with the children after all. They can go as planned. I know they'll be happy with Mother. I shall stay on here as long as I'm wanted doing medical work.'

A puff of sulphured wind whinnied through the corrugated iron. 'This is a terrible place,' he said.

'Neither of us has ever worried about where we lived or worked,' she said, 'so long as we believed we were needed.'

'But you no longer feel obligated in any way to bring to your patients the word of God?' He was incredulous.

'I won't have time,' she said. 'I'll be too busy looking after their poor, broken bodies.'

He pressed her hand and, turning away in silence, began to walk towards the car-park. He was full of despair that was charged with fury. Grail Williams saw himself the victim of a Communist plot, organized by Colonel Bravo who was certainly a crypto-Communist. They were everywhere the Communists; so-called Liberal politicians, land-reformers, organizations like SUCCOUR which were no better than undercover agencies for international Communism, a good part of the Roman Catholic church, infiltrated by Reds who had taken over the Vatican. He had underestimated their cunning, determination, and their terrible patience. Even Mary had been corrupted by their doctrines. They had succeeded in turning his own wife against him.

He stopped for a moment, fists clenched and lip trembling to consider his predicament. Someone must warn General Lopez, he thought. Someone must tell him that the Communists were everywhere—that even his deputy was a Red. He would go immediately. That very night. He started to walk faster, mind made up, resolute, caught up suddenly by a surge of his old combative spirit. If it's to be war, he told himself, we'll see who wins out. In a few minutes he reached the car-park and stopped again, hardly able to believe his eyes. Then he ran shouting to the guard who lay rolled in his blanket asleep by the gate.

Some two hours before this Simon had driven Williams's jeep through the churned-up slime of Los Remedios's shanty town to an isolated shack where he picked up Candido Rosas—also dressed in mechanic's overalls. They then set out on the road to Sosiego.

Rosas had given Simon something like a thin, distraught smile at the moment of their meeting, and thereafter said nothing. After ten minutes the road block at the exit to the town came in sight.

'Buenavista,' Simon said. 'Keep your head down.'

Rosas gave no sign of having heard. He was sitting hunched up, his hand over the lower part of his face. Simon wondered if he could be afraid. He had never seen Rosas before, but knew of him by reputation as brave and resourceful. He was disappointed, sensing something broken about this man.

He braked for the barrier and switched off the headlights. 'Pretend to be asleep,' he said to Rosas.

The day's traffic was at an end, and there were no cars waiting at the road block. Two soldiers were amusing themselves with a bedraggled girl in a miniskirt, and another lay on a bed outside the hut. His arm lay over the side of the bed, and a cat was licking his hand.

'Whatever happens, stay in the car,' Simon said. 'If I have to I'll try and crash through. You won't stand an earthly if you run for it.'

Rosas said nothing, but his hand closed over the butt of the snub-nosed revolver in his pocket. If the worst came to the worst and he saw no hope of escape he would pull it out and shoot himself through the roof of the mouth. Never through the temple, they were always told. One attempted suicide in six survived a temple shot. He was very cold and felt a sudden aching pressure in the sphincter of his bladder.

Simon pulled the car in to the side, and after several minutes one of the soldiers occupied with the girl disengaged himself and came across with a book.

'Where from?' the soldier asked.

'Garaje La Favorita.'

'Where to?'

'Taller Vicente Engineering.'

'Purpose of journey?'

'To fit a new exhaust system.'

'At this time of night?'

'They don't pack up until twelve.'

'Papers,' the soldier said. He was short, with a dwarf's big, serious head, bereaved eyes, and incredibly bowed legs. In his absence the girl and the other soldier had started a more positive sort of horseplay, and he kept looking back.

Simon handed over his driving licence with his identity card and photograph. That finishes me, he thought. It's the mountains after this.

'What's the matter with your friend?' the soldier asked.

'He's asleep. Had a hard day.'

'You're not supposed to be driving this car, are you?' the soldier said.

'How's that?'

'The SM plates. You're not the owner.'

'We service it,' Simon said. 'It has to be repaired, the same as any other car. What happens if we want to check the brakes or the steering?'

'The owner stays with it, that's what happens,' the soldier said.

'I only do what I'm told by my boss,' Simon said.

'And who is your boss?'

'Oscar Martinez. Garaje La Perla.'

'Is he there now?'

'He should be.'

'What's the number?'

'48332. You'll be lucky if you get through.'

'Wait there,' the soldier said. He waddled away towards a low table at the side of the road, on which stood an old-fashioned field telephone. As soon as he turned round the girl had pulled herself free and was patting at her clothes, but what he saw caused him pain. He tripped over a sleeping bitch and vengefully kicked it half across the road. The bitch streaked off howling, and the soldier spat after it in disgust, and picked up the telephone. Simon took the 9mm automatic out of his pocket, cocked it, slipped back the safety-catch and put it away. He felt a sense of elation. The soldier stood with the receiver to his ear, the line, as usual, dead. He wondered how he should deal with the situation. He would have liked to have gone into the hut to discuss this borderline case with the NCO, but the NCO was busy at that moment with a harlot and a bottle of rum. This was a service in which an excess of zeal was ill-rewarded.

He put down the receiver and came back to the car.

'How long's this job of yours going to take?'

'About an hour.'

'On your way, then.' He went to lift the barrier, and Simon threw him a cigarette and went under the raised barrier with a rush. He drove hard and happily on full throttle, slewing and sliding on the bends, and sometimes he would feel Rosas tense up beside him, as danger showed itself and was brushed aside.

Thank God I'm all in one piece, Simon thought. I can take it. He wondered what they'd done to Rosas and longed to ask him, but the movement imposed its iron protocol. No questions and no answers. Simon knew that they sometimes started an interrogation by half-castrating a suspect even before the first question was asked. An ex-comrade called Tarzan had shown him what was left of his sexual organs and the movement had subsequently felt obliged to execute him for suspicion of having given information under torture. They'd taken off one ball and the argument was he must have done a deal to be allowed to keep the other.

Rosas sat slumped in his seat, rolling from side to side on the bends. 'Tired?' Simon asked him.

'I'm all right.'

Was it a fact that the voice turned squeaky after castration, or just another fallacy? Rosas's voice, though weak, was gruff enough. The latest rumour was that the American advisers working with the police had brought a new electrical gadget that did something to the brain—a sort of lobotomy that abolished the will to resist. This seemed to Simon more likely to fit Rosas's case. They had dragged him away through the hole in the prison wall, cutting down the guards with tommy-guns, and the once intrepid Rosas had been strangely torpid. His friends were aghast at his shattered appearance, at those inert eyes, that waxen skin. What had they done to him?

'Where are we going?' Rosas croaked.

214

'The big village down the road.'

'And after that?'

'I don't know. It's not up to me.'

'I'm thirsty,' Rosas said.

'We'll be there in a few minutes.'

At Sosiego, Simon's first inclination was to hide the car and make their way to Sadik's on foot. Then he thought, what's the point? In a place like this everybody knows what's going on. He kicked at Sadik's door and a dog started up inside, and the chickens began to cluck and flutter.

Sadik came in his pyjamas, a sawn-off shotgun grabbed in the hand.

'I'm Icarus,' Simon said. 'I've brought the package.' He pushed Rosas forward. 'This is Mazeppa.'

'Why didn't anyone let me know you were on the way?' Sadik grumbled. He put down the gun.

'There wasn't time,' Simon said. 'Give this man some water. He's thirsty.'

Sadik brought water in a jug, and Rosas took it and began to drink. His hands shook and the water ran down the sides of his mouth. Sadik and Simon exchanged glances.

'How did you get here?'

'In the missionary's car. It's outside.'

Sadik chirped his dismay. 'You weren't told to bring the car.'

'It got too complicated to do anything else. I had to improvise.'

'Does the missionary know the car's gone?'

'He does by now.'

'Anybody see you?' Sadik asked.

'Everybody.'

'You know what that means?' Sadik said. 'It means that this place is done for operationally.'

'You've had a good run for your money,' Simon said.

Sadik went behind the screen, woke his wife, told her to get up and dress the children, pack as much as she could

215

carry and no more, including food for three days, and be ready to leave.

He came back to Rosas. 'I'll want those things you're wearing. You can put these on.' He gave him a shirt and a pair of trousers. 'What sort of shape are you in?'

'I'm all right.'

'Can you take a long walk?'

'If I have to.'

He turned to Simon. 'Your orders are to get back to Los Remedios.'

'I'm finished there,' Simon said. 'I'll be off the active list. They've got my details down in the book at the road block.'

'If you hurry you'll probably still get through,' Sadik said. 'You'll be taking a passenger. He has to get there whatever happens.'

'Not much I can do about that if they've reported the loss of the car,' Simon said.

'You shouldn't have taken it,' Sadik said, 'when you were ordered to get the plates. In my opinion you'll be disciplined. And rightly so . . . Give me the overalls,' he said to Rosas. 'At least you're about the same size, thank God.'

He took the overalls and a torch and went through to the back of the house into the yard. There was a large cage in the yard with a jaguar cub asleep in it. The cage concealed a trap-door and steps leading down to an underground room, and Sadik pushed the cage away, and the jaguar woke up, snarling. He lifted the trap-door, rattled a loose bolt fastened underneath, shone his torch down the steps and whistled. 'Wake up,' he called. 'Time to be going.'

Borda called back, 'Coming,' and soon Sadik heard him moving about, and saw the light of his oil-lamp begin to flicker in the room below. I've got an hour at least, he thought. Mustn't forget to let all the animals go.

21

THE sermon for that Sunday was to be preached by Padre Alberto on the text 'The meek shall inherit the earth,' and it drew a congregation that packed the cathedral. Padre Alberto's sermons baiting the establishment had become famous—an attraction for the jaded rich, ranking almost with a bullfight with a good Mexican matador. Extra police were on duty round the cathedral to help with the traffic and in the parking of the huge American cars. The upper and middle classes of Los Remedios came early and filled all the seats, and after the service there would be whisky parties for the fashionable at which the Padre's attacks on their way of life would be discussed in the spirit of jovial amazement. When the Padre was at his most vituperative he was considered to be in his best form; excellent entertainment value. Those close to the Bishop begged him not to spoil the fun by using his authority to silence the Padre, but the Bishop was beginning to waver.

The sermon started in an unpromising fashion. It was too factual, too devoid of emotional appeal. The Padre produced a string of figures that meant absolutely nothing to his audience and had no impact on them. No one disputed that three per cent of the population owned sixty per cent of the land. No one denied that the mass of the people were illiterate, sick, exploited, destitute and doomed to an early death. These were commonplaces, and dreary fare for those who had come in search of sensation. Padre Alberto mentioned that an average rich family would spent as much on the traditional nougat in celebration of the coming feast as would keep the average poor family in food for a month. The

Conservative point of view shared by the majority of those present accepted that these things existed but that they were part of God's inscrutable plan. A common argument was that the poor and their misery were necessary because otherwise the rich would be deprived of the necessity for practising charity. Beggars had been eaten by dogs, Indians massacred and carried off into slavery, the Padre reminded them, and they stifled their yawns, and waited for the fireworks to begin. The Padre looked down in silence on the rows of scrupulously dressed men and bejewelled women, and not the slightest emotion showed in any face. They were waiting for something better than this. They were waiting for the Padre to call them, as he had done before, a generation of vipers—hypocrites. The Padre began again. His voice, calm and quiet, hardly carried to the back of the cathedral. 'The meek,' he said, 'shall inherit the earth.

'They will inherit the earth,' he said, 'but those who lead them, and who recover for them their inheritance, cannot be meek. They will be led by students and churchmen fighting together wherever they have to fight—in the streets, or if necessary, in the mountains, against the new capitalism, the Moloch which has now become the enemy of Christianity.' The Bishop, Padre Alberto told the congregation, had asked him to preach this sermon—which was to be his final one—on 'the revolution of the non-violent', but he had felt unable to do so. 'Christ tells us to turn the other cheek,' he said, 'but he does not tell us to persuade our neighbour to turn his, nor may we use religion as the church has so often used it, to disarm those who are threatened with oppression and murder.

'A protest cannot be entirely sterile,' said the Padre. 'It must be founded on a hope, however remote. It must contain the germ of a possibility of conversion, of reform, of persuading the wicked man to turn from the wickedness that he has committed. If no such possibility exists—if we are shouting our protest into a vacuum—the revolution of the non-violent is worse than a meaningless catch-phrase. It's no better than a cold-blooded deception—something invented by psychological warfare experts to trick the oppressed into laying down their arms.' His voice strengthened. 'Religion is no longer opium for the people. Pope Paul himself would accept armed revolt with tranquillity if convinced that there was no other way to save the poor from the oppression of the imperialists.'

Stepping down from the pulpit the Padre was seized by pessimism. The congregation was dispersing decorously to their waiting cars, the shrill chatter of their parties, the enormous midday meal, and then the consoling uteri of rooms darkened for the siesta. Why had he ever bothered to attempt to reach them? A protest must not be entirely sterile, he had told them. Surely his preachings in the cathedral had been as ineffectual as the revolution of the non-violent.

Colonel Arana himself had sat in the front row of the congregation, taping the sermon in its entirety, and shortly afterwards the tape was played back to the Bishop, and a copy was flown to the Archbishop in Bogotá. Fateful days followed for the Padre. On the Monday he received a reply from the fifth and last international organization to which he had appealed for help: *The Latin American Committee of the League for the Rights of Man regrets* . . . That afternoon at the Escuela Superior when he lectured the post-graduate students in English Literature, the Principal called him to his office. He warmly congratulated Padre Alberto on his sermon, much of which had greatly appealed to him—but the fact was he was under pressure from several families whose sons were attending the course. Perhaps until the thing blew over . . . the Principal said, and the Padre understood. Next day the Bishop told him of the Archbishop's decision to suspend him from his sacerdotal functions and recall him to Bogotá, where he was to work in the diocesan administrative office.

'I hope,' said the Bishop, 'you'll come back to us one day.'

Padre Alberto's first impulse, as he rushed from the Bishop's Palace to his lodgings at the back of the cathedral, was to refuse to go, to barricade himself in, to defy them to take him by force. Here he began to plan a vague and impractical resistance based on converting his rooms at the top of the ancient house into a bolted and barred redoubt from which he would carry out surprise raids on the cathedral, muster up a congregation however small of chance visitors and worshippers, and preach to them the truths rejected with such indifference by their betters.

That evening, as soon as it was dark, he went down into the street and entered the cathedral by a back door. He was soon able to gather a little group: a caretaker, the woman who looked after the private chapels, an official guide, the woman who sold postcards at the main entrance, a small assortment of nondescripts who had come in and settled down in prayerful attitudes and then gone off to sleep, and a secret policeman who had followed the Padre from his lodgings, and who stood at the back trying to memorize his actual words. What Padre Alberto told his listeners was that the time had come to say NO. There were millions more like them, and all they had to do to remedy the heartlessness of their lives was to stand up together and say NO in one single voice. The small congregation listened with great attention, and were in hearty agreement. Padre Alberto told them to collect all their friends and come to the cathedral the next night at the same time. He had visions very shortly of filling the cathedral with the humble and meek.

Next morning he was awakened soon after dawn by the secret policeman of the night before who asked him with the utmost courtesy to pack his things and be ready to leave within the hour. He had instructions to put him on the eight o'clock plane leaving for Bogotá.

'And if I resist?'

'Be reasonable, Father. There wouldn't be any point. I'm not arresting you. My orders are to see that you get on the plane.'

Padre Alberto went to his window and looked down on a corner of the square where workmen were already engaged in putting up stands for the forthcoming procession. A twenty-foot drop at least. The policeman had pulled up a chair to sit by the door. As he said, resistance was pointless. He realized that his work in Los Remedios had been brought to an end.

'You're a worker, too,' Padre Alberto said. 'You're exploited. You may be better off than the majority of your class, but really you have a miserable sort of hand-to-mouth existence.'

'What do you expect me to do about it?' the policeman asked.

'Stop being a policeman. Take a decent, honourable job.'

'Perhaps you'll tell me where to look for one, Father. All I do is to carry out orders. The ones who give me the orders are the ones who are responsible. I agree with you it would be nice to be able to say NO, but the moment I say NO, my five children will start starving.'

The discussion went on as they drove out to the airport.

'You ought to have known you'd have to go sooner or later, Father. They didn't mind having you around so long as the situation stayed reasonably quiet, but as soon as the guerrillas showed up again it stood to reason you'd have to go.'

'Guerrillas? Didn't we read in the newspapers they'd been liquidated?' Padre Alberto said.

'The ones that came from Ecuador. I'm talking about the latest collection—the city kids who've gone up to Quebradas. The worst so far. There doesn't seem to be any end to it.'

'And there won't be. I can see hard times ahead for you. I wouldn't like to be in your shoes when the real revolution comes.'

At the airport a number of people recognized Padre Alberto, and it seemed that a few of them recognized the policeman, too. They were clearly hostile towards him and, emboldened in some cases by the fact that they would soon be leaving the area, they made offensive remarks about him in voices that could be overheard. At the ticket counter Padre Alberto's one-way ticket had been examined, commented upon and passed from clerk to clerk, and presently the porter who had carried his baggage to the scales came over.

'We'd all like to say we're sorry you're leaving us, Father. When are you coming back?'

'Not for some time, I'm afraid,' Padre Alberto said. 'I'm being sent on a long trip. For the sake of my health.' He smiled and the porter shook his head.

The policeman, embarrassed by the unconcealed hostility of the crowd, their angry stares and mutterings, tried to make it quite clear that Padre Alberto was under no form of constraint. He moved away from him on the bench on which they were both sitting, then bought a paper and buried his head in it. Presently Padre Alberto got up and went to the lavatory and the policeman lowered his paper to watch him, but made no attempt to follow.

Padre Alberto opened the lavatory window. Under it roses wilted in a dilapidated garden, and a few yards away a row of taxis waited at the roadside to pick up fares from the incoming plane. Hoisting himself up, he was just able to squeeze through the window. He walked quickly to the nearest taxi.

'What's the nearest village to the Quebradas mountains?'
'Sosiego.'
'Sosiego, that's right. Take me there.'

A moment later he tapped the driver on the shoulder.

'Do you know any gunshops?'

'About a dozen. What sort of gun do you want?' the driver asked.

'Just an ordinary hunting gun. Nothing complicated. Something about right to hunt jaguars.'

'I'll take you to a friend of mine,' the man said. 'If you want a good hunting gun, you won't do better.'

22

T H E old Cholo Indian had guided Borda in three days to Quebradas—that sanctuary of furtive humanity since Inca times—and at Quebradas he had found a trapper to take him to 'the Arab' he had been told to ask for. Sadik had hidden him for a week and given him false identity papers describing him as a skilled construction worker born in Leticia in 1950. 'As soon as you get to Los Refugios, the orders are to go to Mirones, the builder,' Sadik said. 'You're the new steeplejack he advertised for.'

There had been no difficulty at the road block on the way back to Sosiego, and Simon, euphoric and over-confident, hadn't been able to resist stopping for an unnecessarily long chat with the dwarf-headed soldier. As soon as they were out of sight of the block he drove the jeep off the road into a clump of trees, and there they abandoned it and finished the journey on foot.

That night Borda slept in Mirones's house, but next day he was taken away to be interviewed in a room by someone he never saw—a voice from behind a screen. 'Being a matter of urgency,' the voice said, 'you are justified in working through the holiday. Several loose tiles have fallen in the street and are a danger to passers-by. Your pass will admit you to any part of the cathedral at any time and you will be given the key to the door of the bell-tower staircase. To familiarize cathedral personnel with your presence, you will start work as soon as possible, carrying with you nothing but replacement tiles, cement, and your tools. The weapon will be placed in the bell-tower on top of the main beam from which the bell is hung. You will not go to the bell-tower until 11.30.'

The screen was a Japanese one, a luxury purchase of two generations before, but now faded and frayed to match the rest of the appointments of the mean room : the flaking chromium of modernism in decay, the false grain on plastic surfaces, the cowed-looking Madonna in washed-out blues and greens over the glowing torch-bulb. The two men who had brought him there and who sat on either side, hands stuffed into their jacket pockets, had the faces of gangsters the world over. I'm a prisoner, Borda thought.

A bulge appeared in the silk of the screen as the man behind it shifted his position. There was something about his voice that Borda found disagreeable. He had expected a comradely, man-to-man discussion of the action that lay ahead, but this was the voice of one of those soft-spoken advertisements for chocolates so popular on the Brazilian television—a gentle, insinuating invitation to peril, dressed as an indulgence. 'You will carry out your revolutionary task with absolute coolness, in the knowledge that you are not alone —that a thousand invisible friends are at your back.' To Borda the voice advertised abandonment. Abandonment with a chocolate coating. 'And no thought or effort has been spared, of course, to concoct a foolproof plan of escape.' I'm expendable, Borda decided. I'm to be thrown to the wolves.

'And now,' said the man behind the screen, 'perhaps we should run through the details once more, to make sure nothing has been forgotten.'

They'll do nothing for me, Borda told himself. Just leave me to get on with it. But it's not too bad. I never gave myself better than a fifty-fifty chance of surviving. If only they keep their promise about the car I'll get away. But they won't keep it. As soon as I'm up there on that roof I'll be on my own.

23

T H E great procession of the Virgin of Los Remedios on the first of May of every year was the occasion when civic status and precedence were defined, and a citizen staked his claim to the dignities of the year to follow. This was shown with great precision by one's position in the procession, and the enormous majority who were not included had no status at all. For twelve months of the year people manœuvred, pulled strings and shuffled from power alliance to power alliance in an attempt to move up in the order of precedence, but as these manœuverings had to be carried out in a cautious and oblique fashion, spectacular improvement was rare. There were no hard and fast standards of selection. As a rule, ultra-conservatives of impeccable ancestry marched at the head of the procession, but wealth came into it too. The ladies of the Sisterhood of the Holy Thorn, who tottered along under the weight of heavy lamp standards containing unlit candles immediately behind the image, held their places only while they had at least a few hundred pesos in the bank to back up their rank. If one of these women's family became destitute, she sooner or later slipped back in the procession to join the Sisterhood of the Five Sacred Wounds, where she still took precedence over the wife of the General Motors agent, who was the richest man in Los Remedios. On the whole the members of ancient and powerful families lived subdued, unemphatic existences, and men whose ancestors had crossed over with Pizarro from Spain to plunder the country found all the glory they could digest in these two hours once a year, when they marched with their heads held erect, while others knelt.

The mood of the day was one of bravado, of a traditional, almost pious infatuation with chance. In this one day in the year everyone became a gambler. Great issues were settled once and for all by the flip of a coin; women cut cards to decide whether to leave a husband or accept a lover, men plunged heavily on the stock market. In the cantinas it was double or quits when it came to paying for drinks. For this one day only, stalls were allowed in the plaza where children threw dice for sweets. To be lucky on the first of May was to be lucky for the rest of the year.

This was the day of the Virgin of Los Remedios, a pink and dimpled image, the size of the largest of dolls, dressed in her jewel-encrusted cape for her short journey through the streets, and seen by the hysterical crowd as a sort of Siva of the West, deity of creation and death. It was also the day of the Governor, judged by the populace by his public performance of the rites; the day when he showed himself, walking immediately behind the Virgin under her canopy, alone, slightly ahead of his deputy, and the senior member of his cabinet. The philosopher Miguel de Góngora who had preceded Lopez in office had noted that in its organ-ization and the moods it invoked, the procession resembled a bullfight; with the governor as matador, judged as much by his style as the rest of his performance. De Góngora had written in his memoirs that the people of Los Remedios were more willing to be badly governed by a man who had come up to their expectations on this occasion.

Shortly before midday on April 30th, General Lopez received an unexpected visit from the chief of police, Colonel Arana. Arana, shown in as usual, without formality or delay, found the General reading for the second time a report on the disaster at the Ultramuerte mine. The day had started badly for the General. He had been awakened at dawn to be told of the disaster, and then, an hour later, had no sooner set foot in his study when his favourite possession, the

227

painting on glass, *L'Enlèvement d'Hélène*, had fallen from the wall and smashed to smithereens. The General was inclined to regard this as an omen. He read again: total number of casualties still unknown . . . suspension of operations ordered . . . emergency relief measures for survivors. An aide following on Arana's heels handed him the second edition of *El Diario*. The blank space left in the centre of the front page of the early edition where the censor had removed a cautiously worded report of the disaster, had been replaced by a florid account of a basket-ball match. The General noted with irritation that a photograph of a group of foolishly grinning miners that no longer had anything to do with the rest of the news had been overlooked, and left without explanation on the page.

Arana brought disturbing news. A youth called Juan Simon had been arrested early that morning in connection with the theft of a car belonging to the American missionary, Grail Williams. Simon had admitted that this car carrying Seguridad Militar plates had been used to smuggle the guerrilla chieftain Candido Rosas, recently escaped from prison, out of town. Rosas had been taken to the house of a Lebanese trader at Sosiego, Mustafa Sadik, and there was reason now to believe that Sadik had acted as an agent for the guerrillas, and that Padre Alberto, who had escaped from custody had gone to join them there. By the time police sent to Sosiego arrived, Sadik had fled. Simon had further stated that he returned from Sosiego to Los Remedios with a man who had not disclosed his identity, but who from his description and the fact of his marked Brazilian accent must be assumed to be Orlando Borda who had accompanied the band recently annihilated at Cayambo. Arana read from his notebook what was known of Borda's career: Leader of Brazilian sharpshooters' team to Uruguay 1968. Chosen to lead Brazilian team 1969 Olympiads, but arrested for suspected implication in armed abduction. Escaped from São Paulo prison same year.

228

Since then believed involved in several kidnappings and bank-robberies carried out by guerrilla organizations. Arana thought it best at this stage to make it clear to the General that the unanimous opinion of his department was that a cunningly plotted attempt on the General's life in the near future wasn't to be ruled out.

Listening, the General thought that perhaps it was as well, after all, that he hadn't got rid of the fellow, as he'd intended to do. But I can't allow myself to be associated with this man much longer, he thought. People were beginning to confuse the two images, were saying that he personally devised the tortures, gave the execution squads the order to fire. How tragic it was that only a psychopath could master the arts of repression; Lopez studied Arana with extreme distaste. A grinning, obsequious fellow, he thought. It had recently been reported to him by one of his counterspies that Arana controlled the sale of pornographic films in the province. Quite unconsciously, under his desk, Lopez was tearing a piece of paper into small pieces. It was an act symbolical of his mood.

For all that, it was just as well that Arana had not gone. In Lopez's experience, a humanitarian policeman was not a policeman at all. The General sincerely looked forward to the day when all the repressive apparatus of the police state could be dismantled. It was an ironic fact, as he saw it, that the employment of such as Arana, in this period of discipline and national adjustment, should actually bring the day nearer.

If Borda had come to Los Remedios—as Arana believed he had—charged with the mission of assassinating the General, the only occasion totally favourable to the attempt would present itself at the next day's procession. Arana had several precautionary alternatives to suggest.

His first suggestion—and this was the alternative he personally favoured—was that the procession be abandoned altogether, because it was beyond the police's capacity, he admitted, to provide adequate security measures. Lopez shook his head. It would be regarded as a calamity, he said. Old-fashioned farmers, soaked in the atavism of remote forefathers, would lose hope for their crops. They wouldn't even bother to sow the seed. He reminded Arana that the only time in history that the procession had had to be abandoned was when it had coincided with a severe earthquake.

In that case, Arana said, the General might consider surrounding himself with bodyguards.

Lopez dismissed the possibility. Even in the worst days of the violencia, when an inevitably Conservative governor had been the object of execration of the Liberal forty per cent of the population, such a thing had never been done. Lopez had no objection to Arana's planting armed plainclothesmen, if he could find them, at five-metre intervals at each side of the road all along the route, and ordering the roof-tops to be cleared. But in the procession, he would walk alone. He pointed out that apart from all other considerations, the inclusion of bodyguards—who were bound to be nonentities—would disrupt the finely adjusted social equilibrium of the occasion, since their presence at the head of the procession would be taken as a slight to the distinguished citizens who followed them.

Arana's final proposal was for a last-minute and unannounced change of route. Instead of dragging its way, at the snail's pace of the most ancient aristocratic lady carrying the heaviest lamp standard, through the tight maze of the town's central streets, Aranda suggested that the procession be diverted into modern thoroughfares, where the crowd could be kept at arm's distance and the whole procedure speeded up.

The General objected again. This, he said, would divest the ceremony of its meaning. Its function was to permit the city's patroness to see her people, and to be seen by them. He reminded Arana of the thousands of citizens who had paid down their money for well-placed positions at windows or on balconies that had been advertised for the past three months, and asked him to imagine the frustration and bitterness of the hundred thousand who had taken up their places at dawn, but who would see nothing. If there were a political assassin in the city, Lopez said, Arana had twenty-four hours in which to find him. He would not tamper with the procession.

The General lunched alone, as was his habit, on starch-free rusks and black coffee, after which he lay down for an hour in a darkened room, practising a technique—this time with only fair success—of emptying his mind of its preoccupations. At three-thirty he rose and went back to his study, where he read several reports and signed a number of documents, and at four he called the officer commanding the city garrison into his presence.

Colonel Figueroa was charged with the physical details of the General's usurpation of power, planned to coincide with the end of the procession, ten minutes after the Virgin had been carried back into the cathedral and deposited in her chapel.

The Colonel was a man of rusted political loyalties, once a Liberal but now demoralized by a long subservience to the Conservatives in power locally. He both fought and inflamed a sense of his personal mediocrity by spending most of his spare time at the wheel of a 100 h.p. speedboat, dashing up and down over a small lake in the vicinity, and although he was incapable of any large-scale move on his own initiative he was precise and effective in the execution of orders.

He confirmed that the three doubtful officers in his command had been sent off on leave, and that the garrison had thereafter been alerted, placed on a war footing, and confined to barracks. Five antique Sherman tanks were ready to move to strategic points throughout the city, and Lopez knew that had he asked for more information, Figueroa would have reeled off a stream of details about their armament and crews. With Figueroa in charge of the operation, Lopez understood that these tanks would not run out of petrol or ammunition. Figueroa reported that the local striking force of three Thunderbolts—museum pieces though they were—had been carefully checked over and tuned up, and were ready at the airport to take off. When the moment came they would roar backwards and forwards over the rooftops, creating, as Figueroa put it, a 'responsive frame of mind', and dropping proclamations and leaflets. Figueroa assured the General that the possibility of bloodshed could be ruled out. At 12.15 p.m. the Los Remedios radio station would broadcast the national anthem, and the news of the rebellion's success. This would be the action signal for Lopez's friends in the capital, where an equally painless take-over was expected. The only question mark, the one tiny area of doubt, was provided by the deputy governor, Colonel Bravo, who had seemed enigmatic and aloof to those who had attempted to sound his attitude. But, said Figueroa, he was one Liberal among a hundred Conservatives, a powerless figure, with no following.

Figueroa stayed nearly two hours, until every detail of the operation of the next day had been discussed and approved. When he had gone, there was little more to be done but wait, and for the first time in his life the General found himself prey to an anxiety that was quite foreign to his character. The whole of his life had been a steady march forward of a man charged with a cautious, dogged optimism which, all things being equal, was bound to put him ahead of competitors imbued with the national characteristics of introspection and self-doubt. The General had stolidly refused to notice minor reverses, and this very fact had prevented him from building up the resistance necessary to face a major one like the disaster at the mine, on which so much hope had been staked. At the moment he felt his loneliness like a cutting wind. A man in his position had no intimate friends with whom he could share a weakness. Those who were closest to him remained infinitely separated behind the barriers of servility and self-interest they erected. Removed, then, from the comfort and solace of his fellow humans, Lopez experienced once again the impulse to turn to supernatural guidance.

As he had done so many times before, he dressed himself in a stained and threadbare cotton suit, found a battered panama hat, put on a pair of dark glasses, and a few minutes later was at the wheel of a vintage Opel car on his way to Buenavista. Anybody would have taken him for a ruined shopkeeper, although in the papers he carried he was described as a dental surgeon. At the Buenavista road block he was treated with reassuring insolence by a soldier who snatched off his dark glasses to peer into his face.

Lopez's destination was a shack in the most squalid and disreputable part of the town inhabited by an Indian *brujo*, a witch-doctor who dealt in oracles and enchantments, and who was visited in secret by many whites. When the General got there he noticed a number of flashy cars parked in the vicinity, and he had to wait his turn until several clients ahead of him had been dealt with before a woman with a monstrous goitre appeared, to lead him into the shack. The witch-doctor, a foxy-faced old man, vilely dressed in a saxophone-player's sharkskin jacket, awaited him in a sordid muddle of the bric-à-brac of his trade. He had assumed that Lopez had come for a remedy for impotence and was wondering how much he could charge for one of the fearful concoctions he sold for this, when a second, and closer, look at the General's face sent him into an agitation. Lopez

233

told him that he had come not for a potion or a charm, but for a fortune, and the witch-doctor, trembling violently, pushed a box in front of him and invited him to take his choice.

Lopez understood that what he was being offered was a standard fortune of the kind printed in their thousands locally, and issued by slot machines in packets of chewing-gum and cigarettes, as well as by the caged canaries carried by blind men, who were monopolists in the field of low-priced pre-diction. These fortunes were always composed for realists who had worn out most of their capacity for hope, and were expressed in a negative way, being concerned less with the conquest of love than the avoidance of betrayal, less with impossible happiness than with probable calamity.

The General tore open his fortune, knowing that it would contain little of comfort. He expected to be warned against romantic adventures, travel, lending or investing money, buying or selling—in a word, against action of any kind. But now he found himself staring down at a blank sheet of paper, and was quite unable to repress a slight shudder. This, then, was the sentence of destiny: nothingness. The witch-doctor, grimacing convulsively, foam on his lips, tried to snatch the paper from his hands, explaining that this was the second or third time the same thing had happened that day, due undoubtedly to a fault in the printing machine. He urged Lopez to help himself to a second fortune, but the General shook his head, carefully folding the paper and putting it in his pocket. He left and the man followed him out into the darkness, pleading with him to try again. Could he have recognized me, and if not, what did the fellow read in my face? the General asked himself.

There was only one possible remedy, and Lopez drove from this encounter straight to the cathedral, finding it crowded with the members of the confraternities, and swarming family groups, united in a soft domestic hubbub and the dramatic chiaroscuro of several thousand candles alight in the vast gloomy spaces.

These droning crowds were the aftermath of a succession of ceremonies to mark the eve of the procession. They had begun with the Blessing of the Fire; a piece of respectable Christian shamanism much practised in the churches of the Spanish homeland, but enthusiastically taken over here by the Indians, and incorporated in their own private beliefs. Next on the list had been a mass christening of thirty-three children, all the girls being given the name of Maria Gloria, and all the boys, Salvador. This had been followed by the procession of the tapers, a small-scale version of the next day's procession held within the four walls of the cathedral. The mood of the crowd was happy and relaxed, because the Virgin had been described by a number of persons accepted as specialist observers of this occasion as being 'in form'.

The attraction now was the distribution of the holy water and a long queue waited, slowly filing past the font where a sacristan poured a few drops from a jug into the bottles held up to him. The queue was composed of members of the lower classes. There were back-door methods of access to the water for those who could afford them, and preferred not to come to the cathedral in person.

The General paid a coin of minute value for an empty medicine bottle from a stall at the cathedral's door and joined the slowly-moving queue. Children played under his feet, and Indians who had guzzled down aguardiente in preparation for the fire-blessing ceremony reeled about in a state of sacred intoxication wherever there was an open space. People ahead who had received their holy water scampered away with it into dark corners to drop in talismanic candle-wax, or grains of barley, or even, in the case of the most conservative and pious, to spit into their bottles. It took the General half an hour to reach the font and by that time there was hardly any water left. The sacristan snatched his bottle away, emptied a dribble from the jug into it and gave it back. Lopez held the bottle up to the light and saw that the water had not quite trickled to the bottom. The sacristan waved him on with an impatient gesture. He was immediately accosted by a blackmarketeer who offered to fill his bottle for ten pesos, but Lopez pushed him away.

The General drove back slowly and sadly to his palace, and went straight to his bedroom. He took out the blank fortune, wet it with holy water as best he could, by pressing the neck of the bottle against it, then shaking it. After that he struck a match and set light to it. Most of the fortune burned quickly away, and a second match was enough to consume what was left. Lopez knew it was the most potent act of exorcism he could accomplish. He went to bed and slept peacefully.

24

An army of municipal conscripts worked all night on the city's streets, hosing away the rubbish, the crippled beggars, and the drunken Indians, and snaring the wild dogs to their destruction. By dawn their work was at an end and the advance guards of the crowds had begun to take up their position. It was a day when the sun rose, as the saying was in Los Remedios, that bore malice. The sky was like an unhealthy face, pasty and blotched. A pearly trachoma of cloud formed and dissolved, flinging down a few drops of rain that evaporated like spirit as they splashed on the warm stone surfaces, while thunder rumbled briefly up and down the sky.

By seven-thirty the crowd was solidly packed along the whole length of the processional route, and the Plaza was filling up with late-comers who would see very little. Many of them were carrying small frost-coated bouquets of pansies and wallflowers supplied by ice-cream-sellers. These, if kept out of direct sunshine, retained their colour and crispness for an hour or more. At half-minute intervals the cathedral's great bell crashed out with the sound of buses in head-on collision in space. At eight-thirty a rush took place to a side-door of the cathedral where a deacon scattered ritual handfuls of aniseed and old one-centavo coins. At ten to the minute the main doors were flung open, the procession began to move out, and the waiting crowd fell to its knees.

The procession was led by the garrison band in brand-new American uniforms, trumpets and trombones, fanatically burnished, at the ready. Immediately behind followed the Bishop and his two archdeacons, then the three hooded and bare-footed penitents, then the privileged ladies who scattered rose-petals in the path of the image, then the Virgin herself, carried on her platform by eight men and embowered in lilies sprayed with gold and silver paint, among which little more than her pink doll's face was visible. General Lopez came next. He was dressed in a perfectly-fitting dark suit he had just received from London, and walked with the slow, gliding step still employed for ceremonial marching in the country's military academies. The General seemed to some of the spectators very pale, and they approved of this as contributing to the solemn dignity of the occasion.

Howel, Liz and Hargrave sat in the *preferencia* seats in the grandstand erected in the Plaza. Liz and Hargrave had been there for some time but Howel had only just arrived.

Something distracted Hargrave's attention and Howel bent over to Liz. 'I think it's going to be all right. There was only one man on duty at the Gobernación. I told him somebody had cleared out the inside of the car, and they must have taken the pass, and he just wrote it in a book, and I signed, and that was that. No fuss of any kind.'

'Marvellous,' she said, 'but I still can't believe we're going to get away.'

Hargrave's interest had been aroused by several horse-drawn vehicles rattling into the square nearby. Motor traffic was debarred from the town's centre, and these were the coaches of great families who could not bring themselves to walk, drawn by horses reprieved from the knacker's yard. Suddenly he was with them again. 'Not get away? Of course you'll get away.'

'The plane won't come,' Liz said. 'I'm absolutely certain of it. And if it does come there'll be some awful hold up. On Sunday they suddenly took it into their heads to search all the outgoing passengers and their luggage. In the end the plane took off without about half of them. The weather doesn't look too wonderful.'

'It's clear,' Hargrave said. 'That's all that matters. In any case it's a day flight. They don't bother about weather,'

'I do so wish I could relax and enjoy this,' Liz said, 'but I can't. Have you seen some of the funny people that have been arriving? That's Bravo's girl-friend over there, isn't it? Everybody's falling over backwards to be nice to her.'

'Well, after all, she's the second lady in the province,' Hargrave said. 'Even if she can't walk in the procession.'

Colonel Bravo's Inca mistress, accompanied by the two impoverished gentlewomen who attended her, had been bowed to her seat, and now she turned to smile at each of her neighbours in turn, the natural gold of her complexion deepened by a sallow reflection from the sky.

'It's an amusing place if you don't stay too long,' Hargrave said. 'Just right for a long weekend. I wish I were coming with you.'

'Cedric, really though—why don't you?' Liz said. 'Bob, do make him come.'

'Somebody has to lock up,' Hargrave said. 'Switch off the lights. Have the meter read and so on.'

'You are coming next week, aren't you?' Liz said.

'Well, practically.'

'What do you mean—well, practically?'

'I may be stopping off at Panama on the way back,' Hargrave said.

'That's a new one on me,' Howel said. 'Why Panama?'

'I was talking to Maclaren Frazer. They're in a bit of a tight spot over the Cuna Indians. Maclaren thought I might be able to help out, and I'm going back with him. '

Both Howel and Liz recognized the familiar expression, the sudden earnestness that knitted together the loosening features, an enlivenment of the eye, the bristling upthrust of the beard.

'As you know, these people live on islands. They're fish-eaters and the neighbouring waters are just about fished out.

I happen to know of varieties of beans and squash that will grow in sandy soil even if salt is present. Adequately manured, of course. In this case with seaweed.'

Howel and Liz looked at each other, trying not to smile.

'You really mean that, Cedric?' Howel asked.

'Naturally, I mean it.' There was nothing but sober dedication in his face.

Distantly the garrison band had begun to pump out the Triumphal March from *Aïda* reduced to a tempo that matched the marching speed of the aristocratic old ladies burdened by their heavy lamps. Suddenly the music was drowned by the engine of a plane, low overhead. Everyone looked up.

'That's Williams's Cessna,' Howel said.

'Very low, isn't it?' Liz said.

'For a supposedly careful pilot.'

'Friend Williams appears to be coming unstuck,' Hargrave said. 'At long last. I'm not sure I'd want to be in his shoes at this moment. Did you hear what Bravo said?'

'I wasn't there,' Howel said.

'No, of course you weren't. He said he would insist on a commission being sent down from Bogotá to investigate the disaster. Also the actions of certain foreigners he believed to be contrary to the nation's interests.'

'How can he, when Williams is tied up with Lopez?'

'I don't know, but I still wouldn't want to be in Williams's shoes. They'll never give him another Seguridad Militar plate after the way he lost his jeep.'

'I think the procession may be coming,' Howel said. Beyond the close grain of the crowd at the far end of the square the banners shifted jerkily, and the music of *Aïda* came in thin rhythmic gusts. 'I don't see any cripples throwing away their crutches, or wild Inca antics.'

'Lopez cut a lot of it out,' Hargrave said. 'Bloody security mad. Looks as if it may turn out to be a bit of a frost.' He took a reading with his exposure meter and began to fiddle with the speeds and the diaphragm setting of his camera. 'Don't you want to take any shots?' he said to Liz.

'No,' she said. 'I don't think I will. I really can't be bothered.'

'Last medieval spectacle of its kind you'll probably ever see.'

'I know,' she said, 'and to tell you the truth I couldn't be less worried. I'm afraid that all I really want to do now is to get away.'

'We could go now,' Howel said, 'except there aren't any taxis. It might be difficult to get through the crowd.'

'There isn't all that hurry,' she said. 'I don't mind sitting here while Cedric takes his pictures. I just can't work up any enthusiasm myself, that's all.'

'All right,' Hargrave said, 'I'll get one or two shots and then go to the airport. No point in getting there too soon.'

'No chance of seeing anything of Lopez's take-over, I suppose?' Howel asked.

'We've already seen it,' Hargrave said. 'It's happened. We've had a ringside seat, whether you noticed it or not. Lopez is already president in everything but name. Latin American revolutions are streamlined these days . . . I say, Williams really does take risks, doesn't he?'

The Cessna had appeared over the buildings just across the square coming straight at them and flying lower than the top of a crane on an unfinished skyscraper. It banked steeply away in a curiously slow-motion turn and a flutter of yellow light on its underside, and as it did so the engine cut out, then came back in again in a roar that ended in a cough.

'It looks terribly dangerous, doesn't it?' Liz said. 'Do you think he's in trouble?'

'Could be. Looks awfully like it.' As Hargrave spoke the plane did a half-circle, passed behind the unfinished sky-scraper, came into sight again, its engine popping. There was another snuffed-out roar, and it appeared to hit a barrier of air, and then dropped. Howel felt the thump as it hit the ground in his haunches and thighs, where they were in contact with the seat. Liz screamed, and two puffs of black smoke went up.

Grail Williams died instantly when his plane stalled and crashed in the mean street running parallel to and behind the main Calle Animas. With him was Arana, Chief of Police, who lived on for half an hour without regaining consciousness. The flight was a last demonstration of the thoroughness that had advanced Arana in ten years from his position as a simple investigator in the city vice squad to that of the second most powerful man in the province. As luck would have it, the order for the return of the helicopters lent to General Lopez had come the day before the procession, so Arana had fallen back on Williams for a last-minute inspection of the rooftops, which had been placed out of bounds to the public for the day.

Arana's second-in-command, Captain Navarro, saw the crash and diagnosed it as sabotage. At that very moment he had been called to deal with an urgent but delicate matter. One of his men had reported the presence of a suspicious person in the cathedral, and Navarro, a cautious man only recently promoted and determined to take no chances with his career, proposed to do nothing about it. Navarro would never have considered entering the cathedral with a body of armed men unless given a positive order by Arana to do so. Now Arana was almost certainly dead. He dealt with the situation by sending a single plainsclothesman with instructions on no account to discharge a firearm inside the building. Navarro then began to worry about his future. The secret police were much hated by the regulars, and although Navarro was a regular he had had a foot in both camps.

Colonel Figueroa had a close and unimpeded view of the crash from the top of a bank in the Calle Animas where he

242

was keeping a watch on events. He noted the plane's last-minute attempt to settle like some monstrous dragonfly between the walls of a narrow street that wrenched both wings cleanly away, leaving the fuselage remarkably intact until disrupted by the explosion of the petrol tank. Five minutes later a messenger brought the news that Arana had been in the plane, and Figueroa quietly reprimanded him for the slackness of his salute.

Nothing, Figueroa knew, would ever be the same again. He could almost feel the beginnings of the shift in the currents of favour. With Arana gone, the political equilibrium had collapsed like a spider's web with one of its supporting strands cut through, and Figueroa knew that whoever came after him would inherit little power but much hatred. Figueroa stood at a point roughly equidistant from the tragic little scene in the street, where an attempt was now being made to drag what he took to be bodies from the flaming wreckage, and the distant bustle in the square, which the head of the procession was now about to leave on the way back to the cathedral. At this moment he felt a sensation of Olympian detachment and power. Potentially, with his guns pointed at the city's heart, he controlled the destinies not only of Los Remedios but of the nation. The messenger was back with the news that Lopez's private army, Squadron Three, as it was called, was beginning to withdraw from positions allotted to it throughout the town, and was concentrating defensively in the Victoria Square. Figueroa could put only one interpretation on this move. This force—the SS of Los Remedios—had been under the direct command of Arana, and with their leader gone they were lost sheep, threatened with a terrible reckoning not only by the citizenry but by the garrison troops who had many insults and aggressions to avenge. Figueroa assured himself that if ever he received the order to suppress them he would finish the job in a half-hour. He enjoyed a moment of fantasy in which he saw himself sending his tanks into action. *If anyone ever gave him the order.*

In the procession, General Lopez had marched for over an hour and he was beginning to feel the strain imposed by the unnatural use of muscles in the slow ceremonial step. A number of small mishaps had marred the smoothness of the occasion. Within five minutes of leaving the cathedral one of the elderly lamp-bearers had collapsed, and the head of the procession led by the band had ridiculously walked away from the floundering tail, thrown into confusion by the incident. Then the sudden appearance of Williams's plane flying low overhead just before the crash had sent two horses out of control, and their riders, allegorical figures representing Justice and Liberty, had been unseated. With the roar of consternation provoked by the plane's crash in his ears, Lopez marched on, properly unmoved, eyes to the front. Then the procession had come to a standstill altogether to adjust the position of the Virgin, who appeared to be slipping down sideways in her bower of lilies.

These were matters to the General of scant importance, surface blemishes on a background of gathering gloom. He had grown up in an environment in which suspicion and scepticism were imbibed with the mother's milk, and a mild form of social paranoia struck at random like an epidemic sickness. To the mind of Los Remedios true accidents hardly ever happened, and obscure human agencies could be found if one investigated deeply enough behind most acts of God. To Lopez, Williams's plane had crashed, in his sight and that of the crowd, because someone had decided that it should do so. His intuition, easily leaping the gaps at which his reason balked, told him that the crash was linked with Bravo's non-appearance to walk immediately behind him in the procession on the grounds, confirmed by his doctor, of a heart-attack. Bravo's heart-attack, the plane-crash, the long overdue appearance of the three Thunderbolts on their leaflet-showering mission . . . the disaster at Ultramuerte. Lopez was a master of the arts of trickery and dissimulation, but he was surrounded by many others who were masters too. Who, he asked himself, could have benefited by putting the pumps at Ultramuerte out of action? Would he have been wiser to give the foreigners the 51% interest they'd asked for? Why had the helicopters so suddenly been withdrawn?

Lopez marched on, arms held stiffly at his sides, eyes raised to the Virgin's head at the apex of the triangle of her cope, each gliding pace precisely timed and exactly the same length as its predecessor. Ahead, the trumpets and trombones spluttered into the Triumphal March for the ninth time. The General was fighting off the feeling of unreality, an hypnosis induced by the slow physical rhythms of the march. The eight men ahead carrying the Virgin had gone out of step, shuffling with fatigue, the sweat coursing down wrists and necks. And then, passing the entrance to a side-street, the crowd parted suddenly with a glimpse of a startling sight: a soldier was being attacked, buffeted, stoned.

Lopez was a prisoner in close confinement, utterly isolated from action of any kind by this unrelenting protocol. He had neither ears to listen to reports, nor voice to command. The General had abrogated his authority for two hours to march, as he felt bound to, in the procession, and little by little as he marched on he had felt the power being stripped from him. In an instant of detachment that enabled him to judge his predicament as an outsider, he saw himself the victim of a brilliantly organized plot, of which Arana might have had some inkling when he had come to warn him the afternoon before. He believed now that his life might be about to end. There was something in the composition of the moment common to the drama of political elimination everywhere in his day. Those who killed public men had developed a Roman taste for theatricality and an audience. If he were to die it would be at the hand of some deluded hireling, whose own assassination would immediately follow, together with as many other secret sacrifices as might be thought necessary to remove all traces, seal all mouths, and impose oblivion. For a while people would ask each other, with hints of little-known facts in their own possession, what they really supposed was behind the Lopez affair. There would be rumours of all kinds, then a dying mutter of speculation, then nothing, nothing, nothing. They would change the name of the sports arena, a clinic, a street, a square, knock down a couple of monuments, and in a decade he would be forgotten. A mention of Alberto Cervera Lopez would only be found in the most specialized and detailed history books of the epoch. Dwelling on these lugubrious possibilities, Lopez's feelings were not of self-pity, but those of a father who, looking ahead, experiences a sharp sorrow at the thought of his numerous family deprived of his protection. His loss to the country, to all the people of the province who were his children, would be irreparable. There were so many responsibilities, so many things left unfinished.

Suddenly his spirits lifted. Ahead in the sky the cross of the finial of the great dome of the cathedral had thrust up into sight, and soon the dome rose into view. The cathedral was the inviolable sanctuary that awaited him, and also, with the procession's return and the deposition of the image before the high altar, the General's two-hour exile from authority would be at an end. His subordinates would come running for their orders. He would fix them with a calm eye, and the power would flow back into him again.

The dome with its satellite cupolas lifted gently to fill half the sky. A misted sun had broken through to revive the colour of the ancient tiles, which reminded the General of the dusted blue of a kingfisher's wing in a case of birds that are beginning to fade. Lopez estimated that there were a hundred and fifty paces to go, and he began to count. The approach of the end of the ordeal had animated the procession. It was in order on the last lap for servants to take over the heavy lamps from their exhausted mistresses. Knowing this, the band speeded up its tempo. The bare-footed penitents limped along a little faster. The Bishop, who was flat-footed, with very short legs, was on the verge of breaking into a waddle, and the men leading the horses ridden by the allegorical figures of Justice and Liberty had to tug on their bridles to stop them from breaking into a trot as they realized that they were nearing their stables.

With the dome now sinking behind the cathedral's main façade and perhaps a hundred yards to go, Lopez stopped counting his steps and began to plan. Figueroa and Navarro would be standing in their dress uniforms, cocked hats, swords and sashes, one on each side of the cathedral doors as he approached, and he would acknowledge their salutes by raising his right hand, no more than that. It was the prearranged signal for action, for the posting of proclamations, for the cathedral choir to rise to sing Te Deum, for the twenty-one-gun salute. After that would come the drive to the palace in the open Cadillac borrowed for the occasion; an appearance on the balcony, a television appeal to the nation for calm, for understanding, for trust. Something would have to be done about Bravo. He would send an independent doctor to visit him, and if the heart-attack story proved not to be genuine, order his preventive arrest. And there was the matter of the missing Thunderbolts to be investigated. Where were the Thunderbolts?

In these last moments the crowd had thinned out and come closer. It was also changed. These people were dressed in ragged cottons, and their faces were dark and without expression. Out of the corner of an eye the General was disquieted to see Indians in full tribal garb. They had always been excluded from the plaza, and to find them there now in their animal skins, with their painted faces, could only mean that the police were no longer in control. To one side a

247

little squatting ring ignoring the procession had formed round three shamans, wearing bearskins that left buttocks and sexual organs exposed. Tails hung down behind them, and their faces grimaced through the jaws of bears' heads, with pieces of glittering quartz in place of eyes. They were dancing in a manner that was obscene to the white, but Lopez, who had heard of this dance although he had never seen it, knew that it was the most sacred of the Indian ceremonies, performed only at moments of supreme crisis, and its purpose was to summon the assistance of all the totemic ancestors of the race.

Even surer evidence of the collapse of order was that they were letting off fireworks in defiance of his ban. A mortarete cracked somewhere in the sky, and a horse took fright close behind him with a clatter of hooves and a warning outcry. At this instant the man on the right corner of the rear of the platform let go his hold to stand away from the others and double up, as if taken with a sudden cramp in the stomach. As he did so the platform tilted and the image began to slide. While the General, marching two steps forward as the platform teetered and rocked, wondered if he must intervene, a second man fell, the corner of the platform dropped further, and the thin wires protecting the whole elaborate composition gave way. The silvered and gilded lilies, the banners, the spangled stars, the plaster crosses and symbols of the Passion were torn from their supports and slid to crash in a tinsel avalanche at the General's feet.

He stopped with the music, standing at attention to stare down at the mound of glittering debris, heaped around a broken doll.

The procession had scattered and dissolved as if charged by an invisible enemy. A riderless horse, sliding and kicking sparks, missed him by inches, but something—perhaps a flying stirrup—struck him between the shoulder-blades. The General turned his head slowly, searching for the comfort of a friendly face, but could find nothing but the deadly, withdrawn neutrality of the Indians. The shamans had ceased to dance and put away their snakes, and now, their backs to him, they capped their hands over their mouths to invoke their ancestors with blubbering wolf-howls and the coughing roars of jaguars.

An Indian had planted himself directly in front of the General, and as they studied each other it occurred to Lopez that the Indian's expression was that of a child bewildered by an arithmetical problem. A question was forming in his mind, but it remained blurred and shapeless, resisting all his efforts to bring it into focus. Why? The man swung the incense-burner he was carrying under the General's nose, compelling him to fill his lungs with copal fumes. The scent was sickening, Lopez coughed, and as vertigo rocked him, the earth curved under his feet and all the buildings tilted inwards. He lowered himself carefully to his knees. Above him the cathedral bell crashed out again. He looked up and saw that the Indian's eyes had never left him. And now he thought he could see pity in the man's face. In an Indian it was a look that frightened him.

The whole town had suddenly gone blind, as the shutters banged-to over every window. Two tanks pushed out from behind the canvas that had been screening them. One of them fired a round from its two-pounder into the sky, then they both stopped to await orders. A great wind was sweeping the debris of the crowd from the square, now littered with hundreds of tiny bouquets of flowers thrown down in panic. The sun had come out fully, draping the streets and squares in mourning shadows. The General lay near the two bearers of the Virgin's platform who had been struck down with him. One of them moved and groaned, while the other lay still. A man came running to roll him over on his back, place his hand over the heart, and then shake his head. An-

249

other had gathered up the broken image in his arms, and gone away weeping.

The agitation and bewilderment that had emptied the streets flowed into the cathedral, and the crowd that waited there stirred with panic. Borda, coming down from the bell-tower, found himself trapped among flustered bodies and candle shadows. People were rushing to and fro pointlessly and in silence, like those whose lives suffer an instant of utter dislocation in a severe earthquake. It was a moment when people die instantly, inexplicably, trodden under foot, or crushed in a trivial convulsion of the crowd. The tank's two-pounder belched distantly, silencing the cathedral's organ whining to choristers forgotten in a loft, and a turtle-dove moaning began near the high altar to which the broken effigy of the Virgin had been carried.

Borda steadied himself for a moment against a pillar, then crossed the cathedral and went out through the side door into Animas Street. He stood there looking up and down the street, which was quite empty under the vertical sun. No car awaited him, as he had known with the absolute certainty of revelation that it would not. He felt something like exhaustion, but it was not an exhaustion to be re-pudiated, rather a kind of satisfaction, a feeling that he had lived his life and entered a calm senility—a feeling of completion, that he had fulfilled the purpose for which he had been born.

He began to walk slowly and without purpose along the street and, reaching the first corner, was stopped by a man who suddenly rounded it and stood in his path. Borda expected him, expected the hesitant familiarity, the out-stretched hand and the nervous smile. He'd seen the face before in life, in a dream, in a premonition; a face that could harbour concern. He took the hand, feeling his finger-bones crack in its grip. The smile had changed to a wince of guilt and Borda looked away from him into the distance of the clean, heat-parched street.

Hearing the scurry of footsteps behind him, he knew what was about to happen and made no attempt to move. He was convinced at last that the dead lived, and of his own right to immortality.

25

F o r three hours the airport was empty, and then, when it was past five in the afternoon, the passengers and their many friends began to arrive. They had come from another and more tranquil world, scrupulously dressed in the uniforms of travel, wearing the faces of people happily absorbed in the small-scale tensions of dealing with luggage, reserving numbered seats and gathering information about possible further delays to the flight. A serene girl had appeared behind the ticket counter. Two porters, alternately grumbling and joking, labelled the baggage and were loading it on a trolley. The souvenir shop had opened for the sale of fake Indian beads, toy llamas and costume dolls. There was an absence in this atmosphere of the hysterical relief Howel would have expected. Nor was there any despondency, let alone grief. 'How can anyone who's been through a revolution possibly look like some of these women do?' Liz asked.

'They're used to it,' Howel said.

'Don't they feel anything at all?'

'Very little, I suspect. They've learned to take these things in their stride. They've had to.'

A wave of chatter and laughter reached them with a scornful reminder of their own limpness. 'I feel old,' Liz said. 'I feel as if I'd aged years in the past few days.'

'You're tired,' he said. 'I suppose we're all tired. It'll take a day or two before things begin to look better again.'

Hargrave came back from the ticket counter, looking like a man at the end of a safari through hard country. A trouser-leg was blood-smeared over one knee where he had slipped down in the stampede in the square. He was an advertise-ment among these smooth-speaking well-laundered men for an emergency that had become forgotten history, and again the thought struck Howel: We don't belong here. We're like animals shifted to the wrong environment. Cows in a desert. Camels in a swamp. We don't adapt.

'It's expected to touch down in about an hour's time,' Hargrave said. 'Been waiting at Medina del Campo for the OK to come in. I just saw Lopez's old Mercedes drive up complete with chauffeur and bodyguard as per usual. Wonder who they're meeting? Shouldn't be any trouble about taking off however late it is, the girl says. The weather en route is quite reasonable. Bit of head wind, that's all.'

Across the field, they saw the last of the three Thunderbolts come in to land, settling like a boat on a shallow mirage, then submerged in it to glide to a standstill, propeller scuttering. Two small yellow whirlwinds, hardly taller than a man, mooched towards it. In the exceptionally clear evening light, the western Cordillera lay sharp-edged along the horizon, and as black as coal. 'Just talking to somebody at the counter,' Hargrave said. 'Remember all that bombing and machine-gunning we heard? That was Lopez's private army being seen off. Terrible shambles, apparently. Most of the bombs went wide. A lot of slum houses caught it at the back of the Plaza.'

'I wonder who it was decided they'd had enough of Lopez,' Howel said.

'I wonder?' Hargrave said. He remembered the old Mercedes waiting in the car park. As soon as the plane from Bogotá came in, a barrier would be lifted and the Mercedes driven on to the field to pick up the distinguished visitor or visitors at the foot of the gangway. Hargrave had seen it happen more than once, and recalled that such visitors were usually from North America. 'Someone was very tired of Lopez,' he said. 'We'll never know any more than that . . . Anyway, you saw your revolution after all. Well, counter-revolution, let's say.'

'Heard it, at least.'

'Don't be so literal-minded. All right, then, heard it. That's better than nothing.'

The talk had fallen a little flat. They had exhausted the sentimentalities of the occasion, and now they struggled to fill in the small reproachful silences. For the second or third time Hargrave enquired and was told the time of their expected arrival at Heathrow. England in May would be marvellous, he said, and they agreed.

'I wonder how Charles will take the news?' Hargrave said.

'What news?' Howel asked him.

'Of your resigning.'

'As a matter of fact I may not after all. Liz and I have been talking it over, and we may do one more tour together. Somewhere not too strenuous like North Africa. It's just an idea. Nothing actually decided yet.'

'After which we'll probably buy a farm. Settle down to a quiet life and have a family,' Liz said.

They both overlooked Hargrave's expression of mock amazement. 'Marvellous,' he said.

'We'll be staying with my people in Bristol until the end of the month,' Howel said. 'Try and come and see us. Bring your wife. We'd love to have you if you can make it.'

'I might just about. If I don't get held up in Panama. Be marvellous to see you again.'

'Cable us if you're coming, that's all. Just let us know the day.'

'We'd absolutely adore to see you,' Liz said. 'Do make the effort.'

At the back of the bar, a man had taken down the portrait of General Lopez, removed the back, torn out the photograph and replaced it by one of Colonel Bravo holding a horse by the bridle. Now he mounted a chair to replace the picture. Colonel Bravo looked down at them, responsible and benign.

'Panama should be a rest-cure after this,' Howel said.

'It might be,' Hargrave said. 'I expect it'll be all sweetness and light in Los Remedios for a while. For a few weeks, anyway. Don't know if you've noticed, they seem to have scrapped the Customs and Immigration, and that funny little man who used to take photographs of you with the secret camera is gone.

'Mind you, I don't think it's any use banking too much on a change of heart. Temperament comes into it. Nothing in these countries really changes very much. As a people we learn from our errors and move on to new things. But basically they're static. May shift the scenery about a bit, but by and large things go on much as before.'

While they had been talking the vaguely martial music from the loudspeakers had expired in a whistle and boom, and now a muffled announcement followed. Instantly a reverent silence fell in the departure lounge, and a voice, hammered shapeless by over-amplification, began to speak.

'Ramon Bravo,' Cedric said. 'The new governor's traditional speech.'

'What's he say?' Liz asked.

Hargrave, listening, raised a cautionary finger. Bravo's words, running into one another came to them inflated and deformed.

'He says his first task is to punish General Lopez's assassins. An attempt made by criminal elements to profit by the public confusion provoked by the deed has already been crushed. The rest sounds like the standard stuff: the cry of the oppressed, justice for all men, peace, reconciliation, the binding up of wounds, the kiss of brotherhood, etc., etc.' Hargrave clicked his tongue in exasperation. 'The same old lies under a new label. He's a poet so this time it's put into poetic language, and they're falling for it. They've heard it all a dozen times before, but they're still ready to believe everything they're told. Just look at them.' People standing nearby were exchanging glances of solemn approval and nods

255

of the head, and a middle-aged man had taken out his hand-kerchief to dab at his eyes. 'He's promising them pie in the sky,' Hargrave said. 'His actual words are, 'All our wives will wear emeralds tomorrow.'' '

A new sternness now rasped in the voice. 'He assures that civil disorders, by whomever provoked, will be repressed with exemplary severity,' Hargrave said. 'Those who advocate violence in the pursuit of political ends will be treated as the criminals they are. Those who remain in the mountains in rejection of all peaceful solutions invite their own extermination. Sounds more and more like Lopez. I fear the new governor may prove to be a disappointment to many. A very complicated man.'

The loudspeaker harangue broke off in mid-sentence. There followed a series of hollow tapping sounds like someone testing a live microphone, and a powerful electrical purr. Then a voice said, not loudly but with the utmost clarity: 'Viva la resistencia! Viva la revolucion!' Something cracked with a whine like ice, and a trayful of crockery overturned and shattered. The loudspeakers crackled and thumped into a background voice that muttered away into silence before a hubbub broke out in the lounge.

'They must have grabbed the broadcasting station,' Hargrave said. 'Absolutely incredible! Managed to get on the air somehow or other, however they did it. Sounded as though somebody got clobbered before they cut off the sound. Said something like the fight still goes on, and they clobbered him.'

Liz was weeping. 'I'm running away,' she said. 'I'm a coward. I'm running away.'

Howel had her firmly by the arm, noting through the window with huge relief the sudden animation of the airport staff as the DC6B from Bogotá came in to land. In a week's time, he told himself, all this would seem very unreal—he hoped to both of them.